AMANDA'S BEDTIME STORY

Whit wanted to rip up Amanda's story and throw it out, unread. But he picked it up carefully, by the edges, hesitant even to touch the words.

"The girl sits in the car. She smokes. She puts the window down. She throws the cigarette out. She is nervous.

"She looks around. It is dark out. She sees trees and some tombstones. She gets out of the car. She tries to light another cigarette.

"The big lady in the purple dress comes. The girl tries to get back in the car. The girl screams. The big lady sticks the knife in her back."

Whit let the papers fall from his fingers when Britt phoned. "I'm going to the cemetery," she said. "Where they found Angela. Want to meet me there?"

BEHIND YOU

Thomas Millstead

A DELL BOOK

Published by
Dell Publishing Co., Inc.
1 Dag Hammarskjold Plaza
New York, New York 10017

Dell ® TM 681510, Dell Publishing Co., Inc.

ISBN: 0-440-10420-3

Printed in the United States of America

May 1987

10 9 8 7 6 5 4 3 2 1

DD

September

Chapter 1

"Where will you be?" she asked the last day he saw her alive. Her taut cheeks were mottled with anger.

"Why do you want to know?"

"It might just be nice to know. In case."

"In case of what?"

"In case you get any calls. In case I have to get in touch with you. In case . . ." The brittle staccato of her voice trailed off. "I need you to . . ."

"To what? You needed me to give you a shove, to get you going. That's done. You don't need me now."

"Not so."

"Bullshit!"

He slammed the door and stormed down the four flights of steps, too furious to wait for the elevator, hardly conscious of the weight of the packed suitcase.

He had never screamed like that, never in sixteen years. Maybe that had been the problem. They'd had none of the creative combat that domestic relations experts said kept a marriage alive, kept communications open.

Was "bullshit" creative combat?

Was walking out? He had never done that before, either, even in the last two years of mounting frustration and tightening tensions.

So maybe this was healthy, he told himself, drinking a series of White Labels at the hotel bar. He had forced the issue. Now that the bitterness was out in the open they could examine it: find the *causes, isolate them, and eradicate them. It would take work, but it could be handled logically—like one of the goddam "management by objective" assignments she had learned so well in business school.*

The bar was empty except for three businessmen, here for a convention. They talked too loudly to each other, bellowing with laughter while their eyes continuously roamed the empty room: Where were the city girls? Where was the city action? Where was the city fun?

Exactly what had prompted the bitterness? He had asked himself this question a million times.

Mainly it was her indifference and detachment. But those were symptoms of something else, and he didn't know what.

There were, of course, the demands of her career.

And the never-spoken-of things hovering in the background: the miscarriages, the eroding profits from her shops, the dwindling royalties from his last two books, and the festering doubts that his next would do any better.

He walked to a pay phone. She deserved, at least, to know where he was. To keep his whereabouts some sort of mystery was childish. Childishness would resolve none of this.

He had only a dime. He turned back to the bar to get a quarter.

To hell with it.

The next day he found a furnished apartment. It would be best, he thought, to pick up the rest of his possessions while she was at her office.

It was just past one when he entered their town house. She was hanging from one of the pine beams that crisscrossed their high, vaulted ceiling. She had used the seven-foot macramé wall decoration they had bought at the Old Town Art Fair the summer before. It was three columns of jute knotted into four-inch-thick strands of rope into which, in a naturalistic design, had been worked seashells, corks, and multicolored rocks.

The small butcher block table from the kitchen lay tipped over near her dangling feet. One sandal had fallen to the floor. The other had slipped halfway down her instep and seemed poised to drop at any moment. She wore her designer jeans and polka dot peasant blouse—what she called her "uniform" when she worked at home.

In the first instant he felt absolutely nothing. In the second, shock and horror. Then he heard the strangled sound of sobs that could not be made into words.

The strength drained from his body and he knew he had to sit down or he would collapse. But he could not look around for a chair because his eyes were riveted to hers.

The face was no longer familiar. It was now a lumpy, purplish gourd. But the eyes were still hers. Although the lids had half-closed, the pupils—centered in irises that were a sparkling light green—gazed intently at him. He knew they were like the eyes in some Renaissance portrait: They would follow him no matter where in the room he went. The tongue had protruded grotesquely, mangled by the clenched teeth, and dried blood covered the mouth. But the eyes were calm, serious, accusing.

Exactly as they had been leveled at him the day before. While she said, "In case I need you . . ."

Chapter 2

"Too literal, God damn it, too literal!"

Whit Pierce tore the paper out of the typewriter, wadded it into a ball, and hurled it at the insipid watercolor of a flower-dotted meadow on the motel room wall.

Too literal. That was exactly how it had happened. Incident for incident. Word for word.

But this was supposed to be a novel, a work of fiction. Not an exercise in faithfully reproducing external detail. Not like the goddam meadow of wild flowers on the wall. He was looking for why, not how. The how he already knew.

"Too literal," he said aloud.

He could at least have had the woman in the story OD on sleeping pills. It didn't matter. How she did it was irrelevant. Why she had done it wasn't.

Why Corinne had done it.

The realization poured over him again, scalding, almost as coruscating as the first time, almost as if it were a fresh revelation. Corinne the poised, Corinne the vibrant. She had never thrown out any hints. None, at any rate that he had picked up. Should he have?

He saw once more the glowing green eyes, transfixing him. Never leaving his face. Demanding incessantly: Why didn't you help me? Why did your love turn so hollow, so selfish? Damn you, why did you drive me to this?

"How could I have known? What should I have done?"

He was aware he'd shouted. God, what must they think in

the next room? An hour ago he'd heard the muted voices of tonight's occupants moving in. This would be his own third night in the motel. Already he had fallen into a pattern. Sleep late. Walk the streets for an hour or two. Drive through the countryside after that. Finally, in early evening, sitting down to write.

And, hours later, giving up in disgust. Crumpled paper littering the floor. Half-filled pages, aborted approaches.

She had eluded him again tonight. Even here, in La Soeur, where she'd been born and where they'd met and fallen into a love so consuming that it seemed the full depths of it could never be explored in a lifetime.

Still, he could not put the words on paper that would tell the story. That would purge him and release him.

With fingers spread over the keyboard, all he saw were those dead, hating eyes.

Pierce pushed his chair back from the typewriter and grabbed his herringbone jacket from the tiny closet.

He drove to the Appleland Inn just outside the city. This, too, had become part of his routine. He didn't remember if the restaurant had existed during the two years he'd lived here in La Soeur, but in these few days he'd developed a liking for it.

It was not a franchise operation like every other modestly priced eating place in town. And it was open twenty-four hours a day. He'd never yet been in it past midnight, but after so many years in Chicago he felt uncomfortable in a community that did not have some place to go at four in the morning.

Pierce sat on the usual stool at the corner of the counter where he could look out the plate-glass window at the parking lot. Someone had left a copy of the daily paper beside the remains of a fried chicken dinner. He picked it up and glanced at the front page: HUNT WIDENS FOR KILLER OF GIRL, 19.

Standards had slipped badly at the La Soeur *Sentinel* since his days there, Pierce mused. The seventy-two-point headline was set in two lines, and the top line ended with the word *for*.

Old Charlie would never have let him get away with that. It would've been tossed back in his face with a snarl. "You can't end a line with a preposition, Pierce. Got to be a complete thought. Damn it all, there are rules for writing headlines same as for writing anything else. Observe them!"

Clearly Charlie wasn't there anymore. But, of course, it had been sixteen years, and Charlie had been close to retirement even then. In fact, the whole look of the front page had changed. They'd gone to six columns, and column one was a boxed series of capsulized national and international stories. Somebody at the *Sentinel* had certainly studied what the big city papers were doing.

He folded the paper and pushed it away. But the heavy, black headline caught his eye again, and it occurred to him that he had not reacted at all to the content of the story. It had been a murder story. But the fact that it had been spread so prominently over page one reminded him that he was no longer in a large city. In Chicago, it generally took mass killings to merit a banner headline.

Thinking back, Pierce could not remember having edited or written anything about a murder in La Soeur during his two years on the *Sentinel.* There probably had been the occasional homicide: one of the brewery workers putting too much extra muscle into beating his wife, or a longshoreman pulling a knife and using it during a brawl in one of the saloons along the river. But never a murder-murder, as one of his colleagues in Chicago used to call them when he'd gone to work on the paper there. There had never been a murder-murder in his days in La Soeur, Wisconsin.

Idly he retrieved the *Sentinel.* He looked at the girl's name on the off-chance that she might have been related to someone he once knew here. Angela Karlstrom. It rang no bell. She had been stabbed ten times in the throat and chest two nights earlier. Her body had been found in the Old Military Cemetery, five miles north of the city, lying beside a two-year-old Dodge

12

Dart licensed to her father. The keys were still in the car. She had not been sexually molested. No weapons were found, and it was not known if anyone had been with her when she drove to the cemetery.

Possibly it could have earned a banner headline in Chicago. If it had been a slow news day. But certainly not two days after the fact. Whoever the young man with her had been—there had to have been one—would probably not be too difficult to locate. Pathetic but commonplace.

Pathetic but commonplace.

Corinne had made headlines, too, but nothing bigger than thirty-six point. She'd acquired enough fame to command a dozen paragraphs in both Chicago dailies. Pierce had been unable to prevent the details of her death from being published. But the papers had not exploited the suicide angle beyond reporting that her business enterprises had suffered recent reverses.

"Whit!"

It was a scraping rasp that Pierce recognized at once.

He had not sought out anyone he'd known in La Soeur from his newspaper days. But he realized that someone from those times must at some point notice him, and now he turned with the semblance of a grin.

"Al! Good to see you."

"I don't believe it! Whit Pierce!"

Al Stabo moved his cigar from his right hand into his mouth and extended the hand to Pierce. He had changed little, an almost tall man looking shorter than he was because of a hunched stoop. The stoop was more pronounced than Pierce remembered, the chest more caved-in, and the lenses in the glasses much thicker. But the eyes were the same—squinting and peering with unsatiated curiosity. The wild tufts of hair still projected like insect feelers from the ears and nostrils, except now they were totally gray.

"Sit down, Al. What'll you have?"

"Hot tea. Getting nippy out there. Just came from a soccer game. Junior high league. Nobody even heard of soccer when you were here, did they?"

"Still covering the jocks?"

"Still assistant sports editor. Whit, I'm sorry about Corinne. We sent flowers and a card."

"Yes. I appreciate it."

He did not remember who had sent flowers or sympathy cards. He could barely remember any of the mourners at the visitation or the cemetery. It was a blur to him now, and it had been disjointed even then: waves of delayed shock, pills desperately swallowed, and prayers that the interminable condolences would end.

"We were coming down for the funeral. But I had an assignment."

"Thanks, Al. How's Winnie?"

Stabo pulled at his cigar. "I'll tell her I saw you. Just passing through?"

"More or less. Staying a couple of days."

"Back to God's country, huh? Winnie's going to insist you come over for dinner. It might be good for her."

"Thanks, Al. But . . ."

Stabo wrenched the wet cigar out of his mouth and examined it, scowling as if it had malfunctioned. "Just what she needs. Maybe like old times."

There was a flatness to the comment, and it surprised Pierce.

Corinne and Winnie had been best friends since high school. The first year after Corinne and Whit moved to Chicago, the Stabos had been to visit them twice. Winnie and Al had invited them back to La Soeur several times. It was only a five-hour drive. But there never seemed to be time. They kept in touch by letter at first; then Christmas cards only. Somehow, close to a decade ago, even this pattern had been broken.

Had Winnie been hurt by this? It was the first time Pierce had considered this. He and Corinne had so seldom spoken of

Winnie and Al in recent years. There was just too much else happening. But had Winnie resented it? Corinne, the successful young big city businesswoman. Whit, the successful young novelist. Dumping their old friends.

"Al, I'd be delighted. Tell Winnie to name the day."

Stabo nodded. "I think it'd be good for her. We lost our daughter. Back in April."

"Oh, my God, Al."

"Jennifer. She was eleven. You never saw her."

"No. I think we—"

"Yeah. We sent you an announcement when she was born. And you sent her a present. A blanket, I think."

"My God, Al, I didn't know. I would've . . . we would've . . . because, if it was April, Corinne was still . . ."

"Yeah." Stabo sipped carefully at the hot tea. "Winnie's taken it pretty hard. It's not all fun and games, Whit. Used to seem like it, right? Hey, I'll tell the gang you're here. Those still left over from your days on the *Sewer.*"

It was a family joke. The La Soeur *Sentinel* was known by its staff as the "Sewer *Sentinel*"—and, for short, simply *The Sewer.*

"Can't be many left," Pierce said. "I assume Ralph's still running the outfit."

"From on high. Now they tell me he's thinking of shooting for a seat in Congress. And to think we knew him when."

Pierce finished his salad and wished he hadn't also ordered a patty melt. He urgently wanted to leave. These names from the past were words, mere words. They generated no feeling whatsoever.

Stabo sipped his tea again and asked, "How's the old burg look to you?"

"Fine, Al. Still a great place to live."

"It's changed a lot. But I suppose not so much as a town like Chicago. And maybe not so fast."

Pierce nodded. And some things had not changed at all, he noticed. The waitresses were robust, fair-skinned, blond, and

15

young. Exactly as he recalled the waitresses in every restaurant in La Soeur sixteen years ago.

The French had discovered and named La Soeur. But when the French moved on, it was the Scandinavians and Germans who came to stay. Still, this city of fifty thousand had a long way to go before it came anywhere near being a melting pot. With the exception of the waitress who now brought him his hamburger—she was not as close to her teen years as the others and had red hair pulled tightly back in a chignon—they might easily have been transplanted en masse from a restaurant in Stockholm or Copenhagen or Kiel.

"It's beautiful country around here. The river. The hills. You have to be away awhile to have it really hit you."

"Beautiful, yeah. I always thought so." Stabo beckoned the red-haired waitress for more tea. "A certain kind of beautiful." His laugh this time was self-conscious.

"A kind of gentle beautiful. It doesn't make you hold your breath and say: 'By golly, look at that!' "

He chomped on the cigar so forcefully that his words were hard to distinguish. "But it always seemed you wanted a different kind of beautiful, didn't you, Whit? You and Corinne? Like a bigger beautiful. Something higher, bigger. Big buildings. Big deals. Big cities. A bigger beauty. I don't know, a more dangerous beauty."

"We wanted to . . ." Pierce began, then thought, What did we want? Why did we leave? "Pass the ketchup, Al."

"Sure. You know, whatever you and Corinne were after, I didn't seem to feel it. I wondered why I didn't. I didn't feel the need for a bigger kind of beautiful. I used to think that maybe Winnie and I were better off with this kind of gentle beautiful. And then this happens to Jennifer."

The rasp was gone from the voice, and it was little more than a whisper. "She was murdered, Whit."

"Al! My God!"

"She was eleven years old and she was murdered."

16

From behind his lenses Stabo's squinty glare traversed the room pugnaciously—the counter, the twin rows of booths, the swinging door to the kitchen.

Pierce dabbed his lips with his paper napkin, then draped it over the patty. "How did it happen, Al?"

"Four, five miles northeast of town. By a small pond. Off of County Trunk P. Up in the coulee country. Hilly, winding roads. Remember that stretch?"

"Dimly."

"There used to be an access road to the pond. Back when the loggers used to work it, years and years ago. The road doesn't go anywhere now. Mostly overgrown with weeds and grass."

"I'd like my coffee now," Pierce told the waitress. She looked at the hardly touched beef patty and asked, "Would you like me to—"

"No, thanks."

"You can't see the entrance to the road when you're driving by on P," Al went on. "It's almost hidden, bushes and young trees. You'd have to know it's there to find it. I went out to it . . . later. The pond is tiny. Pretty. Trees thick all around it."

"Al, are they holding anybody?"

"Nobody. They told me—the sheriff's department—that some young people drive in there once in a while. To drink and take dope and lay around the pond. There were some beer cans there. Jennifer went there on her bike. She biked everywhere. She was absolutely fearless. She was going biking with a girl friend. We thought the two of them were together. Turns out the other girl couldn't make it."

His voice grew louder, and three stools away an elderly man wearing a big-billed farmer's cap turned to look.

"Jennifer just wanted to see what went on around the pond, the other girl said, 'to see what the big kids are doing.' So she went there on her own. . . ."

He stabbed out the cigar in the dregs of his cup. "She was adventurous. Curious! I encouraged her. I told her that's how

17

good reporters are made. She wanted to be a reporter! She was—"

Pierce gripped Al's forearm tightly. "Come on," he said. "We'll go for a ride. We'll go for a drink."

Stabo sank heavily against the back of his stool. He shook his head. "I don't want Winnie waiting. I got so many evening assignments. Always have. But I don't like her to be alone."

He grabbed the La Soeur *Sentinel* and gave the page-one banner story a flicking slap. "Especially when she reads stuff like this!"

"They don't think it's the same—?"

"I don't know!" The words ran together with the sudden explosive rapidity of a jackhammer. "They don't know!"

Then the voice fell. "The Karlstrom girl was stabbed. Jennifer was strangled. Strangled, Whit. So they say that there is probably no connection. All I know is that Winnie was up all night when she heard about this new one. It was like pulling a scab off. Up all night. Remembering what happened to Jennifer. Crying. And trying to see if Jennifer—"

He broke off and hurriedly got to his feet, pulling out another cigar. "That soccer's some game, Whit. All action. Really shook me up learning the rules. I mean, what do I know about strikers and rear guardsmen? I spent my life covering shortstops and tailbacks. Where you staying?"

"The Alhambra."

Stabo flattened a sheaf of messy, folded copy paper already filled with scrawled notes and jotted down the name. They shook hands.

"You're looking good, pal," Stabo said. "The hair's gone salt and pepper, so what? Gives a guy some class, right?"

"You're looking terrific, too, Al."

"Yeah. And there for sure is an Easter bunny."

Pierce did not watch Stabo leave. The red-haired waitress smiled down at him.

"More coffee, sir?"

One of the blond waitresses, carrying a casserole dish, inched past her, crooning: "Behind you, dear."

"Sir? More coffee?" the redhead repeated.

He looked up, aware of her for the first time.

"Sorry. No. Thanks."

Already he felt La Soeur closing in on him. He remembered once when he and Corinne had picnicked on one of the small, shoreline islands in the Mississippi. He had put a grass stem in his mouth and swept an arm in the direction of the churning, brown-speckled water.

"Big news, Miss Becky! Me and Huck Finn gonna rescue old Jim, the slave. Float clear out of here on our own raft!"

She had not smiled, Corinne who so loved to join in bantering parodies. Solemnly she'd said: "Rescue me first, please?" She was looking back at La Soeur's squat, ragged skyline. "Sometimes, when I think of going back there, I can't breathe. It's like I'm choking. . . . Oh, take me along on that raft. Take me along, Tom Sawyer!"

Pierce left the restaurant and returned to his car, almost running through the lot.

Chapter 3

It was the first time the phone had rung since his return to La Soeur. Pierce looked at his watch and realized that he had been staring at the blank sheet of paper in the typewriter for more than an hour.

He wasn't looking forward to dinner at the Stabos'. He picked up the phone.

It was neither Al nor Winnie. The voice was male, a lilting tenor.

"That you, Whit? Marvelous to hear you're in town. This is Ralph. Ralph Hungerford."

"Ralph? Oh, yes. How are you?"

"Never better. And yourself?"

"Fine. How'd you know I was here?"

"The word is out. Greatness has descended upon us. The renowned Chicago author has returned to the soil that nurtured him."

It was the same grandiloquent style that Pierce remembered. Hungerford had been city hall reporter, and not a terribly good one, when Pierce worked on the *Sentinel*. Pierce had been mildly astonished to learn that Ralph had become the paper's publisher as well as the owner of both the city's leading advertising–public-relations agency and a major printing company.

"Al Stabo tell you?"

"Yes. Needless to say, I wish you'd given me a call. Whit, my condolences."

"Thanks."

"We read of it in the Chicago *Tribune.* I had a story prepared for the *Sentinel.* Because Mrs. Pierce was, after all, a native. Are you in town on matters regarding the estate?"

"Not really. Corinne's business interests were all in the Chicago area. I'm just looking the old hometown over."

"You aren't from La Soeur yourself, as I recall. Are you?"

"Minnesota. But my two years here were pretty formative. My first real job."

"Well, now that you're here I think it only fitting we renew acquaintances. Review old times. Fortunately the perfect occasion presents itself. I've already scheduled a dinner party Saturday night. We'd be most honored by your presence."

"That's nice of you, Ralph. But—"

"Nothing very gaudy. Ten or twelve people. All of them pleasant. Al and Winnie Stabo will be there. They'd be disappointed if you didn't come."

Pierce looked from the intimidating paper in the typewriter to the insipid watercolor print on the wall to the worn carpet.

"All right, Ralph."

"Splendid. Seven. Cocktails first. It's 801 Kimberley Drive. But forget the number. It's the last house on the drive, the one bordering Meadowbluff golf course. Do you remember where that is?"

"Sure. It's a far cry from that two-flat you used to have down by the river. You rented the top floor, I think. You and your wife—Elaine, Eileen? I'm sorry, it's been a long while. . . ."

Pierce had been vaguely aware of the humming as he talked, and now it came to him that this was an unconscious habit of Ralph's. While he listened to someone else, Hungerford would frequently sustain a soft, steady note as though to insure that when he spoke again, it would be with perfect pitch.

"I'm not married to Elena anymore, Whit," he broke in. "You'll meet my wife, Britt, on Saturday, and I'm sure you'll find her a most accomplished hostess. See you then."

21

* * *

Pierce had no desire to be an early arrival at the Hungerfords'. Before he realized it, he found himself on Northwestern Avenue and the downtown district, and took a once familiar turn at Pine Street.

It had drawn him, inevitably, again: the imposing brick house with sandstone trimming next to the bungalow on the corner. Pierce pulled up at the curb. This had been Corinne's home. He had walked down this street each of these days he'd been back in La Soeur. Above all, he'd thought, this place should touch off recollections, emotions that would explain Corinne to him. Who she really was. And why she did what she did.

The house had not changed—the Corinthian-columned front porch, the catalpa tree in the yard, the tricky S-curve in the driveway. Each time he'd passed it, memories had swept over him.

Now he remembered the autumn day she'd greeted him at the door wearing jodhpurs and an English hunt-club derby. "Tally ho, Whitney!" she'd trilled, satirizing herself, yet defiantly proud of her own pretensions.

Jodhpurs and a derby—to go for a plodding, one-hour trail ride on two dispirited rental horses through scruffy woods bounded by cornfields.

And other memories. The Easter when he'd escorted Corinne and her mother down these steps to services at Emmanuel Lutheran Church four blocks away. Corinne was radiant in parchment white, an orchid on her blouse.

The Christmas season before their marriage—an endless series of trips in and out of the house, gifts, invitations, and excited laughter. And when they'd sat together on the living room floor, the many voices of friends and family loudly caroling, "God rest ye merry, gentleman," he'd held her tightly and whispered in her ear, "I love you, Corinne . . . I love you. . . ."

But none of the memories explained her to him any more

clearly. Each day this week he'd walked away from the house still empty, still believing there was something important to be experienced here. But he had not wanted to linger in the neighborhood. Other people owned the house now. Corinne's mother had retired to Florida eight years earlier.

Now, studying the house from his car, he was flooded by memories of other times he had parked here.

They had not been furtive teenagers by any means. He was a newspaperman with a manner suggesting great sophistication. She was an independent businesswoman. She had managed her father's floral shop for over a year since her father's death.

Yet again and again they would park in front of her house, like high-schoolers back from a date. The bungalow on the corner blocked the streetlight. And the tall elm near the curb cut off any view her mother might have of the car. That elm was gone now, as were the many others that had once lined the block, fallen to Dutch elm disease.

She had kissed him eagerly, tenderly, from the start. The first night, almost sobbing with desire, he had tentatively touched her knee and she had gently removed his hand. How many more nights had they parked there before he dared try again? So many, it seemed to him now. So many nights with her face against his, wet and warm and sweet, and out of the corner of his eye he could see the edge of her skirt just above the knee and watch, with aching tension, as it crept up higher and higher on her thigh as she sank farther back on the seat under the weight of his straining body.

Pierce touched the accelerator and moved the car forward a few feet. It was precisely at this spot they had parked, and he recalled the night it had all changed. It was the dead of winter, and after an hour their breath had totally obscured the windows. She wore a long, black-dyed fur coat, and it had been tightly buttoned when he had taken her in his arms. Much later he became aware that the coat was open, thrown back, and he realized it had not been his doing. Half her thigh was exposed, and with the tips of his fingers he touched her there, high above the knee, lightly brushing. At last he had slid the hand under the skirt, tremulous, kissing her with renewed ardor as if to distract her from what was happening.

His hand had moved to the inside of her thigh and at each gentle movement his throat caught, fearful she would permit no more. But—suddenly—the smooth, tantalizing feel of the silk. And still she had not seemed to notice.

The silk? Had she worn silk then? Probably not. That was only later, when she was Corinne, the president of Corinne's Crocks and Crafts. But whatever she had worn under her dress in La Soeur, it had felt to Pierce to have the fragility, the sheer, forbidden richness of silk.

At that instant—in a delirium he would never know again—he had felt her hand groping wildly at his belt.

Now, seventeen years later, he tried to coax into being the yearning of that love, that lust, that rapture. Not just remember that he had felt it but once more experience the power of it.

But there was no tingling, no stirring. Nothing.

A pedestrian was approaching. Pierce eased his car away from the curb.

Christ, how I wanted you, Corinne!

He headed east, toward the outskirts of the city.

Her skin was so luminescent that she subtly illuminated any room in which she appeared, any group she joined. She was small, with a face so delicate that her features seemed to have been inked on with exquisitely fine brush strokes. All her features, that was, except for the thick lower lip that could droop almost wantonly or thrust itself out pugnaciously.

For a moment he could almost see her as she was. When the green eyes had been flashing and so aware. Then they froze and were again the eyes of last August: dead eyes in a dead face. But dead eyes that were not quite dead.

"I wanted you, Corinne!" he whispered. "From the start! God Almighty, how I loved you!"

And when did it stop?

"It never stopped," he said softly. "Not for me."

To his right the bluffs stretched skyward. He was driving parallel to Frenchman's Pitch. It was the highest point in the county but invisible on a night like this, when stars and moon were hidden.

Chapter 4

The Hungerford home was two and one-half stories tall, and sprawling. There was an unrelieved boxiness to it, reminiscent of an Army barracks. Yet its underlying ugliness was tempered by the cheery naturalism of its facade—a sheathing of reddish, roughly hewn cedar.

The golf course was visible from any of the numerous picture windows and jutting balconies at the back of the house. A long row of chest-high evergreens divided Ralph's property from the Meadowbluff fairway.

The lawn was immense and, to the south, lost itself in a small woods. A nearby flag apparently designated the cup on Ralph's private putting green.

An unbroken line of towering firs and Norway spruce shielded the house from Kimberley Drive. Two magnificent silver maples brushed their branches against the roof.

As he reached for the ornate brass knocker the door opened, and a woman put out her hand.

"Hi. I'm Britt."

"Hello. I'm—"

"I know. You have got to be Whit. Come on in."

"Thanks." He searched for a comment, but she had thrown him off stride. This was no one he would have envisioned as Ralph Hungerford's wife.

Much of her impact, he thought, was due to what she wore. No, he corrected himself, to the way she wore it. This might have been how she dressed for the supermarket—orange polyester pants and black turtleneck sweater. But the pants seemed to have been sprayed on, and the sweater clung so tightly that her breasts were outlined in explicit detail.

Those breasts were generous and her body wide-shouldered, so that she carried them well. Her waist was nipped in, the hips flaring. As she led him through the foyer, her perfume engulfed him. It was pungent and overwhelming, like falling headlong into a field of wild flowers—a dizzying jumble of hyacinth, narcissus, jasmine.

"Sure glad you could make it. Not many alumni from the paper ever come back. Look who's here, Ralph."

"Whit! Handsome as ever! No different. Well, not much. But we've all changed a bit, eh?"

Tall and squarely built, Hungerford had put on considerable weight around his midsection. It gave him a blocky look. Much like his house. But he did not project an impression of corpulence.

"What will it be, Whit? You still indulge at times, I trust."

"Scotch would be fine, Ralph."

Hungerford's neck and jaws were heavily creased, but the eyes glowed like brilliant azure jewels in a setting free of sag or wrinkle. Pierce found himself wondering if Ralph had had an eye job. Preparatory to announcing his intention to run for Congress, if what Al Stabo had said was true.

"You're an author, Ralph tells us," said one of the guests, introduced as chairman of the brewery. "Cloak-and-dagger stuff? That's about all I read, outside the business press."

"Politics," said Britt. "At least the first one. The inside lowdown on what it takes to win an election. I read it and I really dug it."

"Maybe you should take a gander at it, Ralph," teased the president of the First National Bank of La Soeur. "Just in case you develop a need to bone up on the subject of winning elections." He winked at Britt.

"Might be that Whit could help," she said. "He's been through the wars."

"You've run for office, Mr. Pierce?"

"No. I was press secretary for a congressman for a while, after I got out of newspapering."

"Well, we have a most interesting political situation taking form here," Hungerford remarked. "Next year being an election year—"

"Excuse me." Pierce noticed Al and Winnie Stabo for the first time. They were standing by themselves beside the fireplace, watching the crackling logs.

It was a huge fireplace, and the bricks that enclosed it covered a third of the west wall. The living room occupied an entire wing of the house. The knotty wood-beamed ceiling appeared incredibly distant. Pierce felt like he was in a large ski lodge.

"Winnie!" Pierce took her in his arms, hugged her a long moment, then kissed her cheek.

Winifred Stabo put her hand to his face, touched his forehead, and smiled dreamily. She had grown massive. Slightly over six feet tall, she had always been inclined toward plumpness. But it had been becoming to her then, attractively complementing her ruddy cheeks, pink arms, and her bouncy way of walking—as though the floor were a trampoline that could send her delightedly vaulting to the ceiling at any instant. Now she was thick and columnar, rooted to the earth.

Al shook hands brusquely. Cigar in hand, he gestured at the pillow-covered modular units arranged in a U-shape before the fireplace. "Want to sit down, Winnie?"

She moved deliberately, her pace stolid. It seemed a genuine effort for her to defy gravity.

"Whit," she said in her sleepy voice, "who would've thought we'd meet you here. After all these years."

She smiled sweetly and, after a pause, asked, "Have you heard anything from Corinne, dear?"

Pierce looked at Al, stunned, then back to those placid brown eyes.

"Winnie," he began, "I thought Al told me you knew. About Corinne—"

"Of course," she murmured, "but sometimes there are messages. Particularly when the passing has been difficult. Or violent."

"I don't think Whit wants to go into that now, honey."

"Al, could I have another?"

Stabo sighed. "Sure, honey," he said, and left.

"I thought you might have." Winnie laid a hand on Pierce's forearm. "Heard something from Corinne. I have wondered about her. You know how close she and I were."

"Very close." He hoped Al would be quick with the drink.

Winnie's face was still pretty: moon-shaped with deep red, oval lips. "I would have thought I'd've known when it happened to her. It should have come to me. A dream, a feeling, the sudden knowledge that she had made her transition. I wasn't open to it, somehow. But she was trying to reach me, I know. A reader in Mankato told me."

"A reader?"

"A tarot reader. I was visiting her, in fact, the day Corinne died. And she said, 'Death has struck someone close to you.' And I said, 'Yes, my daughter Jennifer. That's why I came to you.' And she said, 'No, someone else, someone more recent.' And I said, 'No, there's no one.' But the next morning Al called from the office and said he'd just heard about Corinne."

"Winnie, you've been seeing people like this? Tarot readers?"

"Oh, it's not the cards, you know. The cards only touch off their innate abilities. You know, Whit, I believe I've found a way to get through to Jennifer—"

Al had returned with Winnie's drink and Pierce noticed that he had refilled his own. "Not here, honey! Not here!"

"If you want me to I'd like to try to reach Corinne. It can be a comfort. Take the young lady who passed over several days ago. Angela. Did you read about her? They found her in the Old Military Cemetery. Stabbed. Many times. Not like Jennifer—"

"Winnie! No!" Al was pleading now.

"Who knows what she might communicate? Maybe even who was responsible. Oh, yes, they can communicate that to us. Jennifer hasn't, so far. But it's my hope—"

Pierce felt his face must tell her how appalled he was. Gratefully he heard Hungerford announce, "Ladies and gentlemen, dinner is served."

"And be warned," Britt sang out, "we are thirteen at table! If that shakes anybody up the nearest McDonald's is two miles down the road!"

Britt steered Pierce through the wide doorway. She sat to his right, the banker's wife to his left. Resplendent in a scarlet host's jacket, Ralph presided at the head of the French Provincial table. Formal damask curtains had been pulled back, and the window facing the golf course had become a mirror reflecting their images.

"Going to get one of the Packers out here to kick off Indian Summer Days, Ralph?" the banker asked.

"We'll get one. Our options depend, of course, on who Green Bay has mobile after they meet the Rams tomorrow."

"Ralph dreamed up the Indian Summer Days," Britt explained to Pierce. "It's the biggest thing that ever hit La Soeur."

"Couple of towns had Oktoberfest," said one of Hungerford's public relations executives. "But this promotion outdoes 'em all. Gets people from all over the Midwest."

"I submit that we need that kind of creative thinking on the national scene," the brewer asserted. "Specifically, in Washington. Interested, Ralph?"

Hungerford laughed, melodiously. "It's a mite early. There are several options at this point."

"One problem," the banker's wife giggled. "Congressmen don't get to play golf every day, do they?"

"Sadly true." Hungerford chuckled.

"Honestly," Britt drawled, "you can't go anywhere without a view of that damn golf course. Ralph can watch golf, think golf, dream golf all day and all night."

"It is gloriously convenient," Hungerford agreed. "Shot eighteen holes this morning, as a matter of fact."

"This time of year?" the brewer's wife asked. "I thought the season was over by now."

"For these kooks the season isn't over until they're standing in snow up to their hoo-ha." Britt laughed.

She looked directly at Pierce—seeming to share the jest with their visitor—and the tip of her tongue darted out. "I'd best see what's going on with dessert," she said. Rising, her knee touched Pierce's, and her perfume swept over him. Her hand brushed the back of his neck.

He steeled himself to keep from swinging his head around to watch her.

When had he and Corinne last made love? It had been at least two weeks before he found her that day in August. Or was it a month? Or longer? There had been such distance between them.

Britt returned, carrying a dish aloft as though it were a trophy. She set it in front of Ralph and ran her fingers over his balding skull.

"Baba au rhum! And the master of the house gets first bite!"

Pierce let his eyes slide over her. All the women but Britt had dressed with some style, most in chic cocktail dresses. Britt, he decided, simply didn't care if what she wore was tasteful or appropriate, so long as it embellished her figure. Clearly she knew her body was close to incredible, and so she dressed to accommodate it.

She caught him looking at her and smiled. Her two front teeth protruded slightly, and when she drew her lips back the tip of her tongue emerged for an instant between them.

It was intensely provocative. A habit, Pierce cautioned himself.

"Well, Whit," said Ralph, "back here to research a book?"

"Why would he want to research us?" Britt broke in. "Must be more exciting things to write about in the big, bad city."

Standing with one hand on the back of his chair, she leaned forward impulsively to address the distinguished-looking attorney across the table. For a moment her breast grazed Pierce's cheek. "But, Max," she cried, "it would be . . . providential! Perhaps Mr. Pierce could help us nourish our own puny little literary efforts!"

"I don't understand," Pierce said.

"Max and I and a bunch of others have had our hopes for greater self-expression very rudely crushed." Britt slipped back into her chair. "We signed up for a creative writing course at the library. But this year's writer in residence cancelled."

"Anyone I know?"

"Doubtful. He churns out too-too precious novels that read like hieroglyphics in search of a Rosetta Stone. I think he had enough of Heartland, USA, and went streaking back to New York." She laughed. "One thing that goosed him along was hearing that his true love—Paul something—was not proving faithful in his absence."

"If you're suggesting I take over this class—"

"Have you ever taught writing?"

"One rocky period after my first book came out. But—"

"It was meant to be! I know the people at the library. They'll jump to get somebody like you. It's only eight weeks."

Her hand fell to his knee.

"Just think about it for now."

He cleared his throat. "All right."

"Did anyone notice that?"

Pierce started. It was Winnie, speaking evenly and almost drowsily. Until then, neither she nor Al had uttered a sound at the dinner table.

"Notice what?" Ralph asked.

"A face. Looking in."

They turned to the window and saw only themselves, a tableau painting in golden light.

"What kind of face?" Britt demanded.

"Just a face. Down in the corner. A white, indistinct face. It might have been a child—"

"Winnie," Al Stabo interrupted.

"Ralph"—Britt's voice was harsh—"let down the drapes, would you?"

"Another Scotch, Whit?"

"Please."

One wall of the basement rumpus room was lined with enlarged snapshots: Ralph shaking hands with golfing companions; Ralph holding a pheasant he'd shot; Ralph and Britt grilling on an outdoor barbecue. There was a framed sign over the foam-padded bar: "Ve get too soon oldt und too late schmart."

Winnie and Al had left almost immediately after dinner. While Max, the attorney, played on the grand piano, Ralph had sung several Irish airs, opening his tenor voice to the fullest. Then he'd invited Pierce downstairs.

"You've done well, Whit."

Pierce raised his glass in salute. "So have you."

"If I can help in any way, Whit. If you just want to talk about it . . ."

"Ralph, I don't think it would help."

A rapid scampering down the stairs and a large dog burst into the room, scrambling and snuffling, nose to the linoleum floor.

Hungerford shook his finger at the dog. "So she's set you loose to plague our guests, has she?" He tossed down some cashews from a snack dish.

The dog slurped them up. It was long-haired, with a body

like an Eskimo husky and face and ears vaguely resembling a fox terrier.

"Yes, she has." Britt stepped down the last few stairs. "Ain't she a bitch? So what's going on? Old war stories? About how it was on the *Sewer* before I joined it?"

"So you served time on the paper?" said Pierce.

"Police reporter. Came on as general assignment, right away switched over to police. And there I stayed. Some amaretto, Ralph. Thanks, sweetie."

"And a damned fine reporter, too."

"I did win a state press association award one year. It's hung up over there in that corner."

"For what?"

"I hopped in the car with these cops just after the downtown savings and loan got held up. A teller got shot. I lucked out because these were the cops that got right on this bastard's tail. Forced him over and he ran in a house. Held the family hostage. I talked him into giving up. But not before I got an exclusive interview."

Pierce shook his head. "And you said nothing much goes on around here."

"Oh, it goes on. Look at the Karlstrom thing. Angela Karlstrom. Our latest page-one homicide."

"And Al and Winnie's daughter."

"I feel so damn sorry for them, Whit. I tried talking to them tonight. But they just sort of climbed into a shell."

Pierce yawned. "Look, it's getting late and I have to run. It's been fun."

Britt ruffled the dog's coat. "Come on, Smokey. You can have the rest of the baba."

At the front door she clasped his hand in both of hers. "Remember, think about that writing course!"

"I will. Good night, Ralph. Good night, Britt."

A mist had fallen, and the fairway was invisible beyond the border of shrubbery. A thin layer of precipitation coated his windshield. Pierce groped through his pockets for paper tissues, found none. With his sleeve he began wiping off the window when he heard the squeal of hinges.

Somewhere in the rear of the house a door had opened, and now Britt was running lightly, silently to him.

"Well," he said, "this is—"

"I need to know, Whit. Will you? Teach that course?"

"Well, look . . . I'd love to. But, really—"

She pulled his head down and pressed her lips hard against his.

Short of breath, her lips on his cheek, she whispered, "Please, Whit?"

"All right . . . my God, yes!"

Chapter 5

He hoped for a minute or two of privacy to go over the sketchy notes he'd thrown together. But when he walked into the library conference room at ten to eight, one member of the class was already waiting.

"Mr. Pierce? I'm Mrs. Siegerson." He took the frail hand she extended. She was seventyish and tiny. A large silver cross dangled down the front of her black, long-sleeved dress.

"I thought you should know we're not all amateurs," she smiled. "Here."

He accepted a thin, pastel-colored book. *Wally Woolly Comes Clean.* The book jacket described it as a "tale for today's children based on an inspirational Biblical parable."

She had inscribed the back of the title page to "My colleague and teacher, Whitney Pierce." The publisher, he noted, was a vanity house. She had paid all of the printing costs herself.

"Thank you. It's very kind of you."

He flipped open his attaché case. It had been a gift from Corinne that he'd never liked—stylishly thin and appropriately initialed just below the handle. It was the sort of case carried by high-powered executives and the twin of one she had bought for herself. Fine for her world, he had thought. But not for his. He had banged it and kicked it until it acquired a kind of weary insouciance, and now he was at least able to tolerate it.

Britt and Max, the lawyer, entered together. She gripped Pierce's hand and gave him a quick peck on the cheek. "So it's all worked out! I told you it was providential!"

At a rear table, Pierce's attention was caught by a tall, attractive young woman with pink cheeks and startled eyes. He was sure he knew her, and then it came to him: the waitress from the Appleland Inn. Tonight she had let her russet hair fall down over her shoulders. He nodded to her.

At three minutes after eight he closed the door and read off the roll. Only one name went unanswered—Amanda Gatliffe.

"To begin with," he said, "I'll discuss some of the principles of fiction writing. Later we'll get into some practical work. If any of you have brought something you've already written— Mrs. Siegerson brought this book of hers, for instance—I'll be happy to check it out while you're busy being creative. In subsequent classes we'll be doing a good deal of analysis of each other's work. That's the only way to learn. Fiction must be practiced, not preached. Having said that, I will now preach."

The door opened, and someone in the back of the class gasped. A grotesque figure gaped at them, a hulking woman, incredibly thick in the trunk and legs.

Her face looked as though two slabs of rough granite had been imperfectly fitted together. One ear projected noticeably; the other lay flat against her skull. The right eye was considerably higher than the left. One cheekbone was pushed in sharply, while the other was puffed out as if from some infection.

She wore an Army overcoat—a brown woolen "horse blanket" that must have dated from the Korean War or even World War II. Her feet were incongruously wedged into elegant, stiletto-heeled suede pumps festooned with saucy tassels.

"Amanda Gatliffe?"

" 'At's right, guv'ner," a voice answered, and Pierce caught sight of someone all but hidden behind her.

"Please come in."

The woman stepped forward gingerly on her high heels. There was nothing in her walk suggesting a physical impairment, but she seemed momentarily befuddled by the staring faces and the bright, overhead neons.

Amanda Gatliffe's escort guided her to an empty chair at the rear table, all the while winking at Pierce. He was young— possibly nineteen or twenty years old—tall and agile. Pale blond hair spilled between his birdlike shoulder blades. The face was exceptionally narrow, like someone seen from the extreme edge of a movie screen, and completely pliable, changing expression continually.

He helped Amanda shrug out of her greatcoat and then, skipping to the door, he faced the class, scratched his crotch, and exited.

Nervous titters broke the sudden silence. Throats cleared in embarrassment. The fortyish housewife next to Amanda Gatliffe moved her chair a foot or two away. Amanda fixed her eyes on Pierce, waiting patiently.

"Well," he said, "to resume!"

He held his notes as he talked, but soon there was no need to refer to them. Conflict. Point of view. Dramatic structure. The ideas flowed easily. He was surprised when he checked his watch and found it was past nine.

"All right, your turn now. I'm going to give you a sentence: 'The sky was a brilliant blue and cloudless.' That's the start of your story. Got it down? Okay, tell me what happens after that."

A few sent pens or pencils scurrying across the paper immediately. Some closed their eyes in concentration. Others sought inspiration everywhere from the ceiling to the map of the world on the wall to their own fingernails.

Pierce picked up the shortest of the already completed pieces on his desk, the submission from a bearded young man. It introduced a character named Hal Lucinate, who spewed out a series of one-liners. Pierce found none of them amusing. There was no theme, no story line.

On the last page the writer had scrawled: "I do ad copy for WLSE but have set my guns on full-time comedy. Could use a boost. Hint! Hint! You don't have any contacts on the *Tonight* show, do you?"

Pierce sighed and permitted his eyes to rest on Britt. Her face was bent close to the paper, and her hand moved at an easy, steady rhythm. She looked up, met his gaze, and the tip of her tongue poked out in a quick smile.

It was stupid. Pointless. And so alien to him. But he continued to stare, wanting her to look up again. To see that smile, that darting tongue.

Then he noticed that Amanda Gatliffe was gawking at him. He was sure she had never taken her eyes from him.

He left the desk and strolled past the tables. Everyone else was by this time writing something.

The tablet in front of Amanda was still blank. She sniffed. Abruptly a large bead of water appeared in her nostril and dropped onto the paper. And then another. She ignored the dripping, her eyes intent on him.

Pierce thrust a handkerchief at her and pointed at the stains on the paper.

"Sometimes I do that," she said. "Froze my nose when I work for some people. Twenty years ago. When I was cleaning lady."

The words—totally without inflection—seemed to float out of an underground cavern.

She dropped her jaw, displaying two rows of chipped and brown-stained teeth, and bobbed her head. He realized she was grinning.

She had written down the sentence he dictated. She had printed it. There was nothing more on the page.

"Just write anything," he told her. "Whatever comes to mind."

"Teacher, I'm finished." Britt waved her story at him.

Pierce crossed over to her, and Max said, "Me, too."

He felt Britt's eyes on him as he leaned back and read what

she had written. "The sky was a brilliant blue and cloudless, and Mae was in heat."

He shook his head, chuckling. There were two pages of exceedingly intimate descriptions of how Mae had bathed and girded herself for what was to be a momentous day. She had enrolled in a scuba-diving class and conceived a grand passion for her instructor, Ray.

"Mae and Ray! Even their names rhymed! What better reason for an affair? Their names were twined in rhyme! There were cosmic reverberations! This was meant to be!"

Mae and Ray . . . Britt and Whit. He hadn't thought of that before. Interesting that she had.

It was cute and it was sophomoric. Pierce shrugged his shoulders.

But his palms were damp and his pulse had begun to quicken. Discreet she was not.

He wrenched his mind away from the fantasy that was beginning to form and glanced at Max Fischer's manuscript. "The sky was a brilliant blue and cloudless. The day, in fact, was too beautiful for words."

That was all.

Yet the attorney had been energetically at work every time Pierce had noticed him. Even now, papers were strewn in front of him, and he seemed fully occupied, scratching out, penciling in.

Then Pierce saw the open briefcase on the floor, and it became quite clear.

Max was preparing a legal brief. Of course. Max Fischer was taking this class to be near Britt.

"Time's up," he called. "Turn in whatever you have. Your assignment next week: an original piece of writing on any subject. Two pages minimum. See you next week."

"Tell me truthfully, do I exhibit signs of talent?" Britt asked moments later, bending over his desk.

"Let's say I saw some potential there."

"Do you think it can be made to blossom?"

"We can try."

"Let's discuss it over a drink."

"Can't tonight. Sorry."

She brushed his hand quickly with her index finger and walked to Max, who held her jacket for her. She smiled, thanking him.

The attorney waved to Pierce as they left.

He was aware that his face was flushed.

My God, was she just a tease? Or worse, was it all just a ploy?

He felt the first stirrings of disappointment and hurt. And anger.

Was this class supposed to be an excuse so that she and Max Fischer could get out of the house on Thursday nights?

Now there was the sting of self-reproach.

"Mr. Pierce . . . excuse me . . . I wonder if you'd . . ."

It was the woman who'd sat beside Amanda Gatliffe. She was holding out a copy of his last novel.

"Please . . . I wonder if you'd autograph it?"

"I'm flattered."

Where the hell had she found it? he wondered. The initial sale was a disaster. It had been quickly remaindered and was selling at a drastic markdown—where it was selling at all. This copy looked fresh, clean, completely unread.

"Would you be stopping for coffee anywhere?" she asked hesitantly.

He'd forgotten. The after-class obligation. The groupies who'd take any course to fraternize with a so-so name or a soon-to-be name or a once-was name. Timorous, fluttering, apologetic, but always pressing in.

"Not tonight. Sorry." He brandished the stack of papers. "Too much homework."

"Perhaps next week?"

"Let's keep it open."

Mae and Ray . . . Britt and Whit. "This was meant to be!"

He had no intention of critiquing their writing that night. Pierce threw himself onto his motel bed, then realized he was too overstimulated to sleep.

The kind of night when sleep was dangerous. When the dreams would not be soothing. Nor erotic. Not of Britt or any other woman. Any other living woman.

No, the dreams, as always, would be of Corinne. The ruined face. The accusing eyes. The dead arms that looked as if they might suddenly quiver, lift, and reach out for him in rage.

He dumped the pile of manuscripts on the dresser and selected a few at random. The first was a bewildering science-fiction vignette. The sky indeed was a brilliant blue and cloudless, but the sky was a painted dome covering a small planet in a distant galaxy.

Next was the story by the red-haired waitress, Sally Berwyn, and it proved a surprise. It was a short character sketch, strung with terse dialogue: the chance meeting of two old friends in a restaurant. Underpinning the outwardly ordinary conversation were echoes of a fondly shared past and intimations of a much more painful present.

Al Stabo and me! She had heard them that evening at the Appleland Inn. By no means had she reconstructed their encounter. The dialogue was different, the characters were not facsimiles. But it was an uncanny feat of building a framework of fiction out of a few fleeting moments of observation.

He laid the story aside for future study. Next was the single sheet with Amanda Gatliffe's name on it.

At his prompting she had at least written something. It was printed, and the letters were like a child's—differing in size, straying off the lines, falling lopsidedly into the margins.

The sky was a brilliant blue and cloudless. And the big lady in the purple dress sees the little girl. . . .

His eyes skimmed the rest of the page.
"Jesus God!"

The little girl has blue overalls on. And a white shirt. And a red scarf like tied around her head.

And the big lady in the purple dress comes around the pond. And the little girl stares. And she runs.

The big lady runs after. She lifts up her skirt to run faster.

Just before she gets to the woods, the little girl stumbles on a log. She falls down. The big lady is over her.

The little girl screams. The big lady in the purple dress puts her fingers on the little girl's throat. The big lady squeezes.

The little girl's eyes get big. Her tongue comes out. The big lady shakes her. The big lady drops her.

The little girl lays there, and the big lady goes back around the pond.

Hastily, revulsion gagging him like nausea, he shoved the single page beneath the stack of other stories.
"Jesus God," Pierce whispered.

October

Chapter 6

The Mississippi was an immense black presence to his left. He passed through one dingy little river village after another, most of them asleep by now. But Pierce knew the river never slept, and occasionally he saw the lights of a barge or other vessel pushing toward the Gulf of Mexico.

The Great River Road was a succession of serpentine curves demanding total concentration. His jaw was clenched and his hands glued high on the steering wheel. He remembered that local boosters used to call this the Rhine Valley of the Midwest.

"The big lady in the purple dress puts her fingers on the little girl's throat. . . ."

Oh, Christ! He ought to burn it.

It had been five days since Amanda Gatliffe had turned it in to him. Each day he dragged it out and read it again. Now he knew it word for word.

Five days in which he hadn't written a word. Dreading the next class he must teach. Having to endure Amanda Gatliffe. And Britt and her tarty, teasing con games. None of it relevant to the only thing that really mattered.

Pierce crossed the river north of Red Wing, where Wisconsin 35 became Minnesota 10. The bridge was a narrow, twinkling strand of lights that seemed to float endlessly in the void between the blackness of the river and the blackness of the sky.

He had come to La Soeur to find the Corinne of old.

The idea had seemed so simple. Getting close to her roots would ignite something within him. So simple. Cause and effect.

47

The effect had occurred in Chicago last August. The cause must be here in La Soeur.

And when he knew the cause he'd go through the catharsis of reliving what they thought was their love and what they experienced instead. Relive it through the act of writing the novel about her. And, in writing it, erase forever the image of those glaring eyes.

The brights of an oncoming car did not dim. They were like eyes drilling into him.

"Damn you!" he yelled at the driver. And again he saw those other eyes he could never hide from.

He pulled into a self-service gas station and turned back toward La Soeur.

He had not found her here. Not yet. But where else could he look?

Not in Chicago. Not in their town house. He'd tried it and failed. There should have been something of her lingering in those rooms. It should have been easier to evoke recollections of her there. But the power of those dead eyes was too strong.

In his wallet he carried a snapshot of the two of them, taken at the opening of her Barrington shop. Frequently he had to refer to that photo to remember what she had looked like. The only memory that came easily now was of the thing suspended from the macramé hanging.

He flipped on the car radio to his favorite country music station. The sequence of tales—lost love, restless wanderings, true faith in the midst of turmoil—was strangely comforting.

He turned off on Wisconsin 82, making the wide sweep around La Soeur's southern edge.

If he could not find the answer here, in this trip back in time, then where?

To his right was Meadowbluff Country Club and, somewhere near its farthest eastern reaches, Ralph Hungerford's home. And Britt's.

Well, there would be no more classes.

He passed the Kennilworth Motel, set fashionably against the western foot of Frenchman's Pitch.

On impulse he cut onto the road that led to the top. He had been up there three times since his return to La Soeur but always during the day. The view of the city and the Mississippi beyond was unrivaled.

They'd called it "The Pinnacle" in good-natured derision. Because it was, after all, only twelve hundred feet above sea level and only eight hundred feet above the golf course and the Kennilworth—even if there was no higher point of land in this county.

Yet, once on the outermost promontory, it was a formidable height. The slopes down to the base were steep and in many places sheer. Pierce had done an obit on an aspiring rock climber who perished trying to scale the overhang just below the summit on the southwestern face.

The twisting road had been built to climb at a very graduated rate, so it was a long drive—Pierce gauged it at a mile and a half—to the flattened crown. There were two cars in the parking lot, five hundred yards from the stone pathways circling the peak.

No overhead lights illuminated the bluff. The county did not wish to encourage anyone to loiter after dark. A sign warned that Frenchman's Pitch was closed at ten P.M.

For the first time that evening a quarter moon grew dimly visible. Pierce sat in the car a long while, as he and Corinne had done in the old Hornet. Not to embrace, not to make out, not the usual reasons for coming to the Pitch.

Here they would hold hands. No more. And talk. For hours.

What a windy, callow, self-centered bore I must've been, he thought. Droning on and on about the minutiae of the job, the odds on getting a reporting berth on a bigger paper in a bigger city, the dreams of fiction writing.

And she had listened patiently. In the moonlight he had studied that exquisite pale profile, cherishing the subtle changes in line and shape as her head tilted or nodded or turned fully toward him.

He half-closed his eyes and left his mind open to his reveries. But he could see not even a flickering, shadowy replica of that profile. Nothing.

Two boys raced each other from the top of the point to the VW parked next to Pierce. Neither looked old enough to possess a driver's license. The Beetle zoomed backward out of the lot.

He remembered Corinne gripping his hand as they sat here and he'd spoken of the far-off day when he would write his first novel.

"After that, of course, we will live on Martha's Vineyard or in the Hamptons," she'd said in a stuffy tone she affected sometimes to mimic a Bryn Mawr accent.

"Sure. And just where are the Hamptons?"

"Somewhere east of here. We'll find 'em. Leave it to me." She'd laughed. "And the dedication?"

"To you, naturally. My inspiration! My muse! My better half!"

"No. To our firstborn." Her voice had grown very soft. "It should say, 'To my first beloved child.' Wouldn't that be sweet?"

"And the second book?"

"To our secondborn."

"And the books after that?"

She'd tousled his hair, chuckling. "Depends on how prolific you are. In writing—and whatever."

Pierce got out of the car and walked up the pathway. Their firstborn? Corinne had spoken of children often in those days. And later. Before and after the miscarriages.

We could still have had children. There was still time, Corinne was still young. . . .

The air was mild and he need not have bothered with his whipcord jacket. He passed the old stone redoubt that had been rubble for a century or more and continued to the highest swelling of land.

The city was a maze of light. Past it, the river glided like a black snake, girded by the three shimmering bands that linked the two states. Farther away, the sparsely scattered lights of rural Minnesota were faint pinpricks.

The world spread majestically before him and the sky magnificently above him. With an almost electrical jolt he recalled how he had felt standing here with Corinne.

He had felt as if it could all be his. The dreams he'd confided to her. Attainable. His for the asking.

Because she was beside him. And she exuded energy and power. A power that filled him with a bubbling sense of near invincibility.

He breathed deeply. Yes. With Corinne he had felt more alive than he ever had before. Or since.

Pierce stepped back on the path and was aware of a tingling at the back of his neck. Something had been scratching at him for attention.

A sound, almost subliminal. He'd heard it for minutes, he realized. So low as to hardly penetrate the conscious threshold. But now it was louder.

At first he thought it was a musical instrument, playing a keening, somber measure over and over again. Then he became certain it was a human voice.

Pierce looked around him.

A five-foot-high cyclone fence enclosed the southern and western perimeters of the bluff and extended a short way to the northern side, where the terrain descended more gently and merged with thick woods. Within the fenced enclosure were a few picnic tables and two weathered, coin-operated binocular machines that had been taken out of service after Labor Day.

The fence was more cautionary than restrictive. There was a gap between the south and westerly sections. It was also a simple matter to slip around the innermost edge of the short span of fence on the northern side of the bluff.

In fact, beyond the fence extensive footpaths led to the farthest extremes of the outcropping. Several times he and Corinne had ventured out to those limits. The place was always littered with beer cans. Obviously many had not been daunted by the fence.

The sound was still relatively subdued, nearly inaudible. But it was insistent and monotonous.

And there was something unnatural about it.

He judged that it came from somewhere near the southwestern ledge, the slab above the steepest drop-off.

He took the northern footpath, picking his way with caution. Near the trees the trail disappeared in darkness. But the curdled yellow of the moon had dissipated much of the solid blackness of the night sky, and when he swung around to the western face, the ground was clearly lit.

It dawned on him that the sound was a chant. He paused, inclined to go back. The chant was high, throbbing, inhuman. The words not just foreign but of another place, another time.

Incomprehensible words. Words of jarring sibilance and thick grunts. "Boibee! Loth! Ngame!"

As he hesitated, the rhythm of the chant changed. The voice glided upward. It became more strident. And another word was added.

One he knew.

And with a sickening wrench he knew the chanter.

Inch by inch he crept forward, toward the ledge above the steepest drop-off. He crouched, eased farther toward the edge, and saw her.

Winnie Stabo gazed upward at the moon, her arms widespread. She was a jutting column of blackness against the sheen of the hazy stars.

She hurled once more into the night the jumbled syllables of her ancient chant. To them she added a screeching coda of petition: "Jenn-if-er! Jenn-if-er!"

Pierce backed away.

He cupped both hands around the coffee, welcoming the warmth. He had fled to the Appleland Inn as to a trusted friend's house, seeking the known, the commonplace.

It comforted him to see the red-patterned chintz curtains, the kitsch of the steer-headed cream pitchers. And, most of all, the cheery, fair-skinned, gum-chewing waitresses in their hospital-like white slacks and patterned brown jackets.

This was reality again. Unlike what he had seen on Frenchman's Pitch.

Al, is this the gentle kind of beauty you and Winnie found here?

Sally Berwyn had smiled somewhat sheepishly when he'd entered. She breezed by, carrying an order to the kitchen, and tossed out, "I don't usually do that, you know."

When she returned, he asked, "Do what?"

She placed a plate of acorn squash—the "harvest special"—in front of a customer and walked back to Pierce.

"That story I wrote for class. I don't usually listen to conversations. Oh, I hear bits and pieces. And you can't help but be interested sometimes. But, really, I wasn't snooping on you."

She hurried back to the kitchen, hurried out again, laden with plates.

"I thought what you wrote was great," he said as she passed.

She scooped up silverware to set another place at the counter, then came over to him, smiling with more assurance. "I was hoping you wouldn't be offended."

"That was a marvelous sketch. I don't care how you got the idea."

"Well, it was a private conversation. You and your friend. And I didn't hear much of it, really. I just got . . . well, impressions. A sense of the situation. And I took it from there.

And, really, when you threw that assignment at us, I had to think of *something*. I was kind of desperate."

She put a glass of water on the counter for a new arrival. Her long hair was pulled back tightly again. It was the color that would begin flickering throughout the countryside in perhaps another week—a deep rust—before autumn burst into the full, brilliant flames of mid- and late October.

"I really did know who you were," she said. "I recognized you right away. From your picture on the dust jacket of *Tidings of Comfort*. So I suppose I was inclined to tune in on your conversation more than I should have."

Her face was lightly festooned with freckles. Although she was only somewhere in her mid-twenties, he noticed that tiny laugh wrinkles already had formed at the corners of her wide hazel eyes.

Absently, she swept a wet cloth over a few drops of coffee he'd spilled. "I really loved *Tidings*. Not just because someone who used to live in La Soeur wrote it. But because I really loved the people in it."

"Miss!" An elderly woman tapped a menu. Sally hurried over to her.

"Anything else, sir?" one of the blondes asked Pierce.

"That's all." He debated whether to tell Sally there'd be no class this Thursday. Or any other Thursday. But she was busy with another customer. Best to let the library inform her. And the others. Especially Britt.

The phone was ringing as he opened the door to his motel room.

"Hi. It's Britt. Can I talk you into having a drink with me Thursday after class?"

He paused and then wondered what he was pausing for. Hadn't he already decided to cancel the class? He remembered

54

the desolation on top of Frenchman's Pitch and the sight of Winnie Stabo imploring an answer from the empty night.

"Sure," he said.

That night Pierce sat up until two A.M. reading last week's assignments.

Chapter 7

"From now on you'll be analyzing each other's work," Pierce told them. "That's the most effective way to learn this peculiar craft."

He looked from Britt to Max, who had again come in together and sat next to each other in the first row.

"Please remember that no criticism is meant to be personal. It's meant only to assist the writer and the class. So let's keep our egos under wraps when we're being critiqued. Who'd like to start?"

The bearded advertising copywriter delivered a stand-up comedy monologue. Then old Mrs. Siegerson favored them with the final chapter of her children's book, in which the black sheep Wally Woolly emerges a pure and spotless white after his immersion in the miraculous waters of the Jordan.

Pierce noted that Max Fischer had once more unloaded the contents of his briefcase and was burrowing into his legal work.

"Next?"

Out of the corner of his eyes he watched Amanda Gatliffe. If she volunteered he would pretend not to notice her. He had hoped she would not return tonight. But again her young escort, prancing and jabbering, had led her to her seat. And she had brought a story with her—her thick, clasped hands resting on the two wrinkled pages.

Pierce quickly nodded to a matronly woman who had raised her hand. In a slow and mesmerizing manner she described in excruciating detail a retired English teacher's trip abroad.

As he had during the first class, Pierce swung his eyes to Britt.

"Through an intricate irrigation system, small channels called levados permit the flow of water from high in Madeira's mountains to the villages below . . ."

This time Britt did not smile her knowing, flirty smile. But her eyes met his, directly, unswervingly, and so they remained until the interminable story ended.

"Next week something new," Pierce announced. "Any subject. But it has to be different than what you did for today. Turn in this week's stories as you leave, please."

Britt, buttoning her coat, dropped a note in front of him. It read, "I'll be waiting." She bent over Max Fischer to speak. Pierce heard him say "But—" as she walked off.

"I wish you'd volunteered," Pierce told Sally Berwyn when she passed his desk.

"Not this soon in the game," the waitress said, laughing. "I'm one of those people that needs a couple of others to go off the diving board first."

Just in time, Pierce saw the worshipful devotee so determined to carry him off for coffee relentlessly bearing down on him.

"Sorry, can't make it tonight." He grinned at her. To fend off whatever other invitations she might have prepared, he touched the shoulder of a burly black man who'd worn a perpetual scowl throughout the evening.

"Mr. Evans. May I have a word with you? I'm quite impressed by the work you turned in."

"That so?" The question was wary, almost suspicious.

"Yes. It's good. Quite good."

It had taken Pierce totally unawares when he'd read it. At least thirty thousand words, written in longhand on legal-size yellow paper. Atrocious and frequent grammatical and spelling errors. But by the fourth page he was engrossed. It was the story of an infantry platoon training for duty in Vietnam. The people were real, the raw material compelling.

"How long have you been at this?"

" 'Bout a year. Grindin' it out inch by inch. What you have is maybe a fourth of what it'll be. I try to give it some time every day. Dependin' on what shift I'm on."

"What line are you in?"

"Sheriff's department. I'm a deputy."

"I'd like to talk to you some more about this book. Editing it and marketing it."

" 'Preciate it."

Pierce closed the door behind him and walked through the empty library, past the towering shelves of books. The janitor had extinguished most of the lights, but there were enough overheads on to find his way out.

"Hi, you," she said, materializing from around a corner.

"Oh, hi. Thought you'd be outside."

"Occurred to me it wouldn't seem too cool, just hanging around your car. I don't care to run into Max out there."

"Can't Max be civilized about this?"

"We'll find out, won't we?"

She pulled his head forward and kissed him quickly, lightly. He put his arms around her, pressing hard against her lips.

Someone began whistling loudly and exuberantly.

Pierce spun around. "The janitor," Britt whispered.

From out of a shadowy section of book stacks far across the room, a figure emerged, sauntering jauntily, hands in pockets. The young man who'd accompanied Amanda Gatliffe stopped, a look of utter astonishment on his face as though he had just noticed them. He extended his arms, seemingly overcome by the grandeur of his surroundings.

"Lordy, ain't it glorious what you can learn in a library?" His high voice produced tinny echoes in the stillness.

"You've got no business here," Pierce snapped.

"Waitin' for Manda. She's in the ladies' room, Manda is." He hitched a thumb toward the rear of the building.

"You ought to be on your way, Emil," Britt said. "You and your mother."

"Soon as she's ready." He gave an extravagant wink. "Can't rush a lady, you know. Not a lady like Manda."

Pierce slammed against the push bar on the front door, flinging it open. He led Britt out.

Behind them, a last shout, "Enjoy yourself!"

Then loud, ugly, sucking sounds, followed by uncontrollable cackling.

"That's Amanda's son?" Pierce switched on his ignition.

"Yep. Emil and Amanda. Quite a pair."

"Just who is she? And why is she in this class?"

"She's a local character. A widow. Her husband was an older man, a retired Army sergeant. A drunk. She and the kid have lived off his insurance and his pension. You don't see her around town much. I don't know why she's in this course. The kid you see everywhere. Do I get to pick the spot where we have our drink?"

"You name it, you got it."

"An old hangout. Down by the river. Just off Wharf Row. You may know the joint. The Ace High."

"Sure, I remember it. You won't meet any of Ralph's golfing cronies there. A couple of us from the paper used to stop in there when we wanted to wallow in the backwaters of life."

"Same place. Probably even tackier now. Hang a left here and keep on this street. Some of the old reporters still come in once in a while."

"You don't mind? If anyone sees us?"

"Sugar, they've seen me there plenty of times before. Single. Married. Alone. At the Ace High they don't bother you if you don't want them to. Oh, it's a helluva spot to pick up leads and tips. I used to consider the place part of my beat when I was Susie Deadline, crime reporter."

The tavern was set well back from the street, next to a rickety warehouse that dated from the great days of Mississippi commerce. There was a front and a side door to the Ace High, and although it had been sixteen years, Pierce instinctively went to the side door. That was how the regulars always entered.

Inside it was exactly how he remembered it, including the huge muskellunge mounted on the wall and the faded nineteenth-century lithograph of the riverboat *Belle of La Soeur.* The building was exceptionally long and narrow, and the bar extended the full length of it. There were no windows. Smoke and the smell of beer were thick in the air. Roger Miller's "Squaws Along the Yukon" blared from the jukebox. It struck Pierce that the same record had been played incessantly back in his days on the *Sentinel.*

Britt indicated one of the high, dark, wooden booths that ran from the side to the front door. "Memories of my misspent youth," Pierce said, taking in the half-filled bar.

"We can talk a bit here," she said.

"If you mean your epic about Mae and Ray—don't bother sending it to *Atlantic Monthly.*"

She smiled, but only the tips of her teeth showed. "That was just for kicks. I'll get serious next time. I damn sure will. I meant it, I hope you realize, about doing something with my writing. I've been a reporter, and a good one, and I'm not going to let that part of me stagnate. I'm having a draft beer."

"Make it two," Pierce told the waiter. "How long have you been out of the business?"

"Four years. Since I married Ralph. The publisher's wife can scarcely spend her days chasing fire engines. Or so Ralph felt. I guess he's right. Besides, I'd done it for years. Much as I loved it, can you be a police reporter in a place like this all your life?"

The beers arrived. They clinked steins and drank.

"There are other papers," he pointed out.

"Other papers. TV. The big city. Maybe I could've made it. I think maybe I could've. I've got the knack and I've got the drive. I mean, a chesty broad who can talk without saying "you know" and can actually write a simple declarative sentence—the big time is supposed to be screaming for somebody like that. Right? But I couldn't be sure. I had to think. What if I flubbed it? What if I wound up in another burg like La Soeur? But without a Ralph?"

She tapped the table with her fingers, and Pierce noticed for the first time that they were long, graceful, and well tended. Her wedding ring was dazzling: an enormous, many-faceted diamond surmounting a cluster of finely cut, smaller diamonds.

"So I got security. But I miss the street action. Sure, now I can nag Ralph to get a reporter after this or that story. But, hell, I'm ten levels removed from the excitement. And Ralph owns the newspaper, he and that cartel of his. But much as I hate to say it—"

"Ralph's not really a newspaperman."

She raised her stein to hide her smile. "No. He doesn't really give a damn how they run it, day to day, as long as the profits are there and nobody's filed a libel suit. That agency of his, the PR, the printing company—that's what he gets off on. That, and maybe politics."

"You'd take Capitol Hill by storm, Britt."

She chugalugged her beer. "I thought of that," she said, wiping the foam from her mouth with the back of her hand. "Christ, have I thought of that."

She drew in a huge breath and let her eyes close. "But that's all chancy, Whit. I need something now. Not just something to keep me busy. There's plenty of that. But something to prove that I am what I know I am: a damn fine reporter. I need to make it clear to this community that I am more than the publisher's wife. That I can accomplish something besides wheedling a wedding ring out of Ralph Hungerford."

Her eyes barely opened, and a self-satisfied smile spread across her face. The tip of her tongue slid lazily back and forth against the edges of her two front teeth.

"And I'm already on to what it is."

He drained the last of his own beer. "What is it?"

"The murder of Angela Karlstrom."

"Oh?"

"The young woman they found in the Old Military Cemetery."

"I know. What about it?"

"I want to crack that case. Crack it and write about it."

"Why?"

"It's a terrible crime. A spectacular crime. A crime the sheriff's department is not about to figure out."

"Why do you think you could?"

"I'm smart and I'm pushy. Whit, it's doing something . . . *fulfilling* for a change! I've already started digging into it, and the juices are flowing again! When I get up in the morning, there's something important to get done!"

She pounced on his right hand, brushed it excitedly. "Why don't you come in on it with me?"

"Me? Why me?"

"You've got the background. The research skills. The writing skills. Whit, if we get lucky, this could be a national article or even a goddam book!"

"Why do you need help?"

She let go of his hand and pushed herself back from the table. "I can't do it alone. I need to bounce ideas off somebody. I need somebody who can be somewhere when I'm somewhere else. Somebody I can work with. Somebody I like to be with. Think about it! Just think about it!"

"Look, Britt, that's a major commitment. Let's have another beer and—"

She picked up his hand again and stroked it. "I have to be going now. I told Ralph I wouldn't be late."

"I thought we might—"

She shook her head. "Ralph wanted to talk about plans for Indian Summer Days. I'm pretty active in it every year. He created it and he gets terribly wound up over it."

They drove in silence back to the library, but she slid her body closer to his and her left hand squeezed his knee.

Finally she said again, "Just think about it. I think we'd make a helluva team."

"Did you ask Max what you asked me? To be on your team?"

"Not as bluntly. But, yes."

"And what did he say?"

"He wouldn't have time. And, anyway, it'd be crazy."

"It would be."

"Here's the lot. That's mine, the—"

"I can guess. The Continental. Mark Six, isn't it?"

"Ralph likes to indulge me. What do you say, Whit?"

He parked and switched off the headlamps. "Were you and Max making it all along, or was that your way of getting him interested in your project?"

She returned his look, levelly, coolly. "Life and business are a series of trade-offs. I learned that early. I bargain with what I've got. What else has anybody got to bargain with? But I never give what I don't want to give, just because there's something I want that bad to get. If I give, it's part of the bargain, all right. But it's because I love the giving, too."

Her hand floated up the inside of his thigh.

"It'd be good for you, too, Whit," she said softly. "I know what you've been through. Sure, it's been hell. But you've got to come out of it. There's something about you that's . . . shell-shocked or something. This would get you out of it. This would be doing a *story!* This is going to get you alive and kicking again, Whit!"

She slipped out the door and peered through the half-open window. "What do you say?"

"I'll have to think about it."

"All right. But think about one thing, Whit: This would be fun!"

Britt dashed to her car.

* * *

The next morning he tossed the pile of manuscripts on the bed, climbed in, and began reading. Neither of the two chairs in the motel room was comfortable for more than ten minutes at a time, and he had gradually turned the bed into his office, library, and snack bar.

He read rapidly, appending his comments in red ink.

Another science-fiction tale from the small man with the tic.

A two-page story of thwarted love that he recognized as a plot stolen from the movie *An Affair to Remember*. It must have been shown on TV last week, he thought.

Again, Sally Berwyn's submission was rewarding. She called it "Gene in January," and it was light, poignant, and professional. A young woman awaits the arrival of the man she met and married during a dizzying holiday courtship at a ski resort. Now they are settling in to begin their workaday lives. And will she, who loved the dashing Gene of December, even tolerate the Gene of January?

It was a pretty piece of froth, and he thought it might sell to one of the slick women's magazines.

He added the new material from Nehemiah Evans to what he'd already been given and spent the rest of the evening slowly absorbing the deputy's Vietnam novel. The story needed more polish and more craft. But he knew his initial impression was right. This would be a book of rare power.

At noon he got to his feet, stretched, and considered the only remaining unread story: Amanda Gatliffe's.

Pierce looked out through the dingy venetian blinds. The day was golden with sunshine, without blemish, crystalline in its purity. The memory of Corinne that had come back to him on Frenchman's Pitch returned once more, insinuatingly. The memory of what Corinne had once instilled in him, just by her presence. A feeling of life surging, overflowing with endless possibilities.

Strange how he had forgotten the effect she had on him.

Once she had quickened his instinct to embrace life. Then, two months ago, she had sought to suffocate it.

"This is going to get you alive and kicking again, Whit," Britt Hungerford had told him last night.

How? When I share my days and nights with those dead green eyes?

He went back to the bed. Without realizing it he had put off reading Amanda Gatliffe's story as long as he could.

Now he picked up the two pages she had written. He held them carefully, by the edges, as if hesitant to even touch the words.

But he read.

> The girl sits in the car. She smokes. She puts the window down a little. She throws the cigarette out.
>
> She is nervous. She sits there a long time. It is hot in the car. She puts the window down some more.
>
> She looks around a lot. It is dark out. Night. She sees trees and some tombstones.
>
> She is in a graveyard. She looks at her watch.
>
> She tries to light one of the cigarettes. She is nervous and her hand shakes. Her thumb keeps hitting the cigarette lighter, but it does not work.
>
> She gets out of the car and looks around. It is hot. There is a bridge. She tries to light the cigarette again.
>
> The big lady in the purple dress comes from around the tree.
>
> The girl tries to get back in the car. The girl screams. The big lady sticks the knife in her back. The girl runs. The big lady pushes her down. Next to a tombstone. There is a lot of blood. The girl says, "No, no."
>
> The big lady in the purple dress bends over and sticks the knife in the girl's throat. And then a lot of other parts.
>
> The big lady goes away.

Pierce let the papers fall from his fingers. He went back to the window and gazed out. He was standing there when Britt called.

"I'm going out to the Old Military Cemetery. Where they found Angela Karlstrom. Want to meet me there?"

"All right."

Chapter 8

He'd never been there before, even during his days on the *Sentinel.* It was a ten-minute drive on the Interstate heading northeast, a few miles on a state highway, and then a long stretch on a county dirt road.

It was still too early these first days of October for the full explosion of autumn foliage. There were swatches of yellow, chestnut, and rust all around him but nothing bright or vivid.

The farmland on either side of the road seemed utterly deserted, not a human figure in sight. A herd of cattle looked inanimate, blurred spots of white, like timeworn boulders. Pale gold lingered in the fields of ripe soybeans, wheat, hybrid corn, and—new since his time—broad patches of sunflowers raised for fall harvesting.

He took a graveled turnoff and after several minutes saw the steepled arch over the cemetery and—as he drew abreast of it—her lemon-colored Mark Six well within the fenced-in enclosure.

He parked behind her in the rutted entranceway.

"Hi, you," she said. She wore striped jogging pants, half-boots, and a tight, fluffy, wool pullover. Her eyes were concealed behind huge, curved sunglasses. "Glorious day!"

"Beautiful."

"I thought we might as well begin at the beginning. Let's talk about it."

They leaned against the hood of the Continental. The cemetery was small, not more than twenty or thirty graves. Most of the headstones were well-worn slabs of slate. Weeds and wild flowers grew in lavish profusion.

"She was parked just short of where your car is. I know. I paced it off before you got here. Sixty yards from the road."

"That's from the newspaper story?"

"That's from the sheriff's department report. I told you I've done some digging already."

The wind felt good on his face. It was insistent but with no real bite, a cool caress, as though this were a day in late summer. An occasional gust lifted the boughs of the poplars and willows within the cemetery. They sighed and creaked.

Britt walked to a spot on the narrow lane. "Right here."

"There wouldn't be anything to mark it. Not after the police. Not after the gapers that must've trampled up the place."

"Nothing. I looked hard." She took seven steps and stopped by a headstone.

"This is where they found her."

Pierce looked down. The slate stone was slightly askew, the words on it badly faded:

ERNEST R. JACKSON, PVT. There was some military designation that was not legible.

"The paper said she was a yard or two from the car. Right beside a tombstone. The homicide report was more specific. It gave the name on the stone. This one. She was on her back. There were stab wounds in her—"

"I'll look at the report later, if you've got a copy of it. When did they find her?"

"Not till noon the next day. And then only because her father got pissed off and thought she'd run off with his Dodge. He described the car, and one of the deputies remembered seeing it parked here earlier that morning."

"Her father didn't get concerned until the next day?"

"Not Hugh Karlstrom. Apparently he kept expecting she'd come tooling in any minute. He told the deputies she'd stayed out all night a couple of times before."

"That brings up the obvious point, Britt. I'm sure it's the angle the cops are working."

"The boyfriend?"

"Of course. Look, this was a ghastly thing. But it's not the crime of the century. The odds are that when they find the guy who was with her, the mystery is over—and it won't have been much of a mystery."

He remembered his first thoughts when he'd read the headline on the Angela Karlstrom murder story: commonplace. Pathetic but commonplace.

"Look, you know how it must've been. They drove out here. To talk. To make out. She wouldn't come across. Or she wanted to break off with him. Or she thought she was pregnant by him. God, you know the whole dreary range of possibilities."

"Well, they haven't found a boyfriend."

"Not *a* boyfriend? Or *the* boyfriend?"

"No kind of boyfriend. She apparently hadn't dated any boys for a year or more. There were some hot and heavy romances in high school. But since she got out, no boys. Anyway, none she was seen with or talked about with her friends."

"Some guy from another town. Some guy she met that night."

"There was no physical evidence of anybody else in the car. Admittedly that doesn't prove there wasn't. But there was nothing tangible to show that anybody else was there. They took the car to the state crime lab for a real overhaul. The ashes in the ashtray—her brand of cigarettes. There also were pipe ashes. Her father's a pipe smoker. He'd used the car that afternoon."

"Fingerprints?"

"All they found were hers and her father's and some from a woman her father dates. Of course, things like door handles and steering wheels do get so smeared, so that a lot of the time there's no way to pull off a good print."

Pierce strolled over to the spiked, cast-iron fence running perpendicularly to the dirt road. From here he could see how the land sloped down to the shallow creek that edged sluggishly past the cemetery. More willows stood in clumps along the banks.

He looked at the bridge—narrow, stubby, with rust-colored steel guardrails—spanning the creek.

"What you seem to make a case for," he murmured, "is that she was alone in the car."

"That's a distinct possibility."

"Then why the hell was she out here? In the middle of the night?"

"Nobody's figured that one out. Her father says she took the car about nine and didn't say where she was going. Never did, evidently. The sheriff's boys haven't found anyone who saw Angela or the car anywhere that night."

"Look," Pierce said, "I want to show you something." He reached into his jacket pocket and, without a word, he handed her Amanda Gatliffe's two stories.

Britt read them and exhaled heavily. She was quiet a moment.

"You got one crazy lady in your class, teacher."

"That's what I think. No more than that."

"No? I don't know."

"She's read about these crimes. Heard them talked about. They're simmering in there, inside her. So, when somebody says, 'Tell me a story,' that's what comes out."

"These are sick, Whit. Too sick to just forget about."

"When I read the first one, it was bad enough. I figured it had to be about Al Stabo's little girl. Well, I thought, as bad as that is, maybe she had some private fixation with that case. But then the next one. Obviously the Angela Karlstrom thing. Two unrelated killings."

"But not in her mind."

"No. That's the really strange part. In a sense she's just reporting what she's heard. Reporting it in her own way. Details

70

she could've gotten in the paper or heard on TV. That wouldn't take much imagination."

He laughed harshly. "But then she got *creative.*"

"The big lady in the purple dress."

"Did she think, 'This is a creative writing class, so I've got to add some original touch'? Is she capable of thinking that?"

"That's one thing we can find out! That's one thing we can begin checking!"

Britt placed her hands on her hips and arched her back, stretching in a smooth, catlike motion. "We're making a start, Whit! By God, we're already making a start!"

They walked slowly amid the headstones, scuffing absently at weeds, arms touching occasionally. Her voice fell to its lowest register, deep and husky, but it grew increasingly animated. The words cascaded from her.

"So we've got to see Amanda. It may be nothing. But then, who knows? This thing just dropped into our laps. We have to follow through. Not just talk to her but other people, too. Anyone who knows anything about her. And don't forget Emil—that kid of hers. God, he's creepy. Last night at the library—what kind of act was that? He is an actor, you know. I mean, instinctively. Amazingly good. We roped him into a play at the Theatre Guild last year. *Charley's Aunt,* of all the old chestnuts. God, he was convincing. Brilliant, really. You should've seen him swishing around in that fright wig and gingham hoop skirt. He's a chameleon. Be anything you want him to be. Be anybody he wants to be. But he'd skip rehearsals. Fake his way through, not learn his lines, act snotty. Absolutely no discipline. So he dropped out of the cast."

"What does he do for a living?"

"Nothing, as far as I know. He got bounced out of school."

"You'd said something about Amanda's late husband."

"A minor story a couple years ago. He came home late one winter night, drunk, as usual. Smashed his skull on the front steps. Amanda found him there in the morning. She was still black and blue where he'd beaten her up the evening before. Apparently he was in the habit of kicking the shit out of her and Emil."

"But it was an accident?"

"Who knows? Nobody saw him fall. Mrs. Gatliffe is a little strange. So there were some raised eyebrows."

"It might be best to pass these stories along to the authorities."

She shook her head. "They wouldn't know what to do with them. Not at this stage. Believe me, I know the sheriff and I know his investigators. Two cars meet head-on at sixty miles an hour and they're able to figure out the cause of death. Anything more complicated than that, forget it! Vigo Lustgarten—he's the sheriff—hasn't learned a new fact since he fell off his motorcycle, back when he used to ride up and down in that big Harley Liberator with the sidecar, giving tickets to speeders."

They had reached the edge of the cemetery farthest from the road. Three fat squirrels were chattering near the base of a tree just beyond the fence. Pierce gazed over the stippled fields and forested hills. A distant stretch of green had the landscaped look of a large apple orchard.

"We'll go to Vigo when we've got enough to spell it out for him in words of one syllable. But right now it's our move. We've got one lead. Okay? It may turn out. It may not. But we're off the dime!"

Her face shone with excitement. She gripped the pointed fence posts with both hands and kicked a light tattoo against the lower rail.

"We're going to do it, Whit. Set this town back on its ass! God damn it, we are already off and running!"

She spun around, mouth open, her breast grazing his chest.

Without thinking, Pierce took her roughly by the shoulders and kissed her.

Instantly she laced her hands around his buttocks and crushed her trunk tightly against his. Her lips were soft, searching, gluttonous. The scent of her lush, feral perfume choked him.

He groaned and bent her backward. She went limp, so that all of her weight was in his arms and he was easing her slowly to the ground. The moment her back touched the earth she clasped his right hand and brought it up under her sweater.

"Britt," he gasped. Prone amid the high grass this far back from the arched entranceway, they could not be seen from the road. But their cars could be. And it was broad daylight. And anyone walking in the adjacent fields or by that nearby creek . . .

She wore nothing under the sweater. She placed his hand firmly on one breast. Pierce felt the nipple ripening under his forefinger, and then the blood was suddenly pounding in his head.

"Sugar," she whispered in his ear.

Then it was too late for any other words, for any other thoughts. Hunger ignited and possessed him. He was one thing only: a need that must be met.

She held him, guided him.

He threw his full weight upon her. She rose up, as if struggling against him, and he ground down hard upon her, with all that he was, all of his hunger. All of his desperation.

Then there was the sound of air inhaled deeply, and he realized it was his own breathing and that the pounding pressure had gone.

Her cheek was against his mouth, and he kissed her. "You okay, sugar?"

"Oh, God, Britt, yes . . . I'm sorry. It must've seemed . . . Christ, so callous. . . ."

"Why the hell should it?" She laughed softly. "I figured it'd been a while for you. I figured there's been a hell of a lot of steam building."

"God, it must've taken me all of . . . What? Hell, it'd take me longer to run a hundred-yard dash."

"Well, it's been a while since anybody's been quite that frantic."

"Britt, I'm so goddam sorry. I've never been . . ."

"I'll take it as a kind of tribute." She adjusted her sunglasses. She had never removed them. There had not been time. "Forget it, Whit. I mean it."

She squeezed the nape of his neck. "You look like a healthy specimen. Quick to recuperate. So I'm giving you a twenty-minute break. Then it's my turn."

"Let's get back to town then."

"Why? It's gorgeous out here today." She dressed swiftly, without rising. She held his hand, and they ambled along beside the fence.

They passed her Mark Six and his Pontiac and looked inevitably at Private Ernest Jackson's weathered headstone.

"Poor Private Ernest," she said. "Whit, I'm going to tell Ralph you're working with me on this. It could head off some problems later."

"Fine."

"I already told him I'm nosing around in this case."

"What'd he say?"

"Not much. As if I said I was getting into another charity drive or a Theatre Guild play. Just another project to keep the little woman out of mischief. All he really said was, don't bother the people on the paper any more than you have to."

"Have you?"

"Not much. I don't think they know anything more than they've put in their stories. Hell, they should've assigned a task force to dig into this thing. Knowing Sheriff Vigo's limitations. But there's never been much initiative on the *Sewer* when it comes to spending a few extra nickels to land a big story. Another reason we've got a clear shot at it."

She opened her car and pulled out a stadium blanket of brilliant aquamarine, crisscrossed with black geometric figures.

"This is for picnics, I tell Ralph." She folded the blanket and slung it over her shoulder.

"What's your source at the sheriff's office?" Pierce asked.

"Vigo himself. He owes me, from the old days when I covered that beat. And he needs the paper's support. We endorse him every election, God knows why. He told me what he knew and even let me have a copy of the Karlstrom file. But he wasn't happy about it, and I can't push him too much more. He wouldn't let me talk to the investigators he's got on the case. Didn't want me bothering them, he said."

"Would Nehemiah Evans be of any help?"

"Deputy Evans?"

"That's right. He's in our class."

"That's Deputy Evans? The big guy with the glare that'd break glass from ten feet away? I didn't realize it. I knew they finally let a black deputy into the department, but I never met him. The official report says a Deputy Evans was the first one on the scene. He's the one who found Angela."

"I'll talk to him. But I wouldn't expect he knows much more that he hasn't already reported."

"It's one more possibility. And that contact could lead to another contact. So we're getting an agenda built up. Let's lay out some ground rules."

They agreed to speak together, at least by phone, a minimum of three times a week. Whenever possible, they would conduct an interview together. They would also put their notes in writing.

"Remember," Britt reminded him, "if an article or a book comes out of this, we've got to do more than nail the guilty party. We have got to be colorfully explicit about every goddam thing we did along every step of the way."

"Including this afternoon?"

They had made a complete circuit of the cemetery and were back at the patch of grass and weeds that had been flattened by the impress of their bodies.

"No." She smiled. "But I would damn well love to see your notes about it."

She snapped the blanket out, and at the sudden movement, a squirrel rocketed up the trunk of a poplar to safety on a high branch. Britt let the blanket fall and then she smoothed it. "God, the sun feels good."

She sat down and began to pull off her boots. Pierce hunkered down beside her.

"Oh, my God, what an experience it was my first time. When I was fifteen. It was an apple orchard, and the smell of the blossoms was so rich. To lie there on the earth and see the branches above you and feel the air on your bare skin. God, it's so marvelous!"

Pierce felt the pulses in his wrist starting their fast, hammering blows. Slow this time, he told himself. *Easy, gradual. There is no urgency. None.*

She rose to her feet, and his heart jumped as, in one swift movement, she pulled off her sweater.

"Jesus, Britt!"

Britt, the road! And anyone in those fields . . .

He had not really seen her before, during their first time. Now he stared, and she saw the quick intake of his breath as he caught his first full sight of her. She smiled at him, fondly, and stood motionless for several seconds.

Then she dropped down beside him and folded into his arms.

Slow. Easy. There is no urgency.

He shut his eyes and let himself drift without hurry into the splendor of her body. It was very gradual. He had mastered the intensity of his need, and he continued to will himself to lessen the tempo, to prolong each sensation.

The sun was soothing on his back and legs. Time was not a threat or a matter of concern. It had ceased to exist. Yet a part of him remained acutely aware of their vulnerability.

Crows cawed suddenly, nearby, and he started. Tense, he peered up. Britt laughed huskily, almost a purr, and ran her hands down his spine. He felt the light graze of her wedding ring sliding along the small of his back.

They heard the low drone of a car—a car moving slowly. She felt the stiffening of his shoulders.

"Enjoy," she breathed, pulling his head firmly onto her up-turned breast.

The car continued on, fading into silence.

Moments later, she cried out in ringing, piercing spasms of pleasure. Again he tensed, in surprise and apprehension, believing her voice must be reverberating far over this still country-side. To anyone within earshot, he thought, it must sound like the victim of some savage attack.

Chapter 9

"I was afraid you'd think it was silly," Sally Berwyn said. "A silly story about silly people." She sat opposite Pierce in a booth at the Appleland Inn.

"I think 'Gene in January' could sell. With certain changes. Cut down on the schmaltz. Get into it quicker. The middle of the second page is probably the best place to begin. There's a real flow to what you've done. I can't believe you haven't been spending your spare moments locked in a garret churning out manuscripts."

She rearranged the straws in the chocolate malt she'd brought over from the counter. The backs of her hands were speckled with the same fine freckles that dotted her face.

"No. I've never seen myself as Sally the Writer. With the W in caps."

"What do you see yourself as—in caps?"

"Sally the Teacher. That's what I trained to be. That's what I am."

Pierce took another bite out of his tuna salad sandwich. It was Friday night. Britt and Ralph were attending some grand function at Meadowbluff Country Club. She and Pierce had left the Old Military Cemetery with the understanding that she would call him in the morning. On weekends it would be risky to call her, since it was likely that Ralph would answer.

She'd smiled, and then her yellow Continental had zoomed out of the graveyard, spewing up a geyser of gravel.

"Then," he said to Sally Berwyn, "you're not really Sally the Waitress."

"Only temporarily. Until there's a vacancy in the La Soeur public school system. Just a matter of waiting it out. I already have my degree," she explained, "and I've taught at one of the city's junior high schools for a year. Then I left to teach in Iowa. When I came back to La Soeur, nothing was available."

"What brought you back?"

"My dad. He needs looking after. Cancer. Terminal. He's been all alone since Mom died."

"I'm sorry."

"It happens. But he's tough, and I know it's made me tougher. I've gotten the chance to get to know him better. I was just a kid before, living at home, and he was just daddy. Now he's a friend." She was quiet for a moment. "How's the tuna salad?"

"Excellent."

"The secret is the sweet pickle relish. I told the manager about it. Something I learned in a cooking class."

She made a playful, rueful grimace. "But you must be getting tired of eating here. It's a neat place. Good food. A lot of real characters hanging around. But still . . ."

"I like it."

"Every night?"

"Got to eat somewhere. I live in a motel. No kitchen, no refrigerator. Hadn't expected to stay in La Soeur long. Now it'll be at least another six weeks. Till the course is over. I'm thinking of finding another place."

She seemed to brighten the instant he spoke. Pierce decided that this was a face that could not readily mask what it thought.

"Hey, I know where you can start looking! My Aunt Amy's house. It's empty. She's gone to visit her kids in California till next spring. She'd love to have someone staying there."

"Look, I don't want to put anyone to any trouble."

"No trouble. She asked me to stop by once or twice a week.

Water the plants. See that nobody's broken in. She'd really appreciate somebody living there."

"Okay. I'll take a look. Tomorrow all right?"

"Sure."

"All these characters you say hang around here—have you ever noticed that large woman in our class? Amanda Gatliffe?"

"Not here. I've seen her out on the street. Just moving along. Kind of in her own world."

She stuffed her paper napkin into the empty malt glass. "But her son comes in at night once in a while. Always alone. Always kind of eyeing everybody, taking it all in. Always kind of half-grinning. Not in a friendly way. Sort of smirking. I only served him once. But I remember it."

"Why?"

"Because he walked off with the salt and pepper shakers, the little stinker." She rose. "Well, it's back to being Sally the Waitress again."

"What a lovely day for a call on Amanda." Britt laughed and snuggled up beside him. "Straight ahead, toward the river. Look what I have for you, sugar: a copy of the report from the sheriff's department and my notes on my conversation with Vigo."

"Thanks."

"He also agreed—reluctantly—to talk to me from time to time about what's new on the case. But he's dragging his feet on giving me copies of the stuff he's getting. It was hard enough to make him turn loose the initial report."

"I thought he needed the paper's goodwill."

"He does. But I am not the paper, and he knows it. And he also knows he does not need an uppity housewife cracking this thing before he does."

"He doesn't sound like much of a source."

"Except he can be prodded to put out more. Like I told you, he's indebted."

"Indebted? How?"

"I was real kind to him once. A long while ago. He's always thought I would be again."

Pierce looked at her closely. Her face was expressionless and her voice matter-of-fact.

"Kind to him? This is the idiot sheriff who hasn't had an original thought since he fell off his motorcycle?"

"He's got a mystique of his own. It's called brute force. I was new here then. And here's this human battering ram with a badge pinned to it, breaking up fights and cold-cocking trouble-makers. I was impressed. Yeah, I was kind to him. Once."

Pierce turned back to concentrate on his driving.

"I don't think we have to tell him you're involved, Whit. If Vigo finds out, okay. But no need to volunteer it."

There were no sidewalks along the narrow, winding streets on the city's southwestern edge. The lawns were ill-tended or nonexistent. Entire blocks of mobile homes, aligned in no particular pattern, like whales stranded on a beach. At times, beyond the trailers and the trees, small snatches of the river were visible and, occasionally, one of the houseboats moored in the Mississippi's many inlets.

"Slow down," Britt said. "I think . . . Yeah, that's the kid."

Emil Gatliffe had just ducked his head under the hood of a late-sixties model Mustang, one bearing the translucent horse-head grille ornament. The coupe had been a bright green, but now it was shot through with rust; rust so extensive, it might almost have been designed as trim. The rest of the auto was a sludgy earth color, like grass stomped into mud.

There was no driveway, but the Ford had been pulled up beside a faintly pink mobile home also in dire need of fresh paint. The house was mounted at each of its four sides on cinder blocks. Three other blocks served as steps to the front door. A torpedolike tank of bottled gas lay alongside the building.

Framed in the tiny window of the front door was a Christmas wreath and a red candle.

"Left over from last year?" Pierce mused aloud. "Or early for this year?"

"Probably left over from ten years ago," Britt cracked.

Emil came briskly over to them. His yellow hair had been tied in a pony tail.

"Hello, Emil," Britt said. "I think you know who Mr. Pierce is."

Emil made a show of pulling out a red rag and wiping engine grease from his hands. He extended his hands, palms up, as if for inspection. Then he boomed, "Put 'er there, pardner!" and gripped Pierce's hand heartily. "Shore glad to have you mosey out this way."

Pierce started for the door, and Emil clutched his arm. "And what, pray, can we do for you today?"

"I'd like to see your mother."

"About what, sir?"

"A matter I'll discuss with her." Pierce forcibly removed Emil's hand.

"Manda don't talk to nobody lest they tell me what about."

He grinned winsomely, as though to belie the hard finality of his words. He had the cleaning rag out again, passing it from hand to hand, fluttering it like a matador's cape. His hands were extremely long and graceful, moving continually and weaving endless patterns in the air.

"All right. I want to see her about the stories she's written for class."

"See her Thursday. She'll be there then."

"I'd like to talk to her now."

"You do that for all your students? Make house calls? Or just some of 'em?"

He batted his eyes at Britt suggestively. He giggled and clapped a hand over his mouth.

"Emil, just you and your mother live here?" Britt asked.

"Yes'm."

"Does she have a job?"

"No'm."

"Does she go out much?"

"No'm."

"Why is she taking Mr. Pierce's course? Do you know?"

"Yes'm. She thinks he'll take a fancy to her. He's eligible, we hear. And she'd love to get hitched up to another husband."

Once more he tittered.

Pierce went up the three steps. There was no bell, no knocker. He pounded on the door.

"What about her stories?" Emil's voice was sardonic.

"I just want to talk to her about them."

"She's not home."

"Whit, I just saw some eyes looking out," said Britt. "In the middle of that wreath."

"That's the cat," Emil said. "Weren't there whiskers? Didn't you see whiskers?"

Pierce banged on the door again.

In one bound Emil's lanky body was atop the cinder block, sidling between Pierce and the door.

"Manda's not home!" he hollered. "Manda wouldn't talk to you if she was! Manda would want you to go away!" The shouts were loud enough so that anyone inside would hear them clearly.

They waited. Through the pane in the door Pierce could see only a few pieces of furniture: a heavy chest, a tall bookcase with glassed-in shelves. All the other windows were curtained. Nothing moved within his limited range of vision.

Emil was wedged so tightly against him that he felt the youth's breath on his cheek: a sickly, sweetish smell like rancid milk. The expression on Emil's face had turned to one of mockery.

"Okay, let's go," Pierce snapped to Britt.

"Bye bye." Emil pitched his voice to a falsetto. "Careful on the steps. Remember what happened to Paw-Paw."

"What?" Britt demanded.

"Paw-Paw fall down and broke his crown!"

Emil doubled over, holding his stomach, laughing.

"God damn it," Britt fumed as they drove away. "I know she was in there."

"There'll be a chance to talk to her Thursday."

"If she shows up again. We may have scared her off. God damn that kid!"

Chapter 10

"Is lasagne okay?" Sally Berwyn asked. "I realize chicken and dumplings would be more suitable for Sunday in La Soeur." She pulled a large bottle of Chianti out of a shopping bag. "You don't object to a glass of wine first?"

"Let me get it."

"The glasses are in there. Just water glasses. Aunt Amy's not a hedonist."

Pierce came back with the glasses, and Sally poured out the dark red wine.

"To happy days at Aunt Amy's."

"Skoal. Now why don't you unpack while I whip up the vittles."

Aunt Amy's house was a stucco bungalow with a mansard roof. Both front and backyards were large. Flower gardens—still blazing with yellow and orange marigolds and other late bloomers—ringed the sides and front of the home. It was a neighborhood too close to the river to be fashionable now, but it clung stubbornly to respectability and tradition.

Pierce had liked the house the moment he'd walked in. It was small and old-fashioned. The stairs to the second floor creaked. There were patches in the kitchen linoleum. But it was immaculately clean, and it almost audibly insisted that "my home is your home."

At once Pierce knew that he need not bother looking elsewhere.

There was a grandfather's clock, stopped at five ten. A

honey-pine Boston rocker. Furniture covered with needlepoint that Aunt Amy had spent years on. Hummel-type figurines everywhere. Even a front porch swing.

The main bedroom was clearly Aunt Amy's and so crammed with her belongings that it would have seemed intrusive even to look it over. He selected the more spartan guest room for himself. It had a bow window overlooking the street and a small but comfortable four-poster bed. The mattress was new and sturdy, bought to accommodate Aunt Amy's grown children on their periodic visits.

"That didn't take long," Sally said when he came back downstairs.

"I didn't bring much with me from Chicago."

"You must love it there."

"Well, I suppose."

"I know I do. I'll be there in a couple of weeks. I drop in on a girl friend of mine from college and we make a weekend of it. Once or twice a year."

"Ah. The Rush Street singles bars."

"No!" Her laugh was as quick and spontaneous as her smile. "We'll take in a show, and I intend to get over to the Art Institute. I'm dying to see the exhibit they've just opened—this collection of prehistoric cave art. Fascinating."

"You know something about archaeology?"

"Well, I've taken some courses."

"I'm impressed."

"Oh, just university extension courses. Here in La Soeur. I tend to do that if something interests me. Sally the Perpetual Student. Even gourmet cooking. Though you might not know it from the lasagne."

"I'm expecting to find otherwise."

Pierce helped Sally set their places.

"What's going to be the next Whit Pierce book?" she asked when they sat down to eat.

He paused. "A multigenerational thing," and he described

the big novel he had been working on for three years. The saga of two families, one Irish and one black, over a century and a half of Chicago's history.

He did not mention that all he had so far was four cartons full of notes. That he had not even begun writing the book. Nor that he could not begin to write it until he wrote another book first. One about Corinne. Until he wrote that book, there could be nothing else.

Afterward they did the dishes together. Pierce praised the dinner and then remarked, "It's funny, when I think of it. My wife wasn't much of a cook. Even if she was in the kitchenware business."

He wondered why he'd made the comment and recalled that he'd had five—no, it was six—glasses of wine.

"Not that she was a poor cook," Pierce went on. "She could cook if she had to, and superbly, just like she could do almost anything well. But there was never the time. Or inclination. Especially once she launched the business. God, I was proud of her. But there wasn't the time after that, you know."

"Dinner plates go in this cabinet."

"Last spring I said, 'Let's go to the Bahamas for a month. I need to get a handle on this whole mess of notes I've got. I need to talk it out. And you could use getting away from the shop.' But there wasn't the time."

She took a pan from his hand and finished drying it. "Maybe she needed to talk it out, too. About her business. About any problems she had."

"She had her management team. Her battery of lawyers. But maybe she did need to talk about it. About . . . about whatever it was . . ."

Sally was quiet a moment. "I'm glad you think you can make do here, Whit." She was hanging towels, closing cabinet doors. "Is that okay? To call you Whit?"

"Of course."

"Garbage pickup is Tuesdays. Will you remember that?" She

slipped into her coat, swiftly, before he could attempt to assist her, then reached into a pocket. "The keys. Front door. Back door. They're yours now."

Britt answered when he called the Hungerford home nine thirty Monday morning.

"What the hell happened to you?" she demanded.

"I moved."

"I know you moved. I called that cruddy motel and they didn't know where you'd gone. I wondered if I was being stood up."

"To the contrary. I'm putting down roots."

"I just had to talk to you! Been picking brains all weekend. Discreetly. Whit, Amanda is a grade-A certified nut! And a violent one! Know why she's in your class? Her shrink thought it'd be good therapy for her. Express her emotions. Vent her hostilities."

"And is she ever venting. In what way is she violent?"

"She beat up someone in the neighborhood. With a shovel. Half killed him."

"Why?"

"Some kind of disagreement. He ran his car over her garden. I know some folks who work at the courthouse. They checked the records for me. She was found too unstable to stand trial. Combination of subnormal IQ and being a borderline nutcase. 'Dissociative hysterical neurosis' is one of the labels they pinned on her. They put her in County General for a while. Now she's an outpatient. Her shrink thought she needed some kind of creative outlet. She can't paint or sing. But she can read and write. So he unleashed her on you."

"Lucky me."

"Whit, she's a goddam psycho."

"Then maybe we ought to stop playing games and tell—"

"And let Vigo and his turkeys flub this? No way. Did you look over that report from the sheriff's department?"

"Nothing new there, as far as I can tell."

"That's just the first-day report. Scene of the crime and all that. We haven't seen what's developed since. From questioning her friends and classmates and whatever. I'm going to call Vigo today, but I don't know how candid he'll be. Have you got anything going?"

"I'm seeing Deputy Evans this afternoon."

"Super! Whatever he tells you, pass it along tonight. Can you make it?"

"Where?"

"The fourteenth hole."

"Where?"

Her laugh surprised him. "The golf course. You've been to the house. The fourteenth hole is four hundred, five hundred yards past us, toward the Kennilworth Motel. You can't miss it. There's a big oak right next to it. Huge. Branches close to the ground. The only tree that size anywhere on that part of the course. What we used to call a 'hanging tree' back home."

"Look, Britt, why there? Isn't there some—"

"It's going to be a scrumptious night. Here it's October and not even nippy yet. There's privacy out there. The air's clean. You can see the whole night sky. You can talk without being interrupted. Just park in the Kennilworth lot and cut through that woods."

"What time?"

"Say, eleven?"

"Okay."

"Listen, Whit, we didn't talk about this before. But if there's anything to that garbage Amanda wrote, if it's not just the ravings of a lunatic or an imagination gone totally haywire—"

"Which it most certainly is."

"But if it's not, it means those two killings could be connected."

"You told me the cops said no way. The—what is it?—modus

89

operandi was different each time. The type of victim was different. The manner of killing different."

"But there were similarities."

"What similarities?"

"Sudden violence. Brutal. Out of control. In a rural setting. And the victim was a female. All right, different in ages: a child and a young woman. But still female. And if there's a connection—"

"Which is most doubtful—"

"It could happen again."

Pierce waited in the sheriff department's Malibu while Nehemiah Evans delivered a summons. It was the deputy's last duty of the day, and this would be the only time he'd be free to talk.

He reappeared around the corner of a sagging barn, marching smartly in his crisp poplin uniform and glistening boots. He must have made a snappy-looking soldier, Pierce mused.

"Found him in his hen house," Evans said with a glimmer of amusement. "Thought his choppers'd fall out. Here's this mean-ass black man packin' a pistol an' poppin' right into his own hen house! Ain't nothin' sacred no more?"

He removed his cap and brushed the visor with his cuff.

"Hell, just a summons tellin' him he's got to go to court about his alimony payments. No big deal. But you never know about these kinky old coots off by themselves in the middle of nowhere. Me, I couldn't live nowhere but the city. Let's get back."

They rode in silence a while.

"I'll return your manuscript to you Thursday. I've made a lot of notes. I think there ought to be some fairly minor revisions."

Evans nodded.

Pierce paused, studying the countryside. Evans, he decided, was a straight-ahead type who would instantly see through subterfuge.

"I understand you're the deputy who found the Karlstrom girl."

For the first time Evans's eyes were on him. "Yeah."

"I've gotten involved in a project. To follow up on that case and possibly do an article or a book about it when it's solved."

"You and Mrs. Hungerford?"

"You know about her?"

"I know she talked about it with Vigo Lustgarten. And that she tried to talk about it with a couple of the detectives. This is not a big department. Word gets around pretty damn fast. I don't know what Vigo told her, but those boys wouldn't tell her diddly."

"Why not?"

"Because Vigo told 'em not to. Nobody talks to Mrs. Hungerford but him."

"What about you?"

"Vigo never said nothin' to me. Mainly 'cause he never thought anybody'd bother to ask me anythin', I guess. But I was in at the beginning, and I read some of the reports. I'd be grateful, Mr. Pierce, if you did not make it known we been discussin' this."

"Of course."

"Because I don't stand that high in Vigo's esteem. It was a helluva battle to get into this department. I even had to take it to court. Vigo finally caved in, but he figures that now he's filled his affirmative action quota through the year 2020."

"I understand."

"What is it you want to know?"

"After you found her was there anything about it that occurred to you? Even days later. That you hadn't reported at the time?"

"No. But it wasn't my case, you understand. Once I saw what happened, I radioed headquarters, and my job then was to see that nothin' was disturbed. To keep people away till the plainclothes boys got there."

91

"Keep people away? You mean a crowd formed? Out there in that cemetery?"

"No crowd. But all of a sudden there was four or five people. I tell you, some folks got a sixth sense. They can smell blood anywhere an' zip in on it like a shark. A couple of 'em lived close by, drivin' along, and they saw the flashin' lights. A couple others was listenin' to police calls on their car radios. They beat the investigators and the medical examiner. I had my hands full keepin' them goddam ghouls from trackin' up the scene. They kept tryin' to sneak over and get a closer look."

"Did you know her?"

"No. But I seen her around."

"Where?"

"Mostly dumpy bars outside town. Hangin' out with a pretty tough breed of cat."

"I understand they couldn't determine if she had a boyfriend. Or even a guy she dated."

"No shit. That's because she didn't go for guys. The crowd she hung with—dykes. Almost all of 'em."

A fact which Sheriff Lustgarten had not seen fit to pass along to Britt. Nor had this information appeared in the *Sentinel.* Out of delicacy or fear of libel? Pierce wondered. Or maybe nobody on the paper had dug deeply enough to be aware of it? "I take it they questioned all those friends of hers?"

"A couple times. Shook 'em all down. They been bustin' their asses on this case, I'll say that for 'em. I mean, they had brains enough to say, 'Okay, if the boyfriend didn't do it, maybe the girl friend did.' "

"Is there a girl friend? One in particular?"

"There is. The great bull dyke of La Soeur herself." His large jaw revolved disdainfully with each syllable of the name. "Miss Ruby Lee Cutler."

"And they questioned her thoroughly?"

"Over an' over. She had an alibi. She was in a bar gettin' stoned between eight an' two that night. In view of everyone most of the time. Except to go to the john every so often. The time of death was fixed at prior to two A.M. Probably some time around midnight. So that appears to let R. L. off the hook."

"R. L. and Angela were close?"

"In-goddam-separable. At least as much as R. L. could be. R. L. even kicked out her old live-in."

"What about R. L.'s ex-roommate?"

"The jealous lover? Jan Laughlin. She was at the same bar as R. L. They more or less ran into each other there, the way she tells it. She was in the bar till closing time, as near as anybody can be specific at a joint like that. Anyway, shit, why would Karlstrom drive out to the cemetery with Jan Laughlin? Why would she drive out there at all?"

"That seems to be the key question. What's your guess?"

"My guess is everybody's too caught up with who's screwin' who. Maybe that didn't have anythin' to do with it."

"Then what?"

Evans turned onto a county trunk. "I don't know. But R. L.'s involved in more than runnin' after jail bait. She's got business friends who are none too savory. And I wonder if R. L.'s personal friends don't get involved with them, too."

"She's into some kind of racket? What?"

"For starters she runs the only porno bookstore in town. The city's tryin' to close her down, but she's got a lawsuit goin'. Claims the council's not properly interpretin' the way the community defines obscenity in this enlightened age, or some such bullshit."

"Sounds like you've got it in for R. L."

"Not on account of her shop. Hell, if people want that, let 'em have it. La Soeur isn't big enough, anyway, to get much of a porno industry goin'. Not that some folks wouldn't get their jollies out of it. But the burg is so small, you're always bein' seen by somebody you know. An' bein' proper means more here than it does most other places.

"What I'm sayin' is a shop like hers is a two-bit operation.

But she seems to make one helluva living off it. She bought a farm out here last year. I'll show it to you. An' you know the price of real estate these days. She's never hurtin' for cash. That's my point."

"Then where's she getting it?"

Evans's thick mustache drooped even farther, accentuating the habitual glower. His hair was little more than a thin carpet of fuzz, and his nose had the mashed-in look of an ex-prizefighter.

"I ask her that myself. There's people pushin' shit in this town—heroin an' angel dust an' a lot more. An' it comes from somewhere. An' R. L. makes a lot of trips to Chicago. She says to see the people that sell those books to her. An' people go out to her farm at real funny hours. I see 'em there when I patrol at night. There it is."

It looked like the home of a highly prosperous and industrious agribusinessman. A glossy white building with shutters of brilliant vermilion. There actually were two houses combined: a tall structure that rose to what was almost a square tower, and a rambling, one-story ranch house extension.

The barn and other ancillary buildings looked as if they had just been whitewashed. A pickup truck and a van were parked in the driveway. A metal rowboat rested on a wheeled carrier on one side of the lawn.

"Somebody's pushin' that stuff," Evans growled. "An' you know who's the first they get to? We don't have much of a black population here yet, but those are the kids they go for."

He spent some time readjusting his cap to a precise military angle. "I was two years a cop in Detroit. I liked it. Good at it. But I seen what my kids had to face. Their best friends doin' dope. How can you expect a kid not to give in to that kind of pressure? I know it don't happen to everyone. I know the right thing to do is fight it where you're at. I know there were other neighborhoods we might've gone to. It might've been all right.

"But I got scared. An' I said, We gotta go. An' I came here because I thought . . . I don't know. That this place would be sort of . . . untouched. You know what I'm sayin'? But it's not, Mr. Pierce. I want you to meet R. L. Cutler."

Chapter 11

Pierce vaguely remembered the building as a chocolate shop during his days in La Soeur. A neat and tidy place of tantalizing odors and genteel ladies. Another casualty of the deterioration that had set in over the western fringes of the downtown area. Another business either gone belly-up or moved to the shopping centers.

Ruby Lee Cutler had covered the large plate-glass window with muslin curtains, to shroud customers from curious passersby. Adult Book Store appeared to be the establishment's only name. A sign in the corner of the window warned: YOU MUST BE 21 TO ENTER HERE!

There was only one customer in the shop—a snowy-haired older man in a business suit leafing through a magazine. When he saw Evans's uniform, he swung around to present only his back.

"Well, lookie," said R. L.

She was tilted back on an old wooden kitchen chair beside the cash register, her feet propped up on the counter. In one hand was an open penknife, and with it she continued paring a fingernail. A cigarette dangled from her lips.

"You're out of your jurisdiction, Sambo. Get back to the pigs and the cows."

"Big day today, R. L.?" the deputy asked tonelessly. "Big bucks in panderin', I hear."

R. L. got to her feet, her eyes nothing but slits. "What the fuck are you trying to start here, mister?"

The customer dropped the magazine and took rapid little steps to the door, trying to bury his face in his collar.

The bookshelves lining the walls looked homemade. Two Ping-Pong tables filled the center of the room and on them piles of periodicals and books were carelessly thrown, like remnants at a discount sale. Color spreads of long-ago Playmates of the Month were taped to the walls.

"Just browsing, R. L."

"Listen, you're off your own turf here. I can have you bounced. I don't have to put up with this kind of ape shit."

She was built like a college football linebacker: husky but not quite massive enough for the pros. Her neck was thick and solid as a stone column, and her jaw jutted pugnaciously forward. Yet her face was surprisingly pink and pretty, the skin girlishly smooth. She had a tiny, upturned nose and eyes that smoldered under her broad forehead.

As she talked she moved ceaselessly, tensing and shrugging her shoulders, flicking cigarette ashes onto the floor. And as she moved, she made noise—jingling keys in her pocket, snorting through her nose, stamping heavily with each step.

Her denim jacket and jeans were faded and grease-stiffened. But her boots were new and expensive, cowboy boots of exquisite hand-stitched leather studded with red and blue beads in a star pattern.

"Go ahead, R. L., call the city cops. You're their little pet, right?"

"I can call my lawyer! And get your black ass reamed for harassing me!"

"And I'll call my lawyer. And charge you refuse to let me patronize your shop, for purely racial reasons."

Pierce scanned the contents of the tables. None of the material would transform the community into a latter-day Babylon. There were some of the raunchier men's magazines. Artistic studies of nudes. Henry Miller and *Lady Chatterly's Lover*. The Marquis de Sade and Krafft-Ebing. Profusely illustrated marriage manuals. More than he would have encountered in La Soeur sixteen years ago. But there was little here that could not be bought through any respectable general audience bookstore, even in this city.

He wondered if she had more someplace else. For trusted patrons with special tastes.

"For Christ's sake," R. L. complained, "haven't you got better things to do?"

"Such as?"

"Such as finding out who the hell . . . Forget it."

She flung down her cigarette and ground it out with the heel of her boot.

"Finding out who killed Angela?"

"I said forget it."

"Matter of fact, Ruby Lee, I come over here to ask you a couple things about that."

"I already been talked to by half the shitheads in your department."

"Did Angela hang around your place sometimes when you were here at the shop? So that if anybody went to your house to do business, she'd be there to help 'em?"

"I don't do business at my house. I do business here. Period."

"Oh? Isn't it true you were in the habit of havin' Angela run business errands for you? All times of day and night?"

R. L. peeled a softpack, non-filter and non-menthol, from her breast pocket. She lit it with a flashing motion of a glinting, silver-plated lighter. She blew smoke out through her nose.

"Get this straight. I don't have business errands to run at night."

"Angela talked about picking up and leaving La Soeur," Pierce said. "Didn't that concern you?"

Her hot, brown eyes blazed at him. "And who the fuck are you?"

"Friend of mine," said Evans. "We got lots of people interested in you, Ruby Lee."

"Well, you can all shove it." She stomped back to the cash register, rolling her broad shoulders, and flopped into her chair. "Take off."

Evans gave her a long, utterly dispassionate look. "I'll be talking to you, Ruby Lee."

Outside, Pierce said to him, "I saw the inventory of what they found on or near Angela after the killing. I didn't see a cigarette lighter mentioned."

"I don't remember. If it wasn't listed it wasn't there."

"Nothing about any matches, either."

"Don't remember any."

"Thanks for the chance to meet R. L."

"Yeah. Ain't she a sweetheart?"

What Britt had called the hanging tree was not as easy to find as she had made it seem. Low-lying clouds blotted out the moon, already partly obscured behind the crown of Frenchman's Pitch.

He had wandered over the links toward a grove of trees looming black against the less intense darkness of the night, only to discover they were slender hardwoods. He trudged on, stepped unexpectedly in a sand trap, and fell.

Cursing, he shook the sand from his shoes.

Disoriented, he sat quietly, listening. There was a slight wind, and he heard an almost imperceptible rustling sound. Straining to locate its source, he thought he saw something tall, needle-like, against the night sky.

The flag on the fourteenth hole?

As he neared it the clouds let a shaft of moonlight filter through. The ground rose, and he could see on the downslope behind the green the murky silhouette of a bulging oak with out-flung branches.

The tree was as wide as it was tall. It stood completely alone and had never needed to compete for the available sunlight. It had been free to grow, to spread, to reach out greedily, without restraint.

"Hi, you."

A pale form, she materialized out of the black of the tree trunk and put her arms around him. He kissed her hungrily.

"You said there wouldn't be a chill this time of year."

She laughed. "We'll warm you. Come."

She tugged him by the hand onto the ground, onto something woolen that he thought was probably her stadium blanket. They sat with their backs to the tree, and she handed him a Thermos. It was brandy. He drank deeply.

"God, I love the idea of it." She sighed. "Here . . . in the night air, the whole sky over us . . . and everybody else locked up inside."

She put the Thermos to her lips. "I must have Indian blood in me. It's like I just feel the earth breathing all around me, breathing through me. I couldn't wait to see you!"

She gripped his hand, pulled it to her, and kissed it. "Tell me about Deputy Evans."

He explained that Angela was apparently having a relationship with Ruby Lee Cutler.

"Goddam that Vigo! That could be the crux of the whole thing."

Pierce went on to describe their meeting with R. L., and Evans's opinion that she was involved in drug trafficking. And that this could have been a key element in Angela Karlstrom's murder.

"If it was, it means the two killings weren't connected. The Stabo girl's death couldn't have any drug angle to it. Unless the killer was just spaced out. That would mean Amanda's stories are fiction, Whit, pure and simple."

"There may be other indications of that." He pointed out that in Amanda's depiction of Angela's slaying, the girl was carrying a cigarette lighter. Yet no lighter was found at the scene of the murder.

"Ipso facto. Amanda made it up."

"Probably. Except for one thing. There weren't any matches or matchbooks found, either. But she had been smoking. They found her cigarette butts in the ashtray."

"Could be a lighter in the car. A dashboard lighter. We can ask Hugh Karlstrom. I think it's time we called on him, anyway. Are you game for tomorrow?"

"All right." He placed an arm around her and drew her close. The moon broke through the cloud cover, and the golf course was awash with tepid light. They were able to see the fourteenth-hole flag, listless but fluttering weakly at times.

"Angela and Cutler," she murmured. "It gives the whole crime of passion theory a new twist."

"There's no more evidence that Angela was there with a woman than with a man."

"But it opens a fresh can of worms. The sordid underside of life in La Soeur that the decent and refined would shudder to know exists. So where do we start?"

"I don't know. Evans said that R. L. had ditched her previous inamorata. Maybe we could start there."

"Did you get her name?"

"Jan Laughlin."

"I can't believe it." She picked up the flask and took a swallow. "What we never suspect about others, right? I know Jan. She's in the Theatre Guild play we're rehearsing now. *The Seven Year Itch.* She plays the dumb blonde. And if anybody was ever typecast! Well, three-quarters of the guys in the cast and crew have been trying to get into her since the first day. No dice. And no wonder! Jan and R. L.! Incredible!"

"Well, R. L.'s got more macho, probably, than most of the guys in your play."

"I wonder why she dumped Jan. I mean, Jan was Miss Indian Summer Days three or four years ago. The closest thing we've got to a professional model. Local TV commercials, ad agency work, posing for photographers, playing hostess for company sales meetings. Put it all together and she makes a good living, just on her looks."

"Evans says R. L. likes her full-time tootsies young. Angela Karlstrom was . . . what? Nineteen?"

"And Jan is all of twenty-two. I'm going to get together with her, Whit. I think she can be made to blab a bit."

She unzipped her jacket. She had nothing on under it. "Come here, sugar, and let me get you out of those things. Quick! Down here. Let me get you warm."

He kicked the brandy flask, and it rolled and spilled. He swore.

She laughed. "Oh, my, sugar. You *are* eager! Here! Pull the blanket up around you. Oh, Whit. Good!"

The moonlight lapped over them. He was aware of it defining her face and hair and breasts. She cried out. Not loudly, but the sound of it had to carry, and he pressed his mouth heavily against hers to silence her.

Later, as she lay in his arms, the clouds formed solidly and erased all sight of the moon.

In the sudden, total blackness the flag on the fourteenth hole had vanished. They heard it faintly rustling, snapping at times, because the wind had picked up.

He awoke the next morning stiff, sniffling, and more weary than when he had gone to bed. He knew he had dreamed of Corinne.

He could not remember the dream. But he recognized the aftereffects. A sensation of utter fatigue. Of confusion. Of horror.

It was another mild, sparkling October day. From his window he could see the neighborhood children racing their tricycles and kicking through fallen leaves.

Had Corinne been staring, as usual, in that dream? In silent, unrelenting fury?

Or had what he'd always expected to happen finally happened? Had she—hanging there, her face a lump, the green eyes dissecting him—opened her mouth . . .

And begun to speak?

He sneezed and groped in his suitcase for the box of tissues he hadn't unpacked yet.

That goddam breeze last night. By the time they'd left the golf course his back and shoulders had felt chilled to the bone.

Britt. Was that the reason for the Corinne dream?

Guilt? More guilt?

No, he didn't think so. He didn't, deep down, feel qualms about Britt.

He'd never been unfaithful during their years of marriage. Even toward the end. And Corinne was dead now. This was no injustice to Corinne.

In front of him on the small desk in the bedroom lay the hasty notes he'd made yesterday about his conversation with Nehemiah Evans and his meeting with R. L. Cutler. He would type them up today, expanding on them, putting them in coherent order.

Why?

The investigation was a pointless charade. Childish to think that the two of them had the whisper of a chance of success.

He went to the bathroom and turned the shower on as hot as he could stand it. The issue then was: Did he want to keep on seeing Britt?

Yes!

There was no real bond of tenderness between them. No sense of fidelity. No love.

But she brought out carnality in him that he didn't know he had. Or hadn't for years. Her body had pumped life and feeling and response back into him.

Until Britt there had been nothing. Nothing but the deadness that Corinne had bequeathed him. And the frustration of not being able to decipher it and translate it from his nightmares onto paper.

Yes, Britt is a phase. Temporary. No more than that.

He smeared shaving cream over his face, slapping it on almost viciously. Britt is temporary. Corinne was forever.

Dammit, I can't handle forever!

He nicked his upper lip with the razor. With cold water he daubed at the button of blood.

He resumed shaving and, with the first stroke of the blade, cut himself again.

"Damn!" he muttered. He examined the razor. It was a Techmatic, which he kept set at "light." The dial was turned to "heavy."

Because of the change in setting, the pressure he was accustomed to using had obviously been too forceful.

He reset the razor and wondered if he could have accidentally jiggled the dial when he'd unpacked. But this was his third morning at Aunt Amy's.

And he'd not cut himself the other two.

He looked quizzically at the razor, and then padded in his bare feet to the top of the stairs, peering down, listening.

All he heard were the faint shouts of the children playing outside.

Pierce went back into the bathroom. "Cool it," he said aloud.

He saw his eyes in the mirror, and they were wild and furtive. More blood, he noticed, was oozing from the cut on his lip.

Chapter 12

They took a table in the far corner of the lounge at the Meadowbluff Country Club. From here they had a view of the back nine. A foursome was still on the last hole, although twilight was giving way to darkness, and the temperature had plummeted into the forties.

Recessed ceiling lights, covered by paisley-stained glass, sprinkled the room with a rainbow of pastels. Pierce gazed into the ornate, chrome-framed mirror behind the bar and encountered the eyes of a number of men staring back. Britt must experience this constantly, he thought. Or was the chief interest in knowing who was accompanying her these days?

One of the curious faces was familiar. A very short man who had been at Britt and Ralph's party. He whirled around on his stool and nodded.

"Len Durban," Britt said, nodding back.

"Ralph's majordomo? I suspect your husband will know within minutes that we're here together."

"Of course, he will. And that's great. We wouldn't show up unless we were in full gallop after Angela's killer. Hell, if we were having an affair, this is the last place we'd dare come to. Right?"

She smiled conspiratorially. "This can only tell Ralph that we're doing exactly what I told him we'd be doing. Strictly business."

From across the room Hugh Karlstrom looked bronzed, jovial, beaming. He had no hips, but his chest was thick and full and his arms almost grotesquely long. He wore a brass-but-toned, madras blue blazer that carefully emphasized the V-shape of his torso. Someone had handed him a drink. He held it high, then quaffed it.

"The father in mourning," Britt said.

"You make it sound like he's not."

"I'm sure he is. But Hugh is Hugh. And he's got to keep up his contacts. He's the pro here, you know. But the year's ending and he's got the winter to think about."

"What happens in winter?" Pierce asked it flatly, dutifully.

"He hustles tours for a travel agency. Golf tours a specialty. Pebble Beach. Palo Mesa. Saint Andrews. How the mighty have fallen. He used to make the pro circuit—the whole tournament scene. And did damn well. A bona fide celebrity, La Soeur's golden boy. We'd see him on national TV once in a while."

"He gave it up? Not good enough?"

"Good enough until he crashed. He used to pilot his own plane. Hop around the country to all the tournaments. He smashed the plane up landing at some little field in Florida. He got pretty banged up. And his wife died."

"That's tough."

"He was probably flying drunk. He was inclined to. Here, have an onion ring. They're too doughy, but what can you expect for the three thousand a year it takes to belong to this club? Well, it ruined his game. Some sort of inner-ear thing that screws up his balance. Some of his students shoot a better game than he does now. And there's the limp. But he's still a fairly competent instructor, or so Ralph and his buddies claim."

"There would be guilt, wouldn't there?" Pierce said. He sipped at the Scotch. "I mean, if he'd been at the controls. And he lived . . ." Pierce paused. "And his wife died."

"I suppose so. Probably asking himself why the hell he took her along. He had a babe in every town on the circuit. And a fair number here in the old hometown. Don't sing no sad songs for handsome Hugh. That golf pro has had his number-one iron in some mighty interesting places."

Pierce smiled faintly. "What would Ralph say if he heard you talking like that?"

"He loves it when I talk dirty. You knew Elena, his ex-wife? Prissy. Even walked like she had a chastity belt on."

"So you pushed her out of the picture?" Pierce saw no need, at this stage, to be anything but frank.

"Ralph wanted something better. And he got it. And he knows he got it. Ralph and I understand each other. Which is more than he and Elena ever did."

"He'd understand about us?"

"He'd just as soon not know, to tell you the truth. And there are little fun trips of his here and there that I'd just as soon not know about. None of that affects Ralph or me or how we get along."

She turned to extend her hand to Hugh Karlstrom. His limp was minimal but quite evident. Perhaps it enhanced his romantic appeal, Pierce speculated.

"Hello, Britt. The bartender said you wanted to see me."

Karlstrom's wrists were immense and the tendons on the back of his hands like steel coils. His hand clasp was overpowering until he made the apparent split-second decision to ease up because Pierce was not attempting to challenge his strength.

"May we buy you a drink, Mr. Karlstrom?"

"Make it Hugh. Sure . . . Maggie! Another Polar Bear."

"I'm so sorry about your daughter. I haven't had a chance till now to offer my sympathy."

"Thank you. It hasn't been easy."

There was a nasal whininess to the voice that Pierce had not expected. His first impression had been deceptive. The face was leathery, beginning to wrinkle badly, and looked flushed and patchy despite the deep tan. The cheekbones were rounded swellings that seemed to bear evidence of roly-poly geniality. But the sour mouth and eyes dispelled this illusion. The natty sportcoat and the modishly styled silver-sandy hair attempted to preserve the old image. But close up it was obvious that Hugh Karlstrom had not broken par in a long, long while.

Britt drew him out about Angela's death as far as she could until she reached the point where it must become apparent that her curiosity was more than normal.

"Hugh, I should tell you that Mr. Pierce is a professional writer. He's going to be doing a book about the case. I'm working with him on it, and we'd truly appreciate your cooperation."

"Why would you want to do a book about something as horrible as this?" Karlstrom sounded confused.

His eyes were liquid brown and the lashes extraordinarily long. He had a habit of closing his eyes for a few seconds at a time in such a way as to seem exasperated.

The case had the elements of an engrossing story, Pierce explained. His publisher was committed to the project, he lied, and a contract had been signed. He did not want to sensationalize what happened. He wanted it to be accurate and fair to all concerned, particularly to Angela.

"You're in this, too, Britt?"

She nodded.

Karlstrom's eyes shut. He would have to deliberate on the fact that she was the wife of one of the pillars of the club and of the city, and that he, himself, was by no means the fixture here he once had been.

"What did you want to know?"

"First," Pierce asked, "was there a cigarette lighter in the dashboard of your car?"

"No, there wasn't."

"Did you smoke?"

"Just my pipe."

"Had you smoked your pipe in the car that day?"

"Maybe. Early that evening. Coming home from the club. I don't remember."

According to Karlstrom, the ashtray in the car had been cleaned a day or two before Angela died. It was filled, running over. Had been for weeks. Mainly from her cigarettes. He'd hassled her about it and then noticed she'd finally gotten the job done.

"Had anyone else been in the car that day or the day before?"

"Just Glenna, my girl friend. I drove her to the Twin Cities airport that Wednesday, to fly to Seattle for her sister's wedding."

"So she was out of town when Angela died?"

"Yes."

"Did Glenna smoke?"

"No."

"Did Angela use the car often?"

"Two or three nights a week. I kept it at the club all day. Most of the time her friends picked her up in their cars."

"Did she say anything about where she was taking it that night?"

"No. Just 'out for a while.' That's how she was. No point asking her any more than that."

"Nor when she'd be back?"

"No. Even to ask that would set off a whole *megillah.* She wasn't a child anymore—that sort of ranting and raving. She left about eight. That's the last time I saw her."

He finished his drink, looking not so much bereaved as very imposed upon. Some household, Pierce reflected. The sulky former golden boy and the tantrum-prone teenager.

Pierce gestured for another round. "Angela wasn't working at the time of her death?"

"She'd had a couple of jobs, but she couldn't hold on to them. Waitressing. Clerk in an office supply store. She'd come in late or not show up at all sometimes. Trying to find herself, I guess."

"She'd talked of going off on her own, hadn't she?"

"Sure. Kids do that. It's natural. But she hadn't saved a dime. I told her she was on her own if she left."

"Hugh," Britt said, looking at him evenly, "Angela was quite an attractive girl. Yet she seemed to have no interest in boyfriends."

He closed his eyes for many seconds. When he opened them, she was still gazing steadily at him. He was the first to break eye contact. He studied the sable depths of his drink.

Once, Pierce was sure, Karlstrom must have come on boldly to Britt. The lion of the links, here in his home lair, matched against the city's sexiest social butterfly. The electricity must have crackled between them. Britt would have encouraged it. And Karlstrom would have gone along as far as she'd let him.

Now his voice could scarcely be heard, and its pitch was waspish and defensive.

"She hadn't had her mother for three years. It's not easy, raising a girl that age without a mother. I had my job. I couldn't just stay home with her. And there are obligations with my job. I couldn't be taking a teenager with me. It's hard enough to raise a daughter these days. But when there's no mother . . ."

"Did she ever introduce you to Ruby Lee Cutler?" Britt said, interrupting.

The ruddy patches in his face flared brightly. They were a vivid contrast with his stark-white, almost albino eyebrows. Still, he would not look at Britt.

"I've met Cutler."

"Angela invited her?"

"Yes. A couple times. Until I knew for sure what she was." He clenched his glass tightly, until it shook with the pressure.

"But when I knew for sure, I told Angela that woman was never to set foot in my house again. Never!"

At last he raised his face to Britt, the weathered, outdoorsman's look of it totally displaced by an unhealthy flush.

"R. L. Cutler is responsible for my daughter's death! I hold her responsible. I've told the police. I've told R. L. Cutler. I don't know how Angela was killed, but R. L. Cutler got her into it, whatever it was!"

The whine in his voice had turned to a snarl.

"She got her claws into Angela. Pulled her down into the slime. Down there with the rest of her crowd. With all the deviates and riff raff and perverts . . . Angela didn't know! She just didn't know! But R. L. Cutler comes around, flashing a roll of bills—"

"Was Angela on drugs?" Pierce asked.

"No! But R. L. Cutler tried to get her hooked. She wasn't, no. Oh, there were a couple of times. I could tell. She came home rambling, you know, not making sense. God, I would not have that! A hophead in my house! I had to use force. I never laid a hand on her before. But I had to, those times. And I did! I will not tolerate this, I told her. And it worked. She was wild, okay? Running with a wild crowd. But she was not any kind of addict. They proved that at the autopsy."

Both of those huge, bronzed hands were trembling. Karlstrom put his glass down and dropped the hands into his lap.

"Why didn't she go to live with R. L.?" Britt said softly.

"Because I told her if she did I'd cut her off. No more financial support, ever. No nothing, ever. No father, ever. If she lived with that . . . that *thing,* then I never had a daughter."

His eyes shut for so long that Pierce wondered if Karlstrom was silently commanding that he and Britt go away. As a child might. So that when the eyelids lifted, the world would be as he wanted it and not as he last saw it.

But they were still sitting there, politely staring. Karlstrom looked at them, aggrieved. "Angela didn't really want to live with Cutler, you know. That goddam bitch had turned her inside out, changed her over. But not deep down. Not all the way. There was no way she could have."

Once more he let his eyes close wearily. "Please remember

that. When you do your book. No matter what they tell you, you remember that."

They kept him only a few minutes longer, learning little beyond what had been reported in the press. When Karlstrom left, he asked to be remembered to Mr. Hungerford. He headed straight back toward the bar.

"I'll give his regards to Ralph, all right. Hugh's been trying to get up a planeload of golf nuts to go to La Costa in January. Pestering everybody. Not having much luck so far. The nineteenth hole can really be the toughest."

"Three things," Britt said when she called Thursday morning. "First, I won't be in class tonight. That'll be a perfect time to talk to Amanda's neighbors. While she's in class. And while Emil's chauffeuring her."

"Provided they show up."

"I'm going to park by the library. When I see that they've arrived, I'll scoot out to their neighborhood. Second, I want to invite you out for a drink today. At lunch. With Jan Laughlin and me."

"You don't waste any time."

"I just happened to run into her last night."

"Where was that?"

Britt laughed loudly. "Just where I thought I might. A lesbian bar out in the boonies."

"I didn't know La Soeur had any."

"It's the only one. That I know of, anyway. I don't think we have a dense enough population to do much better than that."

"Where do we get together and when?"

"The Ramada Inn. It's La Soeur's finest dining establishment, God help us for what that says. We're having lunch at noon. Can you stop by around one? I'd like you to give her the once-over."

"All right. You said there was a third thing."

"I'm going to see Vigo Lustgarten and try to get my hands on the Jennifer Stabo homicide reports. I think we ought to be digging into that case, too, Whit. Because something else occurred to me. There was nothing in the newspaper accounts about Jennifer wearing a red scarf. I checked them all, real thoroughly."

"But in Amanda's story—"

"The little girl wore a scarf. Red. Yes."

"If it turns out she actually did—"

"Then Amanda has definitely got a gift for more than fiction."

Chapter 13

Both Britt and Jan were doubled up, giggling, when Pierce joined them. From an ice bucket beside the table, Britt plucked an almost empty bottle of champagne.

"Have some."

"No, thanks. I'll have a Scotch."

"All the more for us," Britt said, refilling Jan's glass. They giggled again.

"This looker here has her first starring role in our next Theatre Guild production," Britt announced. "But it won't be her last. Take a real gander. You're going to be hearing a helluva lot more about Jan Laughlin. Today La Soeur. Tomorrow La World!"

Britt and Jan clinked glasses.

"Mr. Pierce is from Chicago," Britt confided. "Has all kinds of contacts in advertising, television, show business. Whit, don't you think this kid was created for the big time?"

Britt's voice was coarse, slurred. Pierce thought that if she were feigning drunkenness, she was laying it on far too heavily. But Jan seemed to have had enough champagne not to notice.

"Tell me about your part in the play," Pierce said, and as she talked he studied her closely. Her skin was glossy and her features classically chiseled. She was statuesque and, even seated, towered above Britt. Her saffron hair was frizzed into a halo that made her look even taller.

"You do modeling, too?" he asked.

"Tell 'im about the trade show!" Britt guffawed. "The guy with the key!"

"Oh. Right." Jan tittered. "I worked this trade show, and both the managers I worked for came to me—on their own, you know? And they each said part of the deal for hiring me was that I had to spend the night with them, you know? This was at the Kennilworth."

She spoke in a singsong, nine-year-old's voice. Her coral-colored halter dress displayed impossibly flawless shoulders and arms.

"But neither knew the other guy spoke to me, see? So the one gives me his key and says to come to his room that night. And I gives the key to the other one and tells him it's *my* room and he should come in later. And keep real quiet and not turn the light on!"

She and Britt fell into fresh spasms of laughter. "Oh, God," Britt said, groaning, "I'd love to have seen what happened!" She placed a hand on Jan's forearm.

"Well, what do you think, Whit? I say we start pounding the drums for her right now. She's got the talent. She's got the poise. And, Jesus, has she got the looks!"

Now—to Pierce's surprise—she was stroking Jan's arm. Jan did not move. She looked down modestly at the table, and a sly smile played on her lips.

"Well," Britt demanded, "is this a knockout or isn't it?"

"She sure is," Pierce concurred. "Have you known Britt long?" The question was inane, but no others came to mind.

"Oh, I've known Mrs. Hungerford a while. Here and there. But not particularly good, you know. Not till we . . . well, we found . . ."

"We found we both liked the same little bar."

Both women were seized with another fit of giggling. Britt gave Jan's arm a last squeeze and reached again for the champagne.

"I used to live in La Soeur," Pierce said. "Years ago. Night before last I ran into an old friend. Hugh Karlstrom. Know him? Terrible thing happened, he told me. His daughter got killed."

"Umm." Jan nodded. She brought her glass to her nostrils and sniffed at the bubbles. She smiled through the glass at Britt.

"I didn't know her," Britt said. "You might've, Jan."

"Umm. Angela. Right. We used to kind of hang out with the same people."

"Like who?"

"We had this friend in common."

Britt winked at Jan. "Say, Angela was a close pal of R. L. Cutler. Is that who you mean?"

"Oh, right. We used to all go out drinking and everything. Then I stopped hanging out with them so much."

Pierce pushed someone's empty dessert dish aside and tried to appear disinterested in the direction the discussion was taking.

"Hugh seems to think the kid was mixed up in dope. Like so many kids these days."

"Oh, no, not really. Well, a little. You know, some . . ."

She brought her fingers to her mouth as though sucking a marijuana cigarette.

"And once in a while a little . . ."

Her fingers touched her nose and she snorted loudly. She broke out in laughter, and Britt joined her.

"But that's about all."

"Too bad about the kid," Pierce mused. "I imagine this R. L. —was that the name?—is really broken up."

Jan shrugged as if she could not care less. "That's R. L.'s worry. But she won't be lonely."

"I don't know." Britt chortled nastily. "I heard Angela and R. L. were closer than this"—she gripped Jan's hand—"for quite some time."

Again Jan giggled. "R. L. gets around, no matter what.

Heck, I was seeing R. L. off and on all along. Angela never knew."

Britt barked out a laugh and smacked the table hard. "Then R. L.'s got taste, by God!"

She lowered her voice, leering. "But maybe Angela had some other friends, too. We can't be true-blue all the time."

"Who'd want to be?" the childish voice piped. "A little variety . . . Really spicy, right?"

"So, did she?" Britt asked. "Have another friend?"

"Oh, I don't know. R. L. wondered for a while."

"Who was it?"

"R. L. didn't say. A woman Angela talked about. Some well-dressed woman. With a beautiful sports car. She liked Angela. Took her for a ride once. Is there any more champagne?"

"Did Angela," Pierce asked, "ever describe this woman?"

Jan's interest was wearing thin. "Not to me. She'd never tell me anything personal. What does it matter, anyway? She's dead now, the little snot."

"Hey, you're beautiful when you're miffed," Britt said in a soothing purr. "Settle down, gorgeous. We got lots to talk about. Namely, a quick skyrocket to the top for Jan Laughlin."

Jan sat very still. She cast her eyes down, permitting Pierce to observe the sweep of meticulously applied blue eye shadow across her lids. A demure smile touched the corners of her full lips.

He shoved his chair back and noticed Britt's hand lying on Jan's thigh, caressing with gentle, circular motions.

"Got to be running along, girls," he said.

The members of the class were more comfortable with each other now and volunteered their stories and criticisms much more willingly.

The science-fiction aficionado, face twitching with intensity, read a confusing fantasy about a time warp. Sally Berwyn's

"Gene in January" met with effusive praise, and a chapter of Nehemiah Evans's army novel received rapt attention.

Throughout, Pierce felt Amanda's close-set eyes, like a small animal's, fastened on him.

A portly insurance salesman stumbled through ten single-spaced pages, eight of which outlined a program of life and health coverages designed for corporate executives.

The frail Mrs. Siegerson suggested that while his effort was interesting, it lacked what their teacher, Mr. Pierce, had termed a prerequisite. That is, a plot.

"Wrong," snickered the bearded advertising copywriter. "It's got a plot. The plot is: Take my insurance policy, please!"

Not a bad get-off line, Pierce decided, and seized on it gratefully.

"Next week, an exercise in flexibility. The same protagonist you have in tonight's story. But put him or her in a new situation. See you then."

The woman he'd come to think of as the Coffee Lady was wending her way toward him. He groped for another excuse. Then Amanda Gatliffe dropped a piece of paper on his desk. She continued on, out the door.

He picked it up, glanced over it.

It registered in the back of his mind, and his body felt suddenly weak. But for an instant he could not consciously be sure that what he had seemed to have read was what he had actually read.

He forced his eyes back to the first sentence, to read it all again, speaking each word, distinctly, in his mind.

> The lady is under the tree on the golf course. It is night. The man comes along. He sits down with her. They drink something. They talk. The moon is out.
>
> The lady takes her clothes off. The man takes his clothes off. He kicks something.
>
> The lady says, "Oh, my, sugar, you are eager."

The man lays down with her. After a while the lady yells real loud. She says, "Oh, sugar, oh, sugar."

This is a story about what happens on the golf course at night.

He had the sensation that he had been standing with the paper in his hand for hours. Rooted, incapable of movement, incapable of thought.

But the Coffee Lady was still talking, and he realized it had only been seconds.

"Pardon me, please."

He moved quickly through the semidarkness of the library. He heard the air-cushioned door at the front entrance squeal shut.

Pierce ran to the door and pushed it open.

Amanda and Emil were just turning into the parking lot, heading toward the Mustang.

"Wait a minute!"

They paused. Then Emil took Amanda's arm and resumed walking.

"Wait a minute!"

He ran up beside them, but they did not stop. Pierce grabbed Emil and spun him around.

"I said wait!"

The youth contorted his mime's face into an expression of searing pain.

"Now see what you've done!" he wailed. "Yanked me shoulder out of its socket! And me a minor! You've been mean to a child! Mean! Mean!"

"I want an explanation!" He thrust the paper into Emil's face.

Emil blinked, inclining his face forward, and pulled it back. "Don't see too well without the old bifocals. Gettin' on, you know, sonny."

"You know what it is!"

He whirled to confront Amanda. "Look, this can't go on. You wrote this, didn't you? You know what it says?"

"Oh!" Emil nodded, as if at last comprehending. "That's Manda's story. Is that it?"

"You know goddam well that's it."

"Did you read it in class, Manda?" Emil asked with great interest.

She shook her head, slowly, solemnly.

"Did you put her up to this?" Pierce demanded. "Is this your idea?"

"Manda's writin', ain't it? Her printin', I should say. It's her story. Invented it, she did. Out of the blue. It just come to her, it did. She's really creative. Neat little yarn, eh?"

He beamed at Amanda. Her jaw dropped, and her misshapen head wagged in what took Pierce a moment to understand was a grin.

"Get over to the car, Manda," Emil directed. "I'll be right along."

"No," said Pierce. "I want some answers. Mrs. Gatliffe, I want to talk to you."

"I told you," Emil said, "anything about Manda, you talk to me first." His hands were doing their conjuring tricks again. An arm flew out in one fluid gesture, and Amanda moved toward the car.

"So what else did you want to know about her story?" Emil's tone was polite, his lips sneering.

"How she happened to write it. Why she wrote it."

"I told you. It just come to her. Things come to her."

That smirking face touched off anger in Pierce that he'd seldom felt before. "Look, you don't get off like that. I'm not dropping this thing."

"What are you goin' to do, sir? Show it to the authorities? A story about two people on a golf course? There are no names, are there? Wouldn't the law want to know who the two people are? Or who you think they are? And if you say you don't know who they are, they'll say, 'Why did you bother us with this silly thing?' Won't they now?"

Pierce took a step backward. He was frighteningly conscious that he had been about to smash his fist into Emil Gatliffe's mocking mouth.

Emil realized it, too, and it seemed to delight him. "People who come poking around Amanda—they wind up in her stories, you know."

Pierce's fury was so strong that his words came out as little more than a croak. "I want to know how she wrote that! Now!"

"And sometimes"—Emil grinned broadly—"they wind up dead in her stories."

Footsteps approached. Emil glanced over Pierce's shoulder, and now his smile was beatific. A wave of farewell, a series of balletlike leaps, and he was suddenly opening the door of his car.

Nehemiah Evans drew up beside Pierce and watched as Emil throttled the engine into sputtering life.

"Any problems?" the deputy asked.

Pierce shook his head. Evans was silent as the Mustang lurched into McKinley Street, signaling properly for a right turn, and departed.

"Smartass son of a bitch," Evans commented. "You know, I told you that when I found Angela Karlstrom in that cemetery, some people showed up right away. Hangin' around for a look at the body. That Gatliffe kid—he was one of 'em."

Chapter 14

Now the land was afire with autumn. A profusion of colors throbbing in the gleaming sunlight, prodigal in their intensity.

Pierce drove east over the little used county roads. Across the narrow ridges, past the orchards, and the fields still bordered with wild roses.

Traffic was heavier this Saturday. It was a day to savor this season's brief, bittersweet pleasures: trees of bloody red and brilliant orange and yellow. And still a muted green prevailed, clinging stubbornly to branches, holding tightly to the fading wisps of summer.

A magnificent day, yet he was impatient for it to end. With darkness he would see Britt again. He had not expected to see her this weekend. But now that he knew he would, the hours until then seemed interminable.

"Progress, sugar," she drawled on the phone that morning. "I've got some choice dope about Amanda."

"So have I."

"Blockbuster stuff?"

"Interesting stuff."

"First, Ralph said to ask you to meet him in his office Monday at ten. Okay?"

"Why?"

"Some boring business reason."

"Not about—"

"Our sordid, shameful secret?" She chuckled. "I doubt it. Come over tonight. We've got quite an agenda."

122

"Over?"

"My house. Ralph's going to be gone. Overnight. Something in Chicago. Some arrangements for this big speech he's giving."

"What time?"

"Nine. Bring whatever notes you've got. Want to park at the Kennilworth again? Like when you met me on the course? I know nobody can see our driveway from the street. But it might be best if you weren't parked there. Just in case."

"So discreet. So proper."

"I'll show you how proper."

Just before sunset he drove up the side of Frenchman's Pitch. The parking area at the summit was crowded, and shouts and laughter rang in the crisp air.

Pierce passed the chain-link fence and strolled to the crumbled wall of the old redoubt. A young couple stood nearby, the father holding up a toddler who squealed with joy and apprehension at the sight of the earth vanishing into empty space beneath him.

A soft, golden haze covered La Soeur, but in the west it was darkening rapidly. Above the dying sun, gun-metal clouds were faintly visible—far off yet, perhaps as distant as the Dakotas. Pierce gazed down the long, steep slope vivid with sumac, maple, poplar, and pine, down to the bottom of the cliff and, past it, to the wide expanse of emerald green that was the Meadowbluff fairway.

A few tiny figures inched across it. The course was huge, and it was with difficulty that he finally located what he believed must be Britt's hanging tree near the fourteenth hole. He leaned even farther over the edge, but there was no way to catch a glimpse of Britt's and Ralph's home. It was too near the base of the bluff.

Here he had sat with Corinne. Here they had permitted their minds to expand with dreams that journeyed beyond La Soeur. Here he had held her hand and was warmed by her ferocious appetite for life.

Why, Corinne?

The old question. The ever enduring question.

Pierce swung his eyes along the narrow trail encircling the western face of the escarpment. Farther down that path he had come upon Winifred Stabo crying out in the night for her lost, strangled daughter. The vision of her had been horrifying, pathetic, and somehow repellent.

Yet what had he been doing every day since August but crying out to his lost, strangled wife? Trying to call up some shade of her. Trying to conjure an answer from . . . what? A memory. A wavering image as insubstantial as hazy smoke on an autumn afternoon.

It had been a sick thing—Winnie out here imploring the soul of her dead Jennifer to return.

But, dammit, if I knew how to make Corinne appear . . .

And confront me and explain to me . . .

I would!

God help me, I would!

Shivering, his feet dangling in space, he watched night shroud the Mississippi River and settle on the toylike streets and buildings of the quiet city below.

He was no longer in a hurry. Not after those hours on the Pitch, not with the memories of Corinne fresh in his mind.

Corinne who had once loved him. And died swinging by her windpipe, loathing him.

It was past nine thirty when he cleared the woods. His hands were cold and there was an iciness within him that anesthetized all feeling.

"Hi, you," she purred. But her face held the tiniest touch of uncertainty, a fleeting web of lines clustered just above her eyes.

She kissed him ardently. He knew his response was not what she had expected.

"You okay? God, it's that same herringbone thing again. Is that the only coat you have?"

She led him by the hand over the deep, green pile carpet into the living room. Beside the fire a brandy bottle and two large snifters stood on an elegantly austere mahogany side table with brass corner braces. One glass was full and the other a quarter empty.

He dropped onto one of the handsome love seats near the fire. She hesitated, then sat on a matching unit across from him.

Britt's robe was a simple terry—turquoise, mandarin collar, knotted at the waist. It hugged tightly to her, flattering the lines of her body. Pierce knew with certainty that she wore nothing under the robe. The thought did not produce the dry catch in the back of the throat that was the familiar forerunner to desire.

She kicked off her slippers and tucked her feet under her. "First the bad news. Vigo wouldn't let me see the original report on Jennifer Stabo. So I couldn't find out if she was wearing a red scarf or not. I didn't want to ask Vigo. He'd want to know why I asked, and he probably wouldn't tell me, anyway. So that part of Amanda's story is still unconfirmed. Of course, there is a way to get it answered."

"Yes?"

"Ask Al Stabo. He's your old buddy, no?"

The dog poked its sharply pointed snout up at him. It laid its head—strangely small for the large and bulky body—on his thigh. The collar around its neck was of rich, embossed leather and sprinkled with rhinestones. Somehow it reminded him of R. L. Cutler's boots—the fancy stitching and the inlaid beads fashioned into a pattern of stars.

"Here, Smokey," Britt called. She rubbed the dog's head and the white, fluffy hair of its neck. "He's a Karaelian beardog. They're brave as hell. They used to use them in Finland to chase down real bears. No sport for a sissy. But he's spoiled rotten. Aren't you, lover?"

She kissed the tip of the long, wet nose, laughed, then peered keenly at Pierce. "Now the good news. The goose-pimply part. The neighbors think Amanda is a witch!"

"A witch? In what way?"

"No particular incidents. But once in a while somebody'd come to visit her. Somebody who didn't look like a friend. In fact, they said she had no friends. Sometimes these visitors were better class people, and the neighbors thought they were having their fortunes told. Or having Amanda put a hex on somebody. Emil drops a lot of hints along that line."

"Do they believe Emil?"

"Not really. They think he's a petty criminal of some kind. They've seen him lugging things back at peculiar hours."

Pierce moved farther away from the intense heat of the fire. "What about Amanda? Does she come and go at odd hours?"

"Occasionally. Always with Emil."

"I suppose nobody remembers whether she was out on the night Angela was killed. Or the afternoon Jennifer Stabo was killed."

Britt swished her brandy to and fro. "It was hard to lead into that kind of thing without tipping anybody off about why I was there. But, no, nobody remembers any special night she was out late. There's no particular pattern, evidently, to her comings and goings."

The dog whined quietly, wanting to be petted some more. Ignored, Smokey padded silently away and up the sweeping staircase to the second-floor balcony. Pierce heard the faint click of paws on a hardwood floor.

"One of the neighbors gave me some graphic poop on the crime Amanda got arrested for—beating the bejabbers out of this guy who drove through her garden. He was drunk and couldn't find his own trailer in the dark. It sounds kind of funny. Banging him with a shovel because he plowed some carrots and beans under. But I'm told she split his skull open and kept hitting him and hitting him. And if somebody hadn't pulled her away, another lick or two and she'd've chopped his head clear off."

"All right, but let's look at it this way: She was defending something important to her. That garden. Maybe the guy she attacked set off some kind of deep-down rage because he reminded her of her late husband. A thoughtless drunk stamping out whatever little bit of enjoyment she could call her own."

"Yeah. Maybe she retaliates pretty forcefully when she thinks she's been victimized."

"But that's not the same thing as prowling the countryside, killing indiscriminately."

"It could grow into that. Maybe she thinks the whole damn world's victimizing her now."

"Jennifer Stabo? She was eleven."

"The woman's a lunatic, Whit! Maybe Jennifer looked like some girl who used to bully her back when she was a child."

Pierce reached for the attaché case he'd thrown down beside her. "You might be interested in this." He handed her the last story Amanda had written.

Britt waved the paper back and forth as though it were a fan. "Hot damn! Hot damn! Whit, this is fantastic!"

She sat up straight, kicking her heels on the floor.

"But damned if she hasn't given the game away. This time she's gone too far. Do you know what this means? The implications?"

"I think so."

"It means she was *there*. It means she's writing things that happened, things she saw. Things she was involved in!"

Britt got up, gesturing with the snifter.

"That means the other stories weren't figments of her imagination. She was there. She saw!"

"Or Emil did."

Britt stopped. She drained her drink. "Or Emil did. Either way, one or the other of them knows what happened. To Angela and Jennifer. Either they did it or they know who did. Because God knows you and me making it on the fourteenth hole was not something they read about in the paper. And that means—"

"I understand the logic of it."

"God, Whit, we're *this* close to cracking this thing!"

She walked to him in long, swaggering strides, smiling down in total confidence. "We're gonna do it, sugar."

Pierce swiveled his head to gaze into the flames. If he had put his hand into the fireplace, he knew there would be no searing pain. He was encased in ice. There would be no sensation. Nothing.

"So I'm going to tell the sheriff's department what I know. It's their job."

"No!"

"I'm going to give them her stories. Not the last one. No need for us to embarrass ourselves. But they should see the rest."

"No. We agreed. No!"

Abruptly she spun around, putting her back to him. She placed the brandy snifter on the end table and picked up the decanter to pour herself another. Instead she folded her arms, facing the darkened doorway to the dining room.

"Vigo wouldn't know what to do with the information. I told you that."

"It's his job. I'm finished with it."

"Would you like to see the notes I made? About talking to Amanda's neighbors? About talking to Jan Laughlin?"

"Britt, I'm telling the sheriff what I know."

"Okay. But let's see if we can dig up a little more on our own first."

"Dig up what? No, I'm finished."

Whirling, she gave a startlingly loud laugh. She had undone the buttons of the upper half of her robe.

"Stupid me, Whit! Going off half-cocked as usual. Jumping to conclusions before the facts are in. The despair of my old journalism profs. The thing is, we could be all wrong. Maybe Amanda did see us that night. Or Emil saw us. That doesn't have to mean she still didn't make up the first couple of stories."

She plopped onto the velvet cushion beside him. "Listen, we wait till Amanda does her next story. See if she has any more surprises. Then we'll have a nice long talk with her."

Britt's tapered fingers with their plum-colored nails glided across his back and began kneading his shoulder muscles. "If the next story doesn't make it clear, okay. Then we see Vigo."

Her lips brushed his ear. "That just means waiting a little bit longer."

She kissed him forcefully, pressing his head back against the chair. "Okay?" she whispered. "Agreed?"

She gave him no opportunity to answer.

Britt, it's never failed you before, has it? But it's not going to work this time.

Frantically she sat up, pulling her arms free of the robe. It slid to her waist. She perched on the cushion on both knees, straddling his body. She bent to him. With one hand she cupped a breast and swished it back and forth across his lips.

He tasted her. The heavy, earthy tang of her perfume swirled over him, steamy and suffocating. He let the taut nipple revolve around the perimeter of his mouth. But his arms did not tighten around her. His head sank back even farther, his eyes closed.

He felt her hand moving down his chest, down to his belt. Her fingers pried and tugged.

Then she was kneeling on the carpet at his feet.

He closed his eyes again. "Britt . . ."

Within her mouth he was stirring. He shuddered. She felt it, and her head bobbed more rapidly.

He groaned and lightly touched her tousled, flaxen hair. Now her tongue was everywhere at once, fluttering like the wings of a hummingbird. Pierce thrust himself forward, deeper into her, again and again.

"Britt! My God, Britt!"

A nervous whine intermingled with his shouts. A cold nose

filled his hand. Smokey. The muzzle was shoved first against Pierce, then against Britt, nudging her and licking her cheek. The terrierlike ears stood straight up, alert and quivering.

"Britt!" Pierce called out in one last, uncontrollable convulsion.

The dog's curled, bushy tail wagged with furious excitement, and the tick-tick-tick of its panting was like a previously unnoticed clock in the suddenly silent room.

It was nearly dawn. They were sprawled atop a rumpled, quilted bedspread, their legs still intertwined. They had made love three times. First on the thick carpet. Then Britt had gone for her bedspread, and Pierce had followed her upstairs. He had tried to ease her onto the bed, but she had laughed and pushed him away and run down again to the living room.

"Do I have it right? The bedroom is off-limits for visitors?"

"You may think it's corny. But I couldn't be with you up there. One of my quirks. I cannot shaft Ralph on his own bed. Cornball, huh?"

Pierce smiled faintly. "Ralph need never fear. His marriage bed is sacrosanct. His living room, however . . . Doesn't the mood ever strike you or him down here when the fire starts crackling and it's obvious you don't have a damn thing on under that robe?"

"Are you kidding? Married couples don't do crazy things like this, for God's sake. *You* were married." Her fingertips picked at the matted, graying hairs of his chest. "You've never said anything about her. Your wife."

"No."

"Why not?"

"What were you expecting me to say?"

"Look, I'm an old police reporter. If I'm out of bounds tell me. Why did she do it?"

"Britt, you are the soul of finesse. Why did she do it? My God, if I knew that . . ."

His own voice sounded far away to him. The fatigue had made him vulnerable, he knew.

"Why did she do it? Her business was going down the tubes . . . and the miscarriages . . ."

"She wanted children?"

"She talked about it. A helluva lot. We took tests, to see whose fault it was. Nobody's. They couldn't find any reason."

"How did you feel about it?"

"Children? Fine. Maybe it would've brought us closer. Maybe . . ."

"Could she have learned something you didn't know? That she could never have a baby? Or even that she'd contracted something godawful?"

"I asked them to look for that. In the autopsy. And I asked her doctor that. She'd been to see him only ten days before. There was nothing."

"Did you love her, Whit?"

"Yes. I did."

"I don't mean just at first. We all do then, don't we? I mean, did you still? Up to the last?"

"Yes."

"Is that why . . . Tonight . . . you weren't . . ." Her velvety voice softened, faded. She put her chin in her hands, looking broodingly into the dying fire.

"Britt," he mumbled, "let's spend today in the country. Away from here. Drive somewhere north, way north."

"Ralph's coming home late this afternoon. Tomorrow we kick off the stupid Indian Summer Days. There's a ton of things to do, day and night. For Ralph it's what Coronation Week is to royalty. And I've got to be faithfully at his side every minute of it."

"Then just for a couple of hours today. We'll have lunch somewhere, over on the Minnesota side."

On her hands and knees she crawled to the stack of firewood.

Sparks flew as she wedged a thick, foot-long cedar log onto the smoldering coals.

"Oh, sugar, wish I could. But I've got a guest coming over for brunch. Jan Laughlin. I think I can wheedle more out of her."

Pierce reached for the brandy he had set down hours earlier. He wrinkled his face because now the taste was too sweet, too sickening.

Britt sat cross-legged on the floor, rocking forward and backward.

"We need every scrap we can find, Whit. Every scrap. There's so much more to piece together. That's why I don't want to share anything with Sheriff Vigo yet. So we've got suspicions. But who really went out after Jennifer at that pond? Who went out after Angela at the Old Military Cemetery? Who really went out there, bringing death?"

She laughed resoundingly. "Hey, remember that for the book!"

"Remember what?"

"The Death-Bringer. It has a neat, eerie sound, doesn't it? A great ring to it."

Pierce slowly got to his feet, pulling on his clothes.

Chapter 15

"I know you're busy, Whit. And Lord knows I am."

Ralph Hungerford's cobalt eyes were clear and calm in the oversize, deeply fissured face. "You remember Len Durban?"

"Of course." Pierce grasped the hand of Hungerford's diminutive chief lieutenant and felt the slightest lessening of pressure. Would Durban be here if Ralph intended to confront him about the affair with Britt?

"Delighted." Durban's voice was like the sound of a stereo unit on which the bass has been turned all the way up. It vibrated throughout the room.

"Let's get to the nub of it," Hungerford said. He moved smoothly to his desk and picked up a sheaf of papers. His blue, pinstripe trousers and his crepe de chine shirt were perfectly tailored to lend at least a suggestion of dash and trimness to his bulging, bearlike body.

"A speech, Whit. Merely a speech. But a speech that could represent a turning point for me. I'd very much appreciate it if you'd assess it. Dive into it, tear it apart, give me your candid views. And your creative suggestions. Len, take his jacket, will you?"

Pierce let Durban deferentially remove the coat and bear it to a closet that materialized with the sliding of a panel in the dark walnut wall. The room was long and high, the richness of the walls heightened by discreet track lighting, the two sumptuous rugs Ming wool with dragon patterns. His desk was rosewood, curving in a soft arc, its polished working surface almost barren. On each wall hung an oil painting of an eighteenth-century English sporting scene.

Ralph patted the back of a chair upholstered in fine-grained corduroy and waited till Pierce sat before resuming.

"The speech is for the National Economic Forum. It's to be given December eighth in Chicago. This is a national panel. It's going to focus countrywide attention on me and on my views. And more than that, Whit, I'm going to let the cat out of the bag. Just for you."

He winked. "Len advised me not to be so forthright. But you and I go back a long way together. You're almost family." He ran a hand over his bulbous, balding skull.

"This is going to launch my campaign for this district's seat in the House of Representatives. I've weighed my options and I've made my decision. I'm going for it."

Pierce became aware that Len Durban was peering closely at him, grinning expectantly, as though awaiting his reaction to being present at a momentous occasion in history.

"Well, good luck to you, Ralph."

"Now you see why the speech is so important."

"It can position Ralph as the only candidate with truly national stature," Durban interjected eagerly.

Ralph smiled. "Remember, Whit, I said important for both of us. It occurred to me that it could be a godsend, your arriving in La Soeur at this time. Of course, I don't know your long-term plans. But you are an experienced, professional writer. You know the political milieu. And you know this community. I'm going to be needing people, good people—"

"Whoa, Ralph. I just said I'd read the speech."

"Fine. We'll leave it at that for now. And be candid. Len wrote it, but he's not so overcome by his own brilliance that he won't yield to the wisdom of a proven pro. Right, Len?"

"Absolutely."

"And if you'd like to tackle a rewrite, let me know. We want the best and we'll pay for the best."

Ralph pointed, and Durban handed the papers to Pierce.

"Hark now, Whit. There'll be other speeches, news releases, media contacts. I know you have your career as a novelist. But you might want to consider taking a year or more off to gain some new perspectives."

"Let's keep it open for now, Ralph."

"Maybe not for too long?" Durban put in. "The election's a year away, sure. But the primary's in April, and we want to staff up as quickly as we can."

Behind Durban's *basso profundo*, Pierce was conscious of Ralph's characteristic humming as he maintained the vocal level he would use when he decided to break into the conversation.

"True, Whit. So please ponder it carefully. It could—"

A buzzer sounded. "What line? Thank you. Whit, it's the head of the Association of Commerce and Industry. A crisis in the Indian Summer scheduling. I have to talk to him now. I told you this was the most hectic week of the year. Could you read the speech in Len's office? Len, would you—"

"Certainly. This way."

Durban's office was one-third the size of Ralph's. The prints on the wall—scenes of Paris in the rain—were the same ones Pierce had observed hanging in every discount furniture store he'd ever been in.

When Pierce finished the last page of the speech, Durban blinked anxiously at him through his granny glasses. "Well?" The voice was as close as it could come to a quaver.

Was this poor bastard on the hook? Pierce wondered. The speech was at best adequate. But he had no strong convictions about what it would take to improve it. Nor did he have any real interest in attempting to do so.

"Looks good, Len. It punches hard, but it takes a statesman-like stance."

Durban looked relieved. His voice grew authoritarian again. "Glad you think we're on the right runway for takeoff. Now, about the position Ralph mentioned. We'd love to have you aboard. I'm not sure, though, that Ralph made it clear that as the organization's shaping up, I've been asked to be his campaign manager. And after the election—and, hopefully, the victory—the plan is for me to be press secretary as well. We will definitely need speechwriting support. However—"

"However, the speechwriter reports to you. Tell Ralph I'm pondering my options."

"Excellent." The tiny mustache wiggled cheerfully. "And how are you and Mrs. Hungerford faring in your little—"

"Our little what?"

"Your research project. For—what is it?—an article, a book?"

"We're faring fine."

"Excellent! I'll fetch your jacket from Ralph's closet."

The rain slanted in mercilessly that night, blowing in off the river. Pierce sprinted from the garage to the back door. A clammy chill permeated the house.

He switched off the downstairs lights and climbed the steep stairs. At the door of the guest bedroom he halted.

The floor was a chaos of clothing, paper, and books.

His breath hissed inward. Slowly he swung his head to take in the entire room. The closet door was open, and the interior clearly visible.

No movement anywhere, no sound.

The wind howled, rattling the shutters. But there was no creak on the stairway behind him, no hint of noise downstairs.

Pierce sifted through the litter. Both suitcases had been emptied and the dresser drawers pulled out.

The attaché case had received the roughest treatment. It was upside down, near the bed, its spine cracked, as if someone in haste or anger had stepped on it heavily.

Scattered everywhere were typewritten pages and pages covered with handwritten notes. Most represented the failed efforts he'd made on the book about Corinne. Mingled with them were the notes he'd taken on the Karlstrom-Stabo cases.

Pierce riffled through them. At first glance nothing seemed missing. All three of Amanda Gatliffe's stories were still there.

Nor did anything else appear to have been taken. Flipping light switches, he went back downstairs and checked the front and back doors. No sign of forced entry. Then he checked every window on both floors. All were securely locked.

There was still the basement. He touched the doorknob and realized he did not want to descend those steps. There were two casement windows down there, and the intruder easily could have gotten in through them. And whoever had broken in could still be down there.

He dialed the police and, immediately afterward, the Appleland Inn. Sally would still be on duty.

"It's Whit Pierce. Nothing to be alarmed about, but I wanted to clarify a point. When I got back to the house, I found somebody had gotten in."

"Oh, no!"

"Nothing to be alarmed about. Doesn't look as if they took anything, and the police are on their way."

"Are you all right, Whit?"

"Sure. But the thing is, it doesn't look as if they forced their way in. So I just wanted to check. I do have the only keys, don't I?"

"Yes! They're Aunt Amy's only keys. One for the front door, one for the back. Wait a minute. I remember now."

"Remember what?"

"She had a duplicate. In case she locked herself out or lost the original or anything. I remember she told me about it once when she had to use it."

"Where is it?"

"It's for the back door. It's under the back porch. Hanging from a nail. She always said nobody would think to look there."

"Sally, I'm going to call a locksmith and put new locks on both doors."

"Oh, Whit. This is terrible. You're sure nothing's been taken?"

"Doesn't seem to be. Don't worry."

"I'm coming over."

"No need. I'll tell you about it tomorrow."

On impulse he suddenly asked, "What's the Indian Summer event tomorrow?"

"What? Oh, the crowning of the queen, I think."

"Care to go? With me?"

"Oh. Sure. I think I can switch shifts."

"I'll call in the morning."

He turned on the outside light over the back door, got on his hands and knees in the rain-soaked mud, and groped with one hand under the porch. A sharp piece of wood pierced one finger, and then he touched the nail. A key dangled from it.

If nothing had been taken, why had someone gone through his possessions?

He recalled the razor blade incident of five days ago.

The conclusion was inescapable: What else did he have that would interest anybody in La Soeur but his notes about the two murders?

Any other reason for the ransacking would be farfetched. The rest of the house had been untouched.

Then why weren't the notes taken?

Because we don't have solid evidence of anything, even if we try to con each other into believing we do.

But whoever was so curious wouldn't know that. Not till the notes had been uncovered and read.

He went back to the telephone and dialed. Britt answered.

"Whit, I told you this is the worst of all possible weeks. Ralph's in the next room."

"This is important," he snapped, and told her why.

"Well, hell," she breathed. "Somebody's damn sure scared we're on to something."

"The thing is, they may go after you next. They may think you have something I don't."

"I keep my notes in a manila folder in my den upstairs. Next to the master bedroom. Easy to find. I suppose I could stack them somewhere else."

"That's not the point. Who cares about the notes? What we have amounts to zilch. Except for Amanda's stories. And they weren't taken, although I suppose they were read. The point is: What if they break in and can't find your notes—but find you there instead?"

"Then I'd say we smoked somebody out, sugar. Somebody we've been trying to smoke out."

"Don't be so damned carefree about this. It's gotten out of hand. Somebody else has dealt themselves in. We've got to talk about this."

"Dammit, I can't. Tomorrow we start with the pancake breakfast. Then I judge the Kiddieland parade. Then it's the Lederhosen Luncheon."

"I'm going to tell the cops your home could be a target, too. They can stake it out."

"No! Look, we keep this place locked up tight. And Smokey's one hellacious watchdog."

"It's getting out of hand, Britt."

"It's starting to get results. Whit, that brunch with Jan Laughlin! Incredible!"

"That's not the issue now."

"I had to ply her with champagne again. Then she goes wacko. Tosses her glass in the fireplace. Then—can you believe this?—she picks up a piece of glass and tries to carve on her tits."

"Britt—"

"I kid you not! She was going to notch my initials there! Like

139

on a goddam tree trunk! I had to wrestle the glass away from her."

There was a figurine on the end table that in the half shadows looked to Pierce like a malevolent dwarf slyly sizing him up.

"Whit, she's got all kinds of cuts and scars. All over her boobs. Both of 'em. Most of the cuts are initials."

Pierce picked up the figurine and placed it down again with its back to him.

"Mostly they're R. L. Cutler's initials. I asked Jan whether she or R. L. did it. She said R. L. did, as a way of making her prove her love. And there's more. You know R. L.'s alibi for the night of Angela Karlstrom's murder? She was drinking at the Ace High? Well, Jan was the main witness. Nobody else paid much attention to R. L."

"Britt, the point is, you could be running a real risk—"

"And Jan lied. She said R. L. never disappeared for more than ten minutes. That's for the record. But she told me that at one point R. L. was gone for something like forty minutes. That would have been enough time, Whit."

"Cops are here. I have to go."

"Just a routine break-in. Got it, sugar?"

"Be careful, Britt. Damn careful."

"Whit, we're going to pull this off. By ourselves!"

Chapter 16

Wednesday night was windy, and the thermometer hovered near freezing.

"It's this way every Indian Summer week." Sally laughed. "Local joke. The real Indian Summer weather comes a week before or a week later. Never during. But nobody cares. It's our version of Mardi Gras."

The contest for the new queen was held in the stadium at the county fairgrounds just outside the city limits. Beer booths had been set up by local service clubs, the profits destined for charities. Sally and Pierce sipped from Styrofoam cups and joined in singing along with a polka band imported from Milwaukee. She had pulled a red-and-blue stocking cap low on her forehead. The tassels swished back and forth over her shoulder blades as she tossed her head about excitedly.

"I'd forgotten how much fun it is." She clapped her bushy mittens together to the tune of "Beer Barrel Polka."

From where he sat Pierce could see Britt perfectly. She and Ralph were in the VIP box directly opposite the stage. Britt was wearing a honey-colored stone marten coat. When the two of them leaped up, applauding—as they did frequently—Britt looked childishly small beside him. Ralph's Tyrolean fur cap perched high atop his huge head, and the collar of his shaggy beaver coat was pulled up around his face. Beaming, he waved to well-wishers throughout the stands.

Britt blew a kiss to the Indian Summer contestants. The

crowd cheered. From a scaffold one of the cameras from WLSE-TV trained its lens on her.

"Which one is your money on?" Sally teased.

"I'm waiting for the swimsuit competition."

"Sorry to be the bearer of bad news, but those evening gowns are as much as they peel down to. We don't want our city's finest coming down with pneumonia."

"Well, some of them are sure risking a chest cold."

She groaned and gave him a gentle jab in the ribs.

Later, strolling down State and Main, they debated whether the most talented candidate had been crowned. "I thought the trumpet player had it," he insisted. " 'Malagueña' isn't easy, and she only hit two clunkers that I heard."

"No, they chose correctly. No one who sings 'The Impossible Dream' has ever lost. It's tradition."

Pierce noted the transition the town had undergone in the past few days. Enormous banners now spanned the street. Store windows overflowed with cornstalks, Indian corn, pumpkins, gourds, and bushel baskets heaped high with plump apples— Jonathans, Delicious, McIntosh. From the open doors of the bars, voices and music poured out raucously into the night air. The sidewalks were crowded. Merrymakers carried mugs and pitchers as they weaved from one celebration to another.

Sally took his arm and promised to guide him to the best pizza in town: Mario's.

"Mario's! I know it. I used to go there. At least something hasn't changed."

"A town like this—does it really change much?"

"Doesn't it? Look at that. A gyro sandwich shop. That wasn't here when I worked here. Nobody in La Soeur would've known what a gyro was sixteen years ago."

"I guess you only notice change when you come back. I haven't been away enough. Just those two years teaching in Iowa. Here it is, Whit."

The checkered tablecloths mottled with cigarette burns were the same as he remembered them. One leg of their table was shorter than the other, and he seemed to recall that, too. But he and Corinne had eaten here so often in those days that they must have sat at every table at some time or other.

He and Sally placed their order and shared a carafe of apple-cranberry wine while they waited.

"You came here with your gang?" she asked. "From the newspaper?"

"With the gang. And with Corinne—" He stopped suddenly.

Sally bent forward anxiously. "I didn't mean to bring you here if there are associations. . . ."

"No, it's all right. I've been trying to remember her as she was then. As I felt about her then."

He broke off. There had been that dinner Sally had prepared for him at Aunt Amy's when he had opened up about Corinne much more than he'd intended to.

"What I mean is," he faltered, "I'm trying to see her as she was in those days. What she was really all about. I want to write about it, Sally. That's the only way to get to the heart of it . . . to grapple with it and . . ."

"I think I understand."

"Because, after we left here, what she was and what she did were colored by our life together. So what I was doing got mixed in with what she was doing, and it gets so hard to tell who's responsible for . . . for trying to figure out why . . . I'm not making it clear. Let's drink to Indian Summer Days."

The hot pizza arrived, and Sally scooped a slice onto his plate. "Green pepper on your half, none on mine. We'd have problems if we did this often."

"Amazing. It tastes the same as ever. I would've bet a thousand dollars I'd never have Mario's pizza again. I thought when I left here I'd left here for good."

"Me, too. When I left for Iowa."

"Why did you leave?"

"I was involved. With a man."

She shrugged and busied herself in pouring and savoring her wine. "Oh, my, it was stupid. He was married. It went on a long time. I kept waiting. He said he'd get a divorce but never did. Really, I'm embarrassed to tell a writer this. It is such soap opera. And so dumb. Now, what kind of story could you make out of that?" She bit her lower lip, and Pierce thought she might be close to tears. He put his hand on hers.

"I'd write it as a story about . . . guts," he said. "You had the courage to come back here."

"I had to. My dad. But I'm hanging in there with it. And when a teaching job opens up, I don't care where it is in La Soeur. Even if it's back where I was."

"Is it going to be much of a wait?"

"I don't know. I've always been so awed by those people who seem to know just what's best for them and march right toward it. I never met your wife, but I thought she'd be like that. I'd heard so much about her. 'La Soeur girl bowls over big city.' I thought it must have just happened automatically. The overnight business success. The TV interviews. Every night the Pump Room. Oh, I just assumed it was so natural for her."

He thought of Corinne looking back at La Soeur from the Mississippi so long ago and all but pleading, "Take me along on that raft. Take me along, Tom Sawyer."

She'd needed him then, In the beginning and during those early years. And during the shaky years. But not in recent years. Not the successful years.

"Not so." He toyed with the last slice of pizza in his half.

"I'm sorry, Whit. I didn't mean to dredge up anything you'd rather not go into."

"You're not. Really. No, she wasn't one to wait. But the world didn't fall at her feet with the wave of a wand. Hell, it wasn't till she opened her third shop that she bought the Maserati. That was the validation for her. Proof that she had made it."

"A Maserati? Fantastic!"

"A bone-white Maserati."

"You don't see too many of them, do you?"

"No, and for what one of them costs you could buy everybody in this state a pizza."

"I only saw one once, that I know of. One that I knew for sure was a Maserati. One of the busboys pointed it out. He's a fanatic about foreign sports cars. It was in the parking lot of the A-I."

She touched the rim of her wineglass to her lips, then lowered it. Her eyes squinted strangely as she strained to bring something to the surface of her consciousness.

"And I talked to the woman who was driving it. She was at the counter. She had coffee and pie, and she said she had to drive back to Chicago. It was a white Maserati."

"Well, Corinne didn't have the only one."

"It looked so out of place at the A-I. She was a well-dressed woman. Very attractive. Beautiful, really."

"When was this?"

"Oh, maybe seven or eight months ago."

"Corinne hadn't been back to La Soeur in years."

Sally spoke slowly, almost reluctantly. "I even remember the day. Because the woman mentioned how terrible it was. It was the day that little girl was found murdered, out by that pond in the country. Your friend Mr. Stabo's daughter."

Pierce bent toward her. Suddenly his body had gone rigid.

"We'd just heard about it at the A-I. They'd just reported on the news that a La Soeur child had been strangled. And the woman with the Maserati heard them talking. And I remember her saying how terrible it was for something like that to happen. That's how I remember her and what day it was."

Pierce pulled the wallet from the inside pocket of his jacket.

He flipped through it and removed the photo of Corinne and himself.

Sally looked at it a few moments. Bewilderment fluttered across the long, gently sloping planes of her face.

"Whit, that's the woman."

Chapter 17

Dammit, where was she?

At eight ten he still had not begun class. He waited behind the large desk, shuffling papers, one eye cocked on the door he'd left open.

All day he had been anticipating her baleful presence and, most especially, the story she would hand him. So much hinged on it: whether it indicated she had more than peripheral knowledge of two savage murders; whether he and Britt went to the authorities with what they knew.

At eight fourteen he gave up on her, shut the door, and felt a stultifying sense of anticlimax. Nothing would be decided tonight, and the two-hour span of the class loomed like a desert of nearly infinite proportions.

And so it proved. Another tedious travelogue—about a leisurely lunch in Curaçao—from the retired English teacher. A convoluted explanation by the insurance salesman of the need for replacement-cost homeowners' coverage to offset the inroads of inflation.

And yet another purloined movie plot from the Coffee Lady, Mrs. Blye. A father-daughter team run a confidence game and attempt to bilk the heir to a sizable fortune. The plan disintegrates when the young woman falls in love with the intended victim. Idly, Pierce searched his mind for the title of the original.

In his critique he charitably avoided questioning the genesis of her story. And after dismissing the class he nodded benevolently when she scuttled forward to suggest coffee.

"Fine. Collect whoever's interested and let's be on our way."

"Something happen to your briefcase?" Nehemiah Evans inquired.

"An accident. You've got a sharp eye, Mr. Evans."

"Don't know about sharp," the deputy said, and grunted. "You used to bring a fine-lookin' briefcase down here. Now you're using a big brown envelope. Seems natural to wonder why."

"Will you join us for coffee?"

"No thanks. Like to get a couple hours in on the book tonight."

"Good night then."

Sally, he realized, had slipped out without his noticing it. From the front steps of the library he saw her car in the darkened lot.

"I'll meet you there," he told Mrs. Blye.

Sally saw him coming. She ran down her window and waited.

"I thought you might want to come along."

"Not tonight, thanks." Shadows covered her face and absorbed the rust of her hair. But he could see clearly the doubt in her wide eyes. She looked steadily at him—troubled and totally serious. "Whit, I don't think I should've said what I did last night. I shouldn't even have commented about your wife, even though I meant it to be complimentary. I don't know you well enough to talk about things like that. It was very uncalled for."

"Not so."

"And I don't think I should've mentioned that part about seeing her. About the Maserati. I saw the look on your face. The minute I saw it, Whit, I knew this was something you didn't need to know. I don't know why. But I should've kept it to myself. I should've shown some tact."

"Sally, you were just being open." He lowered his head to her level. "It's just that what you said . . . surprised me. I don't quite know what to think of it. Corinne never mentioned any trips back here. It's probably not important. But, still—"

"Whit! There!"

He jerked upright and whipped around.

Just behind him there had been a noise. He heard it the instant she called out.

Pierce heard a polite, throat-clearing cough. Emil Gatliffe faced him, three steps away.

"Ahem! Ahem! Your pardon, please, excellency."

He stood ramrod straight, his quicksilver face sternly officious.

"It is my majestic duty to deliver to you a document of brilliant consanguinity," he pronounced with mock-heroic solemnity. His left hand had been behind his back. Now he held it out to Pierce. In it was a sheet of paper.

Pierce grabbed the paper.

"Farewell, my liege," Emil intoned.

It was much too dark to make out the words. "Sally, would you turn on your overhead, please?" She nodded and unlocked the door for him.

He sat beside her and brought the single page close to his eyes. It was written with a red pencil on white, ruled tablet paper. He recognized at once the childish, awkward printing.

> The pretty lady opens the door in her home and lets in the big lady in the purple dress.
> The pretty lady looks surprised. It looks like she knows the big lady, but she still looks surprised. She turns around and walks up the little stairway. The big lady follows her and puts her arm around the pretty lady's neck.

With both hands Pierce squashed the paper together.
No! I will not finish this!

* * *

Then, smoothing it, he read on.

> The big lady pulls and squeezes real quick and real hard. The pretty lady just says "oh," and then her neck cracks. The big lady drags her into the middle of the room.
>
> The big lady in the purple dress gets a little table from the kitchen. She pulls down a long kind of rope from the wall. She puts the pretty lady on the table. The pretty lady moves. The big lady in the purple dress ties the rope to the ceiling. She ties the other end of the rope around the pretty lady's neck.
>
> The pretty lady is hanging there. Her eyes are open. Her eyes are green.

He folded the crumpled paper twice and stuffed it in his jacket pocket. He stared through the windshield at the solid cement wall in front of the car.

"Whit?"

He did not move.

"Whit? Whit!"

Sally frantically shook his arm.

"What is it? Are you all right? Is there—"

She was silenced by the anguish in the face he turned to her.

"What?" he said.

"I only—"

He pushed the car door open and vaulted out. He began running.

"Whit?"

Emil. Make him answer. There must be an answer. Must!

Where would he have gone? It was only eight or ten blocks to Main Street. There would be the Indian Summer celebrations again. Noise. Crowds. Confusion.

Of course, that's where. The chameleon. The wraith. Blending into the streams of people. Dodging, taunting, sneering.

But he must find him. He could not live with this. He could not handle the implications of it. He could not think about what it might mean.

He could not. He must act. He must move. He must do something. *Anything.*

He had run three blocks as swiftly as he could, pumping his legs wildly, trying to outdistance the thought he knew lay at the heart of his desperation: Was it possible this was true?

An elderly man stepped out of his way with a frightened shout.

A car horn honked. Pierce ignored it. Then it blasted again.

It was Sally, driving alongside him. He waved her away. But she leaned toward him and said simply, "Whit? Please?"

He let himself come to a stop. Breathing heavily, he walked to her Toyota and got in.

"I'm looking for him. Emil," he said quietly.

She nodded. "Downtown?"

"I think so."

She said no more. She continued on, barely creeping along, so he could scan the faces of the pedestrians as they passed. The side streets were not well lit. Emil could have faded from view almost anywhere along the avenue.

Near the corner of Main and Eighth, a barricade had been erected, blocking all traffic.

"The Torchlight Parade," Sally murmured. "I'd forgotten."

He flung himself out of the car, back on the pavement.

"Whit," she said, "I don't know what this is. But I'll wait for you here."

Almost immediately he was lost in the crowd. Thick rows of spectators lined both sides of Main Street, boisterous and cheering. Others streamed back and forth along the sidewalk, in and out of bars, singing and drinking.

The music blaring through the open tavern doors battled with the ragged strains of the marching bands. Spilled beer, flattened cups, paper napkins, and the remnants of mustard-covered bratwurst littered the pavement.

Pierce shoved his way impatiently through the slow-moving mass, his eyes scanning the crowd. Floats were rolling by on the street, and on one of them the new Miss Indian Summer Days stood at the apex of a pyramid, above a semicircle of male torch bearers. Whistles and applause erupted from the bystanders.

Now he was walking faster than the floats were moving. He flicked his eyes over every clump of onlookers, over every passerby, over those lounging in doorways or against lamp posts or peering out of shop windows, restaurants, and taverns.

"Watch it, numb-nuts!"

He had bumped a strutting, burly youth with an ice cream cone in one hand and the other on his girl friend's neck.

"Sorry." Pierce hurried on. He passed Mario's. It was packed again, but no sign of Emil within. He passed the gyro sandwich shop. He passed the block-long Sears store, and he could see that the parade was turning up ahead at Fifteenth Street. There it would reach its end. This was a small city and a small parade. It shouldn't be that hard to spot one particular individual.

But this was an individual who seemed at times transparent, able to appear or vanish at will.

Frustrated, he stopped to observe the parade a moment while he decided whether to follow it to its end or retrace his steps. An ROTC drill team marched by, twenty white-painted rifles twirling and twisting in something close to unison.

Emil was watching them from across the street.

Pierce shouldered his way through a cluster of spectators and reached the curb. Through the ranks of the drill team he saw Emil's face light up in recognition. Emil waved. Then he was swallowed up in the crowd.

A skinny policeman with scrawny forearms and a Zapata mustache tugged at Pierce's arm as he tried to cross the street.

"Can't do, sir. Can't do."

"I just want—"

"Can't do, sir. Parade going by." The policeman raised both hands, palms out. He smiled in comradely fashion. No doubt he and his brother officers had been instructed to go easy on ornery drunks. This was a friendly city and a family festival.

Pierce attempted to protest, but a university band thundered by playing "On, Wisconsin!" He saw Emil again, a half-block away. One incredibly long arm shot up, and the fingers waggled, beckoning Pierce to come on over.

Gently the policeman eased Pierce back into the crowd.

He moved back to the sidewalk. Certainly he could cross the street elsewhere. But Emil had vanished once more. This was another game to him. He must be hoping Pierce would keep up the pursuit. He'd enticed a grown man into playing tag with him.

But a game had to have a starting point. He remembered then what he'd barely been conscious of when he'd gone to the library parking lot to talk to Sally. An ancient, rusted Mustang parked not far away.

Sometime tonight Emil would be returning for it.

Pierce alternately trotted and walked back to the library. There were only four cars in the unlit lot. One was his own and one was Emil's.

He crouched behind a shiny Seville not more than twenty feet from the Mustang. He was soaked with sweat, disheveled. But he felt a determination he had not known in months.

Pierce touched the piece of paper in his jacket pocket. That was all he cared about. That obscenity that Emil and Amanda somehow thought of as fun.

He would not permit himself to dwell now on those paragraphs. All he permitted was a slow fury to kindle in his mind, to expand and envelop him. When he checked the luminous dial of his watch and saw that it was past one thirty, he was surprised. It had seemed as if he'd been squatting beside the Seville for only a few minutes.

As alert as he was, he did not see Emil approach. Suddenly a shadow stood beside the Mustang, and a key flashed in the darkness.

Pierce covered the distance between them so quickly that Emil, for once, seemed indecisive. He made a lunge as if to run. Then he doubled over as if to leap into the car and pull away. But he had delayed too long.

"Bon soir, m'sieur!" Flustered, his lips twitched uncertainly and finally forced a hasty grin.

"Answers!" Pierce hissed.

"Answers? To what, *m'sieur?* Alas, I am but an ignorant high school dropout."

"Answers!"

Emil raised his arms and limply bent them at the elbow, as if invisible wires were pulling him. "What would I know?" he moaned piteously. "Simple, stupid me, Marcel the Marionette."

"Enough!"

Pierce threw him around and slammed him against the hood of the car so that Emil's chest grazed the horse-head ornament. Pierce's right forearm pressed against the reedy throat. With his left hand he twisted Emil's arm backward and upward.

"Remember the story?" he whispered in Emil's ear. " 'The big lady pulls and squeezes real quick and real hard'?"

"Can't place it. Manda has so many stories. Ain't she a caution?"

Emil suddenly kicked and, at the same time, tried to whipsaw his upper body free. Pierce pulled his forearm back viciously. The gangly youth began to speak, but his words turned instantly to a rattling gurgle. His body became still.

Pierce relaxed the pressure on Emil's windpipe. "The story! God damn you! How did she write it? Why did she write it?"

A smile of delight slid across Emil's face. His eyes sparkled merrily.

"Oh. *That* story!"

"Yes, God damn you, *that* story!"

"Just a kind of joke. The better to tease you."

"A joke? You mean she just made it up? Out of nothing?"

"She made it up. Like she makes up stories all the time. Out of nothin'. Almost out of nothin'."

"You're telling me she knew my wife was dead. Hanged. So she made up this little fantasy. Just out of her head. 'The big lady in the purple dress.' Just something out of her imagination."

"Somethin' like that."

"Bullshit! Then how did she know we have a stairway by the front door? How did she know the kitchen table was dragged into the living room? How did she know my wife's eyes were green?"

"She sees these things."

" 'Sees' them? Bullshit!"

"She does!"

" 'Sees' them? How?"

"It's wonderful! She just has to touch something. Something somebody's used a lot. Used for quite a while. So some part of them rubs off. She rubs her hand on it, and she sees what happened to the people."

"She never knew my wife! She never had anything of my wife's!"

"Let me go to my pocket," Emil said.

"That's not an answer!"

"Just let me. You'll see."

"Go on. Just remember, I can snap your goddam head off!"

Emil chuckled soundlessly and winked. "Watch carefully, *amigo!*"

His slender right hand floated in the air, dived into his pocket, and emerged closed in a fist. Like a magician drawing out the suspense of his revelation, he let his fingers slowly unfold.

A soft key case of tooled, black leather lay on his palm. On it was a monogram: C. P.

Pierce snatched it from Emil. It was Corinne's. He'd bought it for her three years before.

He'd taken Corinne's keys along to La Soeur, but he'd never needed them. They'd been tossed with other odds and ends in one of the dresser drawers. He'd never have thought to check on whether they'd been taken.

"You stole this," he said, his voice thick with outrage.

"Removed it. Was going to return it. That's why I had it on me tonight. I was going to open your car and slip in the keys and then lock it up again. Sort of surprise you."

"You broke in. You tore through my papers, threw all my notes around. It was you!"

"I never! Never tore up nothin'! I just went in and looked around. It's like you invited me. The key was under the porch. I just wanted to take something of yours. So Manda could read it." Emil gave an exaggerated, theatrical shrug. "Thought the key case would do it. I was going to take the razor first, but I just fiddled with it. Changed the setting. Another little joke on you."

"That was a week ago. You came back Monday night. You went through my papers."

"I never!"

"Bullshit!" He swung the youth's arm sharply up behind his back. Emil whimpered, squirmed, and spat out the words, "You hurt me, you'll get it! Like Paw-Paw! You will!"

Pierce pulled his forearm away. The blazing intensity of his fury had run its course.

Emil rubbed his throat. "I was never in your place but just the once. And I didn't make no mess. Just lookin' for something to bring to Manda."

Calmly Pierce said, "I want to talk to your mother. Now."

Emil nodded appreciatively. "Sure, you do! Who wouldn't? The wonders she can show you!"

Then he shook his head, sighing heavily. "But it's too late for gentlemen callers. And Manda's sick. That's why she didn't come to your old class tonight. A shame but that's how it is."

"Now," Pierce said.

"She's sick, I tell you. She gets this way time to time. It lasts a day or two and then she's okay. But she takes leave of her senses. I have to put her to bed. She gets like a baby."

Pierce felt the recoil of a new jolt of anger. He dug his hand into Emil's shoulder just where it joined the fluted neck.

"Now! I want some answers. Or, by God, I assure you I'll go to the police and the judge who handled her case and anybody else I can find! I'll get her sent away, I promise you! I'll raise such stinking hell they'll put her away and never let her out!"

Emil had no mask now to pull over his rubbery face. He stared at Pierce with open incredulity. "No. You wouldn't. Manda can't go back there."

"Just try me. You don't know how far I've been pushed. Just try me!"

The thin body seemed to shrink, to pull inward. Then Emil straightened and clicked his heels together. He beamed an enormous grin.

"I would be honored, sire. Honored!"

"My car." Pierce clutched Emil by the bicep and led him away.

On the drive to the southwest side, Pierce lashed out with question after question.

"Everything she wrote in those stories is something she 'read,' something like that key case?"

"Now you got it. There's even a spiffy word for it. Psychometry. You can look it up. Gives Manda some class. Pip! Pip!"

"What about the Angela Karlstrom case? What did she have of Angela's to read?"

"A cigarette lighter. I picked it up there in the cemetery the next morning. Pretty. Silver-plated. Had a ram on it. 'Fraid the gendarmes wouldn't be too happy to hear I took it."

"Jennifer Stabo?"

"A little coin purse she happened to be carryin' that day. Her momma gave it to Manda, matter of fact. Sometimes people come to Manda for readings like that. I tell her: You were blessed with a blessed gift. Use it. But don't give it away. Put a little something in the pot. Sometimes she sees something, sometimes she don't. But it's ten bucks on the barrelhead either way!"

"She saw what she saw about Jennifer. But she didn't tell Mrs. Stabo?"

"Not on advice of counsel, your honor. Me, that is. Like I told Manda, people like Mrs. Stabo think they want to know what happened to their dear departed. But, no, sir, no, they don't. Not really. Anyway, that's the kind of story Manda and me like to keep to ourselves. We can know about it and talk about it together, and nobody else is the wiser. So she told Mrs. Stabo it was all a blank and she didn't see a bloomin' thing."

"Then why did she make that the first story she wrote for me?"

"Tricky devil, that's you—right? Tossed her a curve, you did. Tellin' all them poor simps they had to write a story then and there, their first class. And start it with something about the sky being blue. Manda was stumped. All that come to her was the Jennifer story. It happened outside and the sky being blue an' all. So that's what she wrote."

"And the golf course story?"

Emil began cackling, and he wrapped both arms around his stomach.

"That wasn't Manda. No, sir," he said at last, gasping. "Methinks thou knowest who that was."

"You. Why?"

"To knock you off your high horse. Show you Manda and me are something special. We know things. We know lots of things people don't know we do."

Pierce coasted down the lane of haphazardly placed mobile homes until he recognized the Christmas wreath in the front door window. The neighborhood was silent but for the yapping of a small dog. A damp, penetrating mist had rolled in from the nearby river.

While Emil unlocked the door, Pierce asked softly, "Does your mother have a purple dress?"

The youth bowed low, lank yellow hair spilling over his forehead as his arms swung wide.

"See for yourself, *mein herr.*" He shut the door behind them and they were in thick, almost total gloom except for the reflection of a distant red light.

Pierce tensed. He felt a sense of confinement, of threatening presences posed everywhere around him. As soon as Emil turned on a floor lamp, Pierce realized why.

It was like being dropped into the midst of a going-out-of-business sale at some jam-packed discount store. Furniture of every style surrounded him: steel office cabinets, bookshelves, wall shelves, chests stacked atop desks, knickknack-laden tables.

There were so many objects around him that they registered on his mind as only a fleeting blur. A battered harmonica, a 1920s steam iron, a Lincoln Log set, a bird cage, an owl clock, an elegant perfume decanter, a turn-of-the-century foot scraper, a miniature chess set, a three-foot-tall pepper mill, a dented bathroom scale, a brakeman's lantern, an Uncle Sam bank . . .

Emil moved farther into the room, along what resembled a narrow passageway. Two persons would not have been able to walk through the room side by side. The trail widened only enough to accommodate three chairs and a footstool. Beside one wing chair badly in need of reupholstering was a laminated snack tray strewn with potato chips.

From beneath a brutally gouged lowboy, a cat's face peered out unblinkingly at Pierce. A mixture of smells clotted the air— the odor of cat, of mustiness, of incense, of chocolate, of burnt grease.

They went through a second cluttered room, but here space

had been hewn out for a davenport, a TV set, and some vinyl-tube lawn furniture. Emil halted before the half-open door beyond, the room from which the reddish light emerged.

"I told you true. She gets this way. They never been able to do anything for her when she does . . . Manda! You asleep, honey chile? We're coming to visit for a while."

He looked in, crooked his finger at Pierce. "See, it's your professor. Here to see if you're gettin' along tolerable enough. How are you, me little darlin'?"

With solicitous hands he raised her massive head, plumped her pillow, and patted the thin curls plastered to her skull.

She rolled her eyes—the right so noticeably higher than the left—over her son, over the room, and onto Pierce. There was no comprehension in the eyes. The jaw fell; the chipped and discolored teeth glinted dully in a mechanical grin.

"I'm sorry to disturb you, Mrs. Gatliffe. But there are some questions I have to ask you."

A drop of water appeared in one nostril and slithered down her sunken left cheekbone. Emil produced a handkerchief and wiped it off.

"Won't do you a bit of good, Colonel. She ain't got the slightest idea what you're sayin'."

"Mrs. Gatliffe, you do remember me, don't you?"

He searched that grotesque face, so like a hastily chiseled bas-relief in the side of a roughly textured boulder. There was no inkling of any conscious perception of his words.

Her enormous body filled almost every square foot of the bed. Her arms were under the covers, which were pulled up to her jaw. The reddish radiance in the room emanated from a brass novelty used as a night-light—an Aladdin's lamp on a stand near the bed.

Other curios rested on the stand, as well as almost everywhere else in her room. A bird feeder, a globe, brooches, dolls, a bud vase, tumblers, hand mirrors, wall mirrors, a fishing pole, corkscrews, rings, a pocket calculator, a golf club, a shaving brush.

An open closet was jammed with dresses and coats on hangers. Other apparel had been flung helter-skelter atop pieces of furniture. The nylon netted floor was a profusion of shoes and boots—mainly women's footgear but some men's also—old and new, presentable and worn. Hats, caps, scarves, and ties were hung or draped everywhere space could be found.

"She's not putting on. She ain't got any idea who you are. Or me, either."

"Mrs. Gatliffe! That last story you wrote! You remember it? About the pretty lady? The pretty lady who died?"

The vacant grin remained. But her eyes were traveling the room now, jumping from object to object. She was oblivious to him.

"And how do you like our little collection of goodies?" Emil rubbed his hands together. "Ain't they truly a treasure? And you know what so many of 'em are? They're *stories*, Mr. Writer. Stories! Manda has touched them and read them. And told me the stories. She raised me on those stories. Night after night she read me those stories!"

"When will she be herself again?"

"Generally a couple days."

Weariness washed over Pierce in a sudden, unexpected wave. "That's all she knows?" he asked, aware he'd reached the end of his string of questions. "Whatever she wrote in her stories for my class, that's all? No more details? No names?"

"She sees her stories the way she writes 'em. She don't hear voices. She don't hear names. She just sees . . . snapshots! Snapshots that move real fast. Snap your fingers and they're gone!"

He nodded wildly. "But you can catch the whole story if you know how to. You can learn a lot from a snapshot, can't you? You can learn all you need to about the people, if you know how to look at it."

Pierce began threading his way out of the room, moving deliberately to avoid bumping against anything.

"So glad you could drop by and have this chat with Manda. Sorry if she talked your ear off, but she don't know when to quit. Now you know all about her, correct? Nothing more bothering you?"

Emil winked. "One last thing. I think you'd be interested. See that? That snowman?"

He pointed to an object on the stand next to Amanda's bed. It was a small dome set on a pewter base. Inside it was the figure of a snowman. If it was shaken, Pierce knew, "snowflakes" would fall.

"Bring it over here, would you?" Emil said. "I want to show you something."

Pierce went to the stand, picked up the dome, and walked to the doorway where Emil waited.

Instantly, behind him, he heard a guttural rumbling. Spinning around, he was amazed to see Amanda struggling out of her bed. Thick, pasty white arms pushing the massive, straining body upright. Saliva trickled from the twisting, gibbering mouth. Her eyes reflected in the red light of the Aladdin's lamp were flecks of glittering madness.

One swollen hand clasped the golf club. She lurched to her feet. Her inflamed eyes were riveted on Pierce.

She raised the club above her head and started unsteadily toward him. A low, growling sound poured out of her.

Emil grabbed the snowman from Pierce. He thrust it at Amanda dramatically, as an actor might stretch forth a crucifix in a vampire movie.

"Here it is, Manda! See! It's all right!"

Wriggling it before her, he returned it to the nightstand.

"Back where it belongs! Just like always! See, Manda?"

Amanda Gatliffe dropped the golf club. Emil took her arm and guided her back to the bed. As the springs creaked shrilly beneath her, she lifted the dome, upended it, and watched an explosion of snowflakes. Her mouth gaped in a contented grin.

" 'Night, 'night, dear." Emil brushed her forehead with his lips. He motioned Pierce into the next room and started laughing, seemingly so overcome that he had to sag weakly against an old ice chest.

Pierce had been stunned by the sight of Amanda. Now he felt nothing but revulsion. He wanted only to leave this place—this place where he'd thought so many answers would be found.

"Oh, my, if you could've seen your face!" Emil whispered, fighting for breath. "Oh! Precious! Precious!"

Emil dabbed at his eyes. "It's her favorite, see. Had it since she was a kid. Given to her by a nurse who used to look out for her at the home. She was raised in the county home, you know. An orphan. No legitimate parents. She sees the nurse every time she reads the snowman. The lady's long gone now. Dead. But Manda—she still sees her there. Oh, she wouldn't let nobody run off with that thing. She has a temper when you try to take what's hers!"

Pierce followed the passageway back toward the front door. The cat, gray and fat, leaped out of his way and back under the lowboy.

"Oh, come on now, just havin' a bit of sport with you. Had you going there, didn't I? But what fun's life if you can't shake people up a little? What else is there?"

Pierce opened the door, and Emil called, "I let you talk to her. You got no call now to keep after her. You got no call to try to send her away."

Then, in a voice that might be that of an entirely different person, he piped cheerfully, "You see all her dresses? Such pretty colors. Violet, indigo, heliotrope. Purple."

Chapter 18

He made a pot of coffee, taking as much time as he could with each small detail of the task. It gave him something tangible and immediate to focus on. He consumed half the pot, sitting at Aunt Amy's kitchen table, pouring a jigger of White Label into each cupful.

The central question remained, and he had no idea of how to deal with it. What if Corinne had not taken her own life?

He went upstairs and showered. Afterward he was just as weary, not at all refreshed, and totally unable to sleep. He paced through every room of the house, including the basement, checking the new locks on both doors and satisfying himself that all the windows were fastened tightly.

Had Emil lied about not having slipped in here a second time? Why would he lie about a second visit, since he admitted the earlier entry and the theft of Corinne's key case?

Why would he lie? Because he was obviously an incorrigible liar. A trickster, a changeling. Possibly schizophrenic. Determined to torment and confuse. "What fun's life if you can't shake people up a little?"

Still, it was not yet dawn. He brought the coffeepot and the Scotch bottle into the living room and sank into the cozy rocker beside the front window. From here he watched the final Friday of October come to Lindner Street in La Soeur.

Lights winked on in one house after another. Two middle-aged joggers huffed by. Husbands and working wives began departing for their jobs. A trio of high school students piled into a friend's car, tossing a football. Smaller children, including the Sorensons' next door, straggled out of their homes. Many wore witch, ghost, or pirate costumes. Sunday was Halloween, so today there would be parties and games at school.

There had been no visible sunrise, and by nine the day was still bleak and gray. Yet it was daylight, humdrum reality, and Pierce finally acknowledged that the previous night had receded forever.

With it ebbed some of the night's obsession. Now it almost seemed like some irrational adventure he had dreamed: Amanda's story, the confrontation with Emil, the bizarre home that was a teeming library of inanimate objects to be "read."

Read. Or imagined?

A hideous picture—Amanda and Emil gleefully exchanging fantasies evening after evening, savoring every tidbit. But could it really be more than that—two wholly unstable personalities conjuring up sick fantasies?

The phone rang, and Pierce frowned. No longer was he anxious to talk to Britt. Somehow, abruptly, Britt had become part of his past.

The issue now was Corinne.

"Hello, Whit? It's Sally."

He remembered then. She'd said she'd wait. Last night. Downtown. It had completely escaped his mind.

"Sally, I'm so sorry. I must apologize."

"Are you all right?"

"Yes. You must forgive me."

"You're sure you're all right?"

He was conscious of talking very slowly. There had been enough shots of Scotch in enough cups of coffee to make speech difficult.

"I'm fine, Sally."

She did not press him further. "If I can help . . ."

"Thanks, Sally. Call you soon."

The coffee in his cup had turned cold. He dumped it down

the drain in the kitchen and refilled the cup with three ounces of Scotch. The phone rang again, and this time it was Britt.

"Only got a minute, sugar, but I have to know. What did Amanda come up with last night?"

"Nothing much."

"What does that mean, 'nothing much'?"

"Just some gibberish. Nothing to do with Jennifer or Angela. But I found out why she writes what she writes."

In a droning monotone he described his visit to Amanda's, omitting only the reason he had gone there.

"Whit, that's wild!"

"Isn't it?"

"We got a helluva lot more to do on her, once she gets over this fit or whatever. And on Emil. God Almighty, what a character she'll make in our book—whether she's the breakthrough or not. Lord, think of Amanda holed up there in that trailer and rubbing stuff that's been taken off the bodies of murder victims and spinning yarns about how it was done! Talk about local color. That lady's soaking in it! Hey, you were going to check on the red scarf."

"I will tonight. Al and Winnie Stabo asked me over for dinner."

"Great! Anything the matter?"

"Why?"

"You sound so goddam laid-back. Just when we're getting close to paydirt. All week you've been calling me, hot to talk about the break-in. Now it's pulling teeth to get two words out of you."

"Emil admitted he'd been in here and gone through my things."

"Even more interesting. I'm sorry I had to leave you on your own this week. The Indian Summer merry-go-round is over Sunday. I'll see you then, okay? Sunday night. Miss you . . . Whit?"

"Yes?"

"We're still going this alone, correct? I mean, what good would it do to tell Vigo Lustgarten that Amanda sees things in cigarette lighters?"

"Not much."

"We're going to find some answers, Whit. Whatever it takes!"

"Whatever it takes."

"See you Sunday."

"Whatever it takes," Pierce repeated into the dead receiver.

The issue was no longer Angela Karlstrom or Jennifer Stabo. Or some book he'd write with Britt.

No, dammit! The subject is Corinne.

The conversation over dinner was light, jocular, superficial—much like the atmosphere at Al and Winnie Stabo's in the old days. There had been no reference to Corinne during dinner. Or to Jennifer. It was as if the three of them had agreed beforehand on a set of conversational ground rules.

The Stabos' canary trilled in accompaniment to their voices, just as Pierce remembered. There had been several canaries since his last visit here. But it was the same bird cage in the same corner of the dining room. And its purpose was the same: to amuse Winnie during her household chores.

She had always been an excellent cook, and sauerbraten was her specialty. It had never been better, Pierce insisted, and her large moon face glowed.

"Whit's right, honey. You outdid yourself tonight."

"Save room for dessert. Angel food with raspberry topping."

Winnie disappeared into the kitchen, and Pierce followed Al into the living room. Al sat down in the big recliner by the end table and lit up a cigar.

Pierce eased himself onto the faded sofa. He had come tonight for one specific purpose. To ask one question. Now he fumbled for some opening, some path to it.

Then there was no need. Al Stabo lifted a framed portrait

from the table. He studied it a long while and passed it, word-lessly, to Pierce.

"She looked a lot like Winnie, Al."

"Yeah."

The child in the picture was chubby-faced and mischievous, with bright eyes that brimmed with curiosity.

"This was taken only a month before."

He put the cigar in his mouth and chewed it viciously. Pierce handed back the photograph and saw that Stabo's arms were trembling.

"Damn them, Whit." Al's voice was that of a man afflicted by laryngitis, barely able to croak.

"I'd kill them, Whit. Whoever touched my girl."

"Al, that last day. Was Jennifer wearing anything distinctive? Like a cap or anything?"

"A cap? No." He did not seem surprised by the question. His eyes were fixed on the portrait.

"Anything unusual? Anything colorful?"

"A red scarf."

"You're sure?"

"Oh, yeah. We both remembered it, Winnie and me. How Jennifer looked when she left that morning. Pedaling away on her bike. She wore it to keep the hair out of her face when she was riding. Like a pirate."

"The little girl has blue overalls on. And a white shirt. And a red scarf like tied around her head . . ."

Amanda was right.

But if the details about Jennifer were accurate, what about Corinne?

What about Corinne?

Pierce walked to the kitchen. The refrigerator door was open, and Winnie had stooped over, taking the cake out.

"You knew Corinne so well," Pierce said.

"We were best friends, Whit."

"Did you ever see her do anything or say anything that

would make you think: Here is a person capable of taking her own life?"

She rose, stiffly, to her towering height, a dreamy smile on her lips.

"Corinne had one of the strongest wills to live I've ever seen. I don't think she was ready for her transition."

"When she was a girl, was there the slightest hint? Anything at all? Can you remember?"

Her voice sounded far away, so distant that Pierce could barely catch the words.

"I remember a girl in high school who got pregnant. She killed herself. Carbon monoxide in her parents' car. I remember so well Corinne saying that she would never do that if it ever happened to her. And, of course, she didn't."

"Didn't . . ."

"When it happened to her."

Winnie kept smiling at him. Drowsily, absently, she said, "It would never have occurred to her. The life force in her was too powerful."

"Are you saying . . ."

"That's how she was, Corinne. Our Corinne."

He went to her swiftly, gripping her by both shoulders. "Winnie, are you saying that Corinne . . ."

Al appeared in the doorway, his cigar belching smoke. "What's going on?"

Winnie's soft, pink face was suffused with a kind of sweet, detached fondness.

"But they're together now, Whit. That's the important thing. I know with all my heart that Corinne is with Angela. Comforting her. Loving her. Together now as they couldn't be in life."

Pierce stumbled backward, tipping over a chair. "Angela? What do you mean, Angela?"

"Winnie," Al begged, "come back in the other room."

"Angela Karlstrom?" Pierce whispered. "Angela Karlstrom . . . Corinne's daughter?"

"Whit, it was a long time ago." Al tried to place a glass in Pierce's hand. "Here. Have a drink. What difference does it make now, Whit? Please, Whit. Here."

Winnie stared at both of them, slightly puzzled but not at all disturbed. "They're together now, Whit—Corinne and Angela. I think you should try to reach them. If you wish, I know some people who can help."

It was just past three thirty A.M. Pierce, at the far end of the counter at the Appleland Inn, motioned for more coffee.

He had been there since leaving the Stabos. During the early-morning hours the A-I became something of a trucker's hangout, since it was on a main highway and no other restaurant in the vicinity stayed open all night. Even now there were about a dozen customers.

At the other end of the counter two truckers traded loud boasts about how many miles they'd logged today. A third, beside them, had laid his head down to snatch a few minutes' sleep.

Pierce wished he felt tired enough to do the same. But there were too many questions, too many images.

All evening he had attempted to push them aside. Much later —when he was less dazed, less shaken—he would pick them up and examine them. One by one.

Beginning with the fact that Corinne had once been the mistress of Hugh Karlstrom. And was the mother of Angela Karlstrom.

His Corinne. The Corinne he knew so well.

And that pathetic girl. Angela, that pathetic, brutally murdered girl.

The girl who had been just a name to him. The girl who had been the lover of Ruby Lee Cutler. And the daughter of Hugh Karlstrom.

And the daughter of Mrs. Whitney Pierce . . .

No!

No, he would not go around and around with it again. Not again.

He drew in his breath, slowly and deeply, willing his fingers to stop their drumming. The blond waitress bearing the coffee-pot shook her head in amused understanding. Of course, he had to be another of the drunks who filtered in after the taverns closed and sat there so stiffly, so broodingly. The blondes on the eleven-to-seven shift were tougher, with a more worldly-wise air than those who worked the daylight hours.

Pierce had forced himself to examine the face of everyone in the restaurant. Who were they? Why were they here? Where would they go when they left? As long as he could occupy his mind with idle questions, he could stave off those thoughts that shrieked for his attention.

A newcomer entered, and Pierce looked up, glad of the opportunity to have still another distraction.

"How goes it, R. L.," one of the truckers said in greeting.

"Shitty."

Pierce realized Ruby Lee Cutler had recognized him as quickly as he had her. She stomped along the length of the counter, keys jingling, slapping a hand against her hip with every step. She swung her leg over a stool three away from Pierce.

Ignoring him, she placed her order. "Anybody tell you what a sweet little ass you got?" she told the waitress, voice devoid of humor or warmth.

"Oh, can it for once, R. L."

Without looking at Pierce, she said, "Can't leave her alone, can you?"

"What's that?"

"Angela. I hear you were talking to Jan Laughlin. Trying to worm stuff out of her. That bubble-headed cunt!"

She snorted disgustedly, stubbing out her cigarette, bearing down until it was pulverized.

171

Pierce stared at her intently, but still she did not turn to face him.

"Angela," he said. "What did she . . . look like?"

Cutler snorted again. "Her picture was in the paper. She was . . . really something. Not like most of the dogmeat pieces of tail in this town. What the fuck is it to you, anyway?"

Pierce moved one stool closer to her.

"Did she look like her mother?"

"Her ma? No, she didn't." Cutler lifted her chin high, tilted her head back at a precarious angle, and slowly turned toward him, seemingly aware of his presence for the first time.

"What the fuck you want to know for?"

Just visible below the brim of her Stetson, her glazed, drunken eyes flared in hostility.

"I took you for a weirdo from the start. When you and that jig deputy come into my shop." She laughed loudly, sneeringly. Then she struggled to her feet, swept an arm toward Pierce, and bellowed, "Here's the guy that's making it with that colored deputy. Any of you guys want to get in on the deal?"

"Shut up, R. L.!" the waitress snapped.

The two truckers looked up from their coffee and laughed.

Pierce got up, nodded to the waitress, and left.

"They probably got a date together now!" he heard R. L. hollering behind him.

Back at Aunt Amy's he noticed that the neighborhood children had soaped up the windows of the garage. He remembered that this was Halloween day.

Chapter 19

Hugh Karlstrom's home was a modest aluminum-sided ranch house in a development fifteen minutes' drive from the Meadowbluff Country Club.

He held the front door open for Pierce, a can of beer all but hidden in his outsize hand. Karlstrom led him through a neat, plum-hued living room to a more untidy family room. It was crammed with golfing trophies, golfing photos, golfing mementoes. A gargantuan television set was tuned to a golfing tournament.

"Care for a beer?"

"No, thanks."

"Anything?"

"No, thanks."

Karlstrom jabbed an elbow at the television set. "Take a look at that, then go look out the window. And this is only the end of October. But down there it's seventy-two degrees. Look at that sunshine. I played that course many times. Do you play?"

"No."

"The kind of winters we get up here, there's nothing like a golf vacation. Even if you don't play."

He was doing his utmost to project a picture of bronzed, confident cordiality. The chipmunk cheeks blossomed with affability. Both men sat in leather recliners with vibrator attachments. Karlstrom rested his long, wide loafers on a footstool in front of him.

"We've got a good group going to La Costa in January. Some

of the greatest guys in town. Still a couple openings, if you'd like to think about it. A bang-up time, first to last."

"I came here for another reason."

Pierce had not slept for two days or nights. He knew he looked ashen, bleary-eyed, probably on the verge of collapse. He had no plan. But he was aware that before he did anything else, he had to come here.

"I don't know what else I could tell you that you could use for your book." The petulance that Pierce had so disliked initially surfaced again. Karlstrom's lustrous brown eyes were reproachful and suspicious. "Like I said to Britt at the club, that's all I know."

"It's not about the murder. That's not why I'm here."

"Not about Angela?"

"Yes. It's about Angela."

"What, then?" Karlstrom said, impatience rising in his carefully modulated voice.

"Was Corinne her mother? My wife Corinne?"

Karlstrom slowly straightened in the chair and kept rising until he was on his feet. His eyes narrowed to slits, and the cords in the meaty forearms bulged. With a plop the beer can in his hand collapsed.

"Why?" he asked, almost plaintively. "She's dead. They're both dead."

"I have to know. I have to confirm it."

"Does Britt know you're here?"

"No. This doesn't concern her. But I have to know."

Karlstrom closed and opened his eyes several times with almost insufferable languor. When he finally spoke, the words came slowly.

"You wouldn't put it in your book? About your wife?"

"I only want to know if it's true."

"Why should you care? You didn't know her then. She was a high school girl."

"I only want to know if it's true. Is it?"

"Hell's bells, I guess more than a couple people know about it. We tried to keep it a secret. But—a town this size . . . And the gossips can't ever shut up about it. Not if my name's involved."

Christ, it's true!

"It happens to a lot of girls." Karlstrom peered warily at Pierce, his body tensed. "It's not like, you know, somebody cheating on you after you're married."

When Pierce did not move from his chair, Karlstrom grew less defensive. "That's just the way it goes sometimes. And at least I shot straight with her. I didn't deny it. I didn't tell her to go take a long walk on a short pier."

"How did Corinne . . . react?"

"No hysterics. Never." From the first, Karlstrom said, Corinne was determined to have the baby. She had even wanted to keep it and bring it up herself. But her pregnancy occurred at a time when Karlstrom's wife had been anxious to adopt. She was physically unable to conceive, and they had already been listing themselves with a number of agencies. Eventually he had been able to convince Corinne that it would be better for everyone if she gave the baby up.

Karlstrom's wife had not been thrilled to learn that he had impregnated a teenager. But since it happened, she preferred to raise his child rather than some other man's. Not all women would have gone that route, but that was just the way she was.

And Corinne had let the Karlstroms have her child, and she had not intruded in Angela's life?

With new understanding he recalled her driving need to leave La Soeur. Yes, there was a bigger world out there that beckoned. But there was a reality in this city that she could no longer bear. *Corinne, God damn it, I'd have understood. You could have told me!*

"She never saw Angela again after she left here?"

"Oh, yes.".

"What?" Now Pierce was on his feet. "When?"

"A year after the plane crash." Once more the lowered lashes, the long pause that seemed to signify exasperation at the injustices of fate. Exasperation appeared to be as near as Karlstrom could come to sorrow or pity.

Corinne had called him from Chicago. Many times. She'd heard of the accident and insisted that Karlstrom, without his wife, could not provide Angela with a real home. She had asked that Angela be allowed to come and live with her in Chicago.

He'd refused. Again and again. Angela was his child. He would do his duty. But Corinne persisted. And it was true he was busy at the club. And it was true that since the plane crash and his injuries, his career had slid downhill. He couldn't make the pro circuit anymore. He had to depend on what he could make at the club.

So he'd agreed to let Corinne pay a visit and meet Angela. She'd done so. Several times. Three, to be exact. But he was still reluctant to let Angela go.

It was a ticklish situation. He didn't know what to tell Angela. That this was her real mother? How would he explain that to her at this late date?

"Who did she think Corinne was?"

"An old friend who used to live in La Soeur. A well-to-do lady who came back once in a while to see her old friends."

"Did she like Corinne?"

"She seemed to. The second time Corinne came, she took Angela for a ride in her . . . what was it? A Maserati? Angela got the thrill of her life. She talked about it for months.

"In fact, the next time Corinne drove up, Angela asked if she could take the Maserati for a spin by herself. It took a lot of gall. Angela could be real pesty sometimes. But Corinne didn't mind. Corinne and I had plenty to talk about, and this got Angela out of the house."

"When was this?"

"Oh, sometime last spring."

"April?"

"Yeah. Probably."

The day that Sally Berwyn had waited on Corinne at the Appleland Inn. It would have to be, Pierce thought. The day Jennifer Stabo died.

"Did you see Corinne again?"

"That was the last time. I still hadn't made up my mind. She called a couple of times after that. I was half-inclined to go along with it. You know, Angela was pretty well mixed up with . . . well, you know about it."

"When was the last time Corinne called?"

"Two, three months ago. Early August, I think. I said it was a deal. If she'd drive up here we'd finalize it. She said she'd make it the next weekend. She never showed up, and then I read in the paper that she was . . . well, I read about her." He paused. "I have to wonder"—the voice drifted with an aggrieved piteousness—"what would have happened. If I'd gone along with it from the start. If I'd let Angela go. She wouldn't have gotten in with Cutler. And if she hadn't . . ."

Pierce went through the living room and out the front door.

Chapter 20

He ignored the phone, going wearily past it to the closet, hanging up his whipcord jacket.

There was nothing to be said to Britt at this point.

Not now.

Still the phone rang. The shrillness of it was more than he could endure.

"Yes."

"Whit. Thank God I got you!"

The purr was gone. Her voice was husky, unpleasantly rough-grained. She sounded as if she were panting, swallowing words as she tried to catch her breath.

"Listen, we're going to have our book. Goddam, we're going to do what we said we'd do! I found it, Whit!"

"It?"

"The purple dress. *The* purple dress! The one that belongs to— It is! There's bloodstains all over it."

"Britt, can you back up and start over?"

"No time now. But I have to see you. We've got to decide which way to go on this. And right away. God, I knew we'd do it! Look, meet me at the hanging tree. At the fourteenth hole. At seven. Got it? I'll have the dress. Whit, we're going to bring this off!"

"Hold on. Just tell me—"

"Later! The hanging tree. At seven."

The line went dead.

Pierce looked at his watch. Almost five. Dusk already was falling.

He sank into the rocker by the window and tried to keep his thoughts in order. One fact at a time.

The purple dress . . . Corinne and Hugh Karlstrom . . . Corinne and her daughter Angela . . . Corinne's trips to La Soeur . . . Angela riding in Corinne's Maserati . . . Britt . . .

Within seconds he was asleep.

A sudden sound awakened him. He leaped up, bewildered, heart thudding. There was total darkness in the house. He groped for the phone. But, no, it had not been a harsh ringing. It had been a pleasant tinkling. Two tones.

Chimes. The door? Blindly he advanced across the room. No one had rung the front door chimes since he had moved in.

He pulled the door open, and high-pitched shrieks detonated in his face.

"Trick or treat!"

A half-dozen children in masks, witch's hats, ghostly bed-sheets. Pressing forward against him, stretching out hands and bags, giggling, uttering spectral moans. Still only partially awake, Pierce blinked blankly at them.

"Trick or treat!"

He dug into his pocket, gathered up change and put coins in each of the hands. With shouts of laughter the tiny revelers skipped back down the stone steps. By the light of a streetlamp, Pierce checked the time.

Almost seven.

"Damn!" he mumbled, threw his jacket on, and hurried to the car. He drove with the window partly open, letting the cold air wash over him.

He parked again at the Kennilworth rather than have his car seen anywhere near Ralph's home. The night was even blacker than it had been when he and Britt had made love under the boughs of the hanging tree. He removed the flashlight he kept in the glove compartment. It was cheap and tinny, and he couldn't remember the last time he had used it. He tried it and it worked, but the beam was weak and the batteries could go at any time.

Pierce walked briskly into the two acres of woods that began on the grounds of the motel and petered out at the edge of Kimberley Drive.

The blackness was intense, the tree trunks invisible everywhere around him except for the pallor of an occasional birch. The feeble beam of the flashlight fluttered dimly over the crooked path. The dead leaves snapped underfoot, like a string of small firecrackers.

His foot struck something large and yielding. The flashlight picked it out: half of the face of a shattered jack-o'-lantern.

He kicked it away, and a deep silence fell. Then there was a flurry of very faint rattling in the underbrush somewhere to his right.

Pierce switched off the light. He trotted forward along the black path. A branch slashed his cheek, but he lowered his head, ignoring it, aching to see the beacon lights of the Hungerford house.

Then the woods were behind him. Pierce swerved sharply to the right, out onto the golf course. The upstairs lights were on at Ralph's. He would have to fumble his way along the fairway, but he did not want to risk being seen.

He flashed the light on and off, remembering his earlier tumble into a sand trap. Now he had a better feel for the terrain, and his progress was rapid.

Quite distinctly he heard two thin, crunching noises.

He halted. A light wind was blowing. But the sounds were somehow more than leaves tossed against each other.

He continued on, his stomach tightening.

No louder than a whisper, dried leaves gave way and broke. It was not a rustling sound. This time he was sure that it wasn't just the sound of leaves scattered by a breeze. Some weight had been put on them.

How far away? Noise traveled far at night. It might be some distance off. Far off.

Now there was a swish-swishing. Through piled leaves. Then silence. Then a swift padding, almost felt rather than heard.

Pierce swung around. Movement rushed toward him out of the darkness.

He braced, crouching.

He extended the flashlight in front of him, as if pointing a weapon. He pushed the switch forward.

A dog bounded up to him, eyes glinting in the sudden cone of light.

"Smokey!" He laughed. "Damn you!"

The animal stared up, tongue lolling, bushy tail wriggling frantically.

He ran his hand over its head and neck. The pelt was ice-cold and damp with frost. Smokey fidgeted and pulled away.

"All right, let's go."

The dog bolted. Pierce zigzagged the beam around. He was approaching a flat, close-cropped expanse. He was on a green, though he couldn't see a flag.

Pierce hurried down the slight incline on the other side. Smokey came back to him, frisking and leaping. Against the distant lights of Kimberley Drive he saw a thick silhouette. Britt's oak. The lower branches—all he could make out in the gloom—had become stark and bare since he'd last been here.

"Hi, you," he called softly.

He sent a ray of wan yellow light at the trunk of the oak. No one there.

"Your idiot dog just about—"

Smokey was whining. Something was standing on the other side of the tree. Something like a very long, very thin, upright shadow.

He stepped toward it.

It was the triangular fourteenth-hole flag. He flashed his light down the length of it.

The dog's head was lowered, and it whimpered quietly.

Then he saw Britt.

Her arms were outflung, her legs crossed at the ankles. Her stone marten coat was ripped to tatters and crisscrossed with blood.

The spike at the end of the flagpole had been driven into her throat.

He let the light rest on her face. One eyelid had fallen, but the right eye was open. It shone brilliantly in the beam of light. The eye seemed to gaze directly at him in a look of surprised, searching inquiry.

A leaf crunched.

He flicked off the flashlight.

It was not Smokey. The dog stood stock-still, suddenly silent. Alert and listening.

The crackling sounded as if it were on the other side of the green.

Another leaf snapped. It seemed closer. And then another.

Considerably closer.

Pierce ran.

November

Chapter 21

Late Tuesday morning, Pierce opened the front door to Deputy Nehemiah Evans.

"May I have a few words, Mr. Pierce?"

"Come in."

Evans cleared his throat, as if thinking of some appropriate way to begin.

"Please sit down." Pierce gestured at the Boston rocker.

Evans sat very straight, holding his visored cap in his lap with both hands. The ever-present scowl deepened.

"Meadowbluff Country Club is in La Soeur County, you know. It's Vigo Lustgarten's turf."

"Yes."

Evans seemed consciously trying to avoid any movement that would rock the chair.

"Hungerford's putting the screws on him. You read the editorial?"

"No."

"Well, there was an editorial. Even with the Stabo murder and the Karlstrom murder, the paper didn't take out after him personally. But that's over, I guess. No surprise. Shit, not when the wife of the publisher gets herself killed on the most exclusive golf course in La Soeur."

"Yes."

"And the district attorney's started putting the screws on too. So Vigo's feeling it. And the son of a bitch was already so touchy he'd kick your ass around the block if you so much as said 'How's it going' to him.''

"I see."

"What I'm saying is that Vigo is one mean motherfucker."

He pinched the top of his cap, bringing it to a sharper peak. "I wasn't sure you'd be here when I stopped. Thought you might be at the funeral."

"No. I was at the visitation last night."

"Yeah, I know."

"Oh?"

"A couple of the detectives were there. And Vigo himself, for a while."

"And they know me?"

"They asked to have you pointed out."

"I see."

"I'll tell you, Mr. Pierce." Evans looked up at the ceiling. "When I heard about Mrs. Hungerford, I felt I had to go to Vigo and report what I knew. What you told me. About the research you an' her were doin'. I didn't think I had a choice. Not to report it could be construed as concealing evidence."

"Of course."

"Turns out Hungerford reported it, too—that you an' her were workin' together. Vigo already knew she was gettin' mixed up in the Stabo-Karlstrom cases, naturally. Hungerford gave Vigo all his wife's notes. So Vigo would like to talk to you."

"When?"

"Now. Since I know you, he told me to come an' get you."

"All right."

"And bring your notes."

Pierce went upstairs and took the folder from a dresser drawer. He removed from it the stories Amanda had written about the couple on the golf course and about the "pretty lady" who had been hanged in her living room. These pages he folded four times and put back in the drawer, under his socks.

He brought the folder down to Evans and said, "There's a

page in here about what I learned from you. About R. L. Cutler. And her bookstore and your suspicions about her. You want me to include it?"

The deputy grunted. "Yeah, include it. Vigo's goin' to be pissed, me shootin' my mouth off to you like I did. But we got to include it. It's evidence."

"Pierce?" Vigo Lustgarten did not raise his eyes from the papers on his desk. "I'm looking at your notes here. This all of it?"

"Yes."

His voice was a flat drawl, punctuating every sentence with indiscriminate emphasis. His frame was immense, but clearly there had once been considerably more flesh padding it. A blue flannel shirt flopped limply across his chest. There were suspender straps over both wide shoulders. An electric orange-yellow tie had been loosened, baring a stringy throat.

"You and Mrs. Hungerford were running around and checking all this out for what—a month? Trying to second-guess me and my department! And what you got here isn't worth a fiddler's fuck! When did you last see her, Pierce?"

"About a week and a half ago. We had lunch at the Ramada."

"Talked with her since? On the phone?"

"Several times."

"Talk to her Saturday?"

"Yes."

"When? About what?"

"About four o'clock." A beefy plainclothes detective in a far corner pulled out a notebook and was apparently jotting down Pierce's answers. "She said she'd found the purple dress. If you've read those stories there, you know they mention a woman in a purple dress."

"Amanda Gatliffe? That psycho! Do you know how many loonies come out of the woodwork every time there's a murder?

187

To confess to it or claim God told 'em who did it? So she said she found a purple dress? Well, what of it?"

"She said she was sure it was the one worn by the woman in those stories."

"How did she know?"

"She said there were bloodstains on it."

"But how did she know they were from the Stabo or Karlstrom cases?"

"She didn't say."

"Didn't you ask?"

"She said she'd explain when we got together to plan our next move."

"When was that?"

Pierce hesitated. "Sunday. Sunday evening. After the end of the Indian Summer Days events."

"Where?"

"At her home."

"That's all she said about the purple dress?"

"Yes."

"Where'd she call from?"

"She didn't say."

"You didn't hear anything? In the background? Any kind of music or noise or anything?"

"No."

Lustgarten took a full minute to run his rheumy eyes over every inch of Pierce's face. "Where were you Saturday night?"

"I took a long drive."

"Where?"

"All over. East and then back over on the Minnesota side."

"Why?"

"It was Halloween. I didn't want to be up and down all evening with trick-or-treaters."

"Stop anywhere?"

"No."

"What time did you take your car out Saturday night?"

188

"I don't remember. Maybe about eight."

"You were home alone until then?"

"Yes."

"It was just before seven when you left. According to the neighbor who saw you! Mr. . . . ."

"Kendrick," the detective in the corner prompted.

"It might've been seven."

Lustgarten yanked open a drawer and removed a package of appetite-suppressant mints. He plopped one in his mouth. One hand began massaging the acorn-size knuckles of the other. Because his face was so shrunken, his elephantine ears stood out conspicuously.

"I'm going to impound your notes. You want 'em back anytime soon?"

"No."

"Anything else that's not in your notes on her?"

"No."

"Come on, Pierce. Anything she said the last week or so that maybe there wasn't time to write down?"

"One thing. She had a second interview with Jan Laughlin. She said Miss Laughlin told her she'd misrepresented something in her original statement. She said that on the night Angela Karlstrom was killed, it wasn't true that Ruby Lee Cutler hadn't left the Ace High for more than a couple of minutes. She said Miss Cutler was gone at one time for something like forty minutes."

"That doesn't put her at the scene."

"I'm only reporting what Mrs. Hungerford told me."

"Your wife died recently, Pierce."

"Yes."

"Suicide, the Chicago police told me."

"You've talked with them?"

"You bet! She was from La Soeur?"

"I think you know she was."

"She knew Britt Hungerford?"

189

"No."

"You going to do any more 'research'?"

"No."

"With Britt Hungerford dead, no more book?"

"That's right."

"Me and the department have got to solve all three of these things on our own now. Is that right?"

"I suppose."

"Just between us, Pierce, what's your judgment here?" He softened the stridency, but his voice exuded sarcasm. "The same one killed all three? What's the connection? Mrs. Hungerford was stabbed. Like the Karlstrom girl!" He looked over at the detective in the corner. "How many times?"

"Twenty-eight," the detective said. "Counting the wound from the flagpole."

"Two stabbed. But the Stabo girl was strangled! You been investigating this, Pierce. All related? Two related? None related? Give us some help here!"

"I don't know."

"Damn right! You and Britt Hungerford hadn't done diddly-shit!"

"Yes."

Lustgarten held the papers up in Pierce's face. "You think anybody'd kill Britt Hungerford over a mess of crap like this? You think that's why she got killed—these notes she collected?"

"I don't know."

"Think she was killed because she was about to crack this thing wide open?"

"I don't know."

Lustgarten glared at the detective taking notes. "You ever take a good look at Britt Hungerford? You know when a woman like that gets killed what's the first thing you expect the case to revolve around?"

"Well, sir . . ."

"Pussy!"

Lustgarten stood up in front of the three-color topographical map of the county that filled half the wall behind him. The suspenders were a necessity because his baggy trousers were more ill-fitting than his shirt. He leaned forward, placing his weight on the hands splayed out on his desk. His square, haggard face was contorted.

"Did that ever occur to you, Pierce? What? Speak up!"

"I said, of course."

The sheriff sat down again and threw another appetite suppressant into his mouth. He squinted angrily at Pierce and loudly cracked his knuckles. "She could get a guy frantic! Twenty-seven stab wounds! And then whoever did it walks all the way over to the green, gets the flag, and brings it back. Rams it through her throat so hard, it sticks in the ground. Does that sound like anyone you know, Pierce?"

"No."

"Come on. You got together with her. Doing all that crime solving. Planning your blockbuster book. Don't tell me it was all business!"

"No."

"Weren't you getting some, Pierce?"

"No."

"You had to be. Don't lie to me."

"No."

Now he was shouting with all his power, his sunken cheeks beet-red. "It's so! Has to be so! Isn't it so?"

"No."

"Then what'd she do? Call it off? Tell you to kiss off? Is that it?"

"No."

"You are on the record now! If we prove you're lying we prove your whole damn story is a lie! Understand?"

"Yes."

"Now will you give it to me straight? You and her were doing it, right? Nothing so terrible about that. But it's so, isn't it?"

"No."

"When did you know she was dead?"

"Sunday evening. I heard it on the radio."

"You knew we were looking for people who had information."

"I didn't think I had anything to contribute."

"You had your notes. You had those stories. You talked with her that day. Why didn't you come forward?"

Because I ran.

"I had nothing substantial to contribute."

"You were her partner. Investigating murders together. Then *she* gets murdered. Why did you wait for us to come and get you?"

Because I ran.

"I didn't think I could be of any help."

Because I saw her staring.

Like Corinne.

"Pierce, I want you around. And the grand jury's going to want you around until this thing's settled. Savvy?"

"All right."

Chapter 22

"I just called to tell you I can't make it to class Thursday," Sally said. "I had to switch with one of the other girls because I'm taking a long weekend in Chicago."

"Class. I'd forgotten."

Britt's empty chair.

Amanda staring at him.

"But please include me in, Whit, if the class wants to do anything about Mrs. Hungerford. Send a card or flowers or donations to charity or anything."

"I'm cancelling the class. In view of what happened, I don't feel it would be—"

"I think you're right, Whit. It's so absolutely horrible. Did you know her well? I mean, outside class?"

"Yes."

"She seemed so vivacious. Honestly, it makes you shudder to think that could happen."

Pierce said nothing.

"Are you okay, Whit?"

"Yes. I'm okay . . . Sally . . ."

"Yes."

"I'll give you a ride to Chicago. I have some odds and ends to take care of. And I need to have a couple of days away . . . from here."

"Great! Look, I've got to get back to work now. Call me."

He ate at the kitchen table, reading and rereading Amanda's last story.

If it held any cargo of truth Corinne did not plan what happened. It was not a final, contemptuous statement. She did not die with eyes burning with hate for him.

He began washing the few plates and utensils he'd used. Out of the corner of his eye he detected movement.

A face.

He spun around. It was gone. Detergent dropped, and green granules spilled across the floor.

Then the face was back. Eyes starting out, tongue protruding. *The face of someone hanged.*

Then the face went blank. A mocking grin appeared. It was Emil Gatliffe. A skeletal forefinger pointed to the back door. He vanished.

Pierce picked up the detergent box, swore, and opened the door.

"What is it?"

"It's opportunity, sire. That's what me an' Manda are—opportunity!"

Like a foggy apparition, Emil seeped past Pierce into the kitchen.

"Don't know if me an' Manda really want to do business with you. Depends on how friendly you are. But Manda does kinda fancy you. We just might do you a favor."

"I don't want your favors."

"You know, your friends the deputies come to see us. Said you told them about Manda's stories. Manda told them about what she told you—naught, naught, zero, zero. Couldn't do nothin' else. Still sick. Couldn't talk."

His hands fluttered incessantly, touching every object within reach.

"But I told 'em the straight goods. Manda gets visions. She sees things sometimes. And were they enchanted to hear that? Not them clods. Not about the stories. Only about your lady friend comin' to see us Saturday."

"Who? Britt?"

"Ah! Weren't she a beauty. What a wench!"

He plucked two apples from a bowl on the table and began juggling them.

"Britt went to see Amanda Saturday?"

"Saturday morning. All breathless. Said she had a dress she wanted Manda to read. Right then. 'Purple?' says I. 'You got it,' says she. Manda can't, says I. Too sick. Come back later. And then she runs off. That's all. Like I told the deputies . . . Oops! Ah! Got it!"

He dropped one apple back in the bowl and bit into the other.

"No, they didn't care much about Manda's little tales. Did want to know where she was on Saturday night, though. Saturday night at seven. When the foul deed was done. So I told 'em Manda was right home in bed at seven, bein' temporarily out of her wits an' all. Me, I was out. It was Halloween, you know. Night when spirits sashay forth an' caper! Me, I was out in it. Where? Everydamnwhere!"

He flipped the apple core into the refuse container. "Do you know what'd be fun?" he asked with a conniving, sidelong glance. "Really fun?"

"What?"

"Have Manda do another story. About your late, late lady friend. Manda's gettin' better. Almost her old self again. Wouldn't you like to know what Manda sees happening out there on the golf course? With the flagpole?"

Pierce walked back to the sink, gripped the counter heavily, and looked down at the dirty dishes, not seeing them.

"More 'big lady in the purple dress.' That's all."

"We'd find out, wouldn't we? Wouldn't we, hmmm. . . ." His voice trailed off.

"No," Pierce muttered.

"Do you have anything here, by chance? It should be something she had on her. That night. Otherwise it probably won't work."

"I don't have anything."

"I thought I might find something myself. At the funeral parlor. A ring or something that just might slip off while I was standin' there. But they shut her up good and proper, didn't they? Closed casket. Only to be expected, I suppose, when you think of the state she was in."

"God damn you, get out!"

"But it would be fun, Professor! Another story!"

His pliable face filled with cherubic delight.

"Get out."

"Wait. One moment! Just think, Herr Doktor. Some little thing she had on her, some doodad. That's all it takes, and Manda will come through. You can get it from her husband, can't you? You know him, don't you? Stop by for a visit. See if there's something that fits the bill."

Pierce started toward him, fists clenched. "Damn you, get out of here!"

Emil leaped to the door, giggled, and disappeared into the night.

Jesus, to team up with Emil Gatliffe!

They drove in silence for hours, but it was not an uneasy silence.

Pierce had taken Interstate 94, which skirted long stretches of forest as it swung them toward the Illinois border. It was a clear, nippy day of azure skies and milkweed clouds. The high-intensity colors of autumn had faded. But there were evergreens to mitigate the sameness of the landscape. And there was the abiding stolidity of the black, leafless trees that stood defiantly on hillsides, awaiting the onslaught of winter.

Sally left him to his thoughts, content to watch the country-side glide past. The russet hair fell loosely to her shoulders, brilliant and fiery as they drove southeastward into the molten, early-morning sun.

At last Pierce said, *"The Lady Eve."*

"What?"

"The movie the coffee lady lifted her plot from. The last story she wrote for class. I knew I'd seen it. Barbara Stanwyck and Henry Fonda. It just popped into my mind."

Sally laughed, and for the rest of the trip they talked—about the next story she was working on, about the things they would see and do once they got to the city.

Chicago wore the look it had so long ago when he and Corinne had decided to make it their own. Sparkling—alive with enterprise and boldness and creativity. The golden spires vaulting into the sky. The lake a breathtaking blue. The air crystalline and energizing.

Pierce dropped Sally at the Drake, and they made plans to meet in an hour to see an exhibit of Cro-Magnon painting at the Art Institute.

There was an awesome pile of mail held for him at the postal substation, including two royalty checks. He filled out a card that would forward future mail to his La Soeur address, and he deposited the checks in his bank account. There was also a letter from his publisher urging him to call regarding the advance paid for the novel long overdue. Of course, Pierce reminded himself, not a word of it had been written yet. He dropped the letter in a trash can.

Later, at the Art Institute, Sally chattered excitedly about the Ice Age animal figures. "It's believed they were used in hunting rituals," she said. "The magician of the tribe—the sorcerer or whatever—would capture the . . . oh, the *spirit* of the animals by making a likeness of them. Somehow that meant he could enter their souls, so they'd make themselves accessible to the hunters."

"Turn them into happy victims."

"Victims? In a way." She gave a rueful shake of her head.

"Ready to eat? Wandering back twenty centuries can give you an appetite."

"Ready."

"Let's try Cricket's."

197

He would have to put on a suit, a dress shirt, and a tie. It would take only a few minutes.

They turned off Lakeshore Drive at the La Salle exit. The early dusk of November had already covered the city, and the high-rises were aglow with lights.

His town house was six blocks west of Lincoln Park, a quiet neighborhood of quaint older homes—now priced at astronomical sums—and upper-middle-class condominium developments. He and Corinne had bought a four-bedroom unit on the top floor—the fourth—of an elegantly refurbished corner building.

Pierce parked in front of Gypsy's, a small pub on the other side of the street.

"Be right back," he told her. In the lobby he saw a plump woman in her eighties leading a sweatered poodle on a leash. He knew she owned a unit on the second floor, and they nodded. On the elevator they said nothing. He did not know her name, nor did she know his. Nor would she have been aware, or interested, that he had been away for two months. It was that sort of building.

Pierce let himself into the apartment, rattling the metallic camel bells that Corinne had hung on the door. He flipped on the hallway light and steeled himself before climbing the steps to the main level.

It was from here that he had first seen Corinne. Looking directly at him. Hanging from that very beam.

Here where he'd clearly seen, even from halfway across the room, the vivid green of her accusing eyes.

How many days had he lived with it here? Letting it smother him again and again, surprising him at odd moments with its unabated fury, so that he'd fled this place at last in haste and desperation? Seeking answers elsewhere, seeking absolution elsewhere.

Now he walked across the parquet floor to the bedroom that had once been intended as the baby's room. He had moved in here after Corinne's death, abandoning the room and the double bed they had shared.

He pulled a blue worsted suit from the closet. There was so much here, so much he'd just walked away from. He'd pack tomorrow.

Pierce tucked in his shirttails and faced himself in the full-length mirror, carefully knotting his tie. He remembered the man he used to see in this mirror months ago. The man he saw now was thinner, slightly grayer, with dark patches faintly visible under the eyes. Eyes that were wary and more deeply recessed under the wide forehead.

He went back into the living room and noticed the plants that lay drooping and wilted. He would dump them tomorrow. It couldn't be helped. He had left here so quickly in September.

He found himself stepping around the spot in the middle of the living room floor where he'd seen her hanging that day.

Suddenly he knew he could not stay here tonight. He would find a hotel room and come back in the morning to pack. Maybe call a realtor and put it up for sale.

He couldn't hack it here anymore. Not even one night.

Pierce pushed open the French doors to the balcony, permitting fresh air to enter. He stepped out. Corinne had loved the balcony in the summer. She would spread her work out on the patio table, holding the papers down with a conch shell.

Often they ate on the balcony. The last meal they'd had together had been out here.

There'd been no mention of Angela Karlstrom then. Angela, the daughter she was even then hoping to bring to live with them. Her daughter, who must have consumed her thoughts. About whom she said nothing. Never.

I'd've understood! If you'd told me!

He heard the front door open, the clanking of the camel bells. And then the door slammed shut.

Chapter 23

Footsteps ascended the eight stairs leading to the living room.

Loudly. Briskly. No attempt at stealth.

Sally? he thought.

The steps clicked across the parquet. No hesitation. Into the bedroom that had once been his and Corinne's.

In a few seconds they returned to the living room and went at once into the bedroom where he had just changed.

Sally would have said something. Not come barging in without a word.

He tried to call out. But his voice choked in his throat.

The footsteps rang out on the parquet again and proceeded directly to the bathroom. The sound was the sharp, staccato click of high heels. He heard the bathroom door thrown open. A few moments passed. A few moments of total silence.

Then the steps—at a firm, steady pace—went to the room he used as a den. His office. There was no wavering, no·indecision. Whoever it was seemed to know the layout of the apartment inside out.

Another few moments of silence. Then the footsteps headed toward the master bedroom.

Next would be the balcony. Inevitably.

There was nothing to use as a weapon. Pierce's eyes darted wildly about. After Corinne's death, even the Weber grill had been wheeled back inside. The balcony was bare. Not so much as a flowerpot.

He moved to the very end of the ledge. He gripped the iron railing and looked down.

Please! Someone!

No one walking by. No one loitering below. One side of Gypsy's Pub was visible. But not the front entrance. He could see the back of his own car, around the corner.

One shout was all he'd have time for.

One shout might not be enough. Would anyone even hear it? Sally? Sitting in the car with the windows up?

And if she heard him, it would be all over by the time she got out of the car.

His mind raced, ticking off possibilities.

The balcony below? Too cumbersome to climb down. There would not be enough time.

Jump?

Four flights and cement below.

The heels echoed loudly, smartly against the parquet once more.

Approaching. Crossing the living room.

There was no need for stealth, of course. No need to disguise the object of this visit. Only the need to do what the visitor came to do.

Pierce turned to face whoever it was who would now appear.

No!

Something irrational—naked fright, a thirst to survive, if only for seconds more.

Keep your back to the door! Don't look!

As long as he did not know who it was, he did not possess the knowledge that required his death on the spot. He could be spared for another time.

If it could be made to seem that he did not know who was there, behind him.

The footfalls reached the balcony door and stopped.

Don't look!

His knuckles whitened on the railing. He breathed in. It was a gasp, a rattle.

"Sally!" he shouted.

He waved, as if to someone directly below.

"I dropped my keys. See them down there? Got 'em? Good! Sally, listen carefully! I can't explain. But keep standing there. Right there where you can see me! Okay! Good! Now keep looking up!"

There was silence on the threshold of the balcony.

It would be logical for whoever waited there to assume that this was a bluff. But what if it weren't?

"That's it! Where you can see me! Just stand there! Like that! Keep looking up!"

Utter silence. Behind him someone was weighing a course of action. Deliberating on whether this was a desperate gamble or not.

A slight tinkling of the wind chimes attached to the roof over the balcony. More silence.

The sweat coursed down his back. Should he holler again? Could he? He was struggling for breath. The blood pounding in his temples at triphammer speed. Deafening him.

There was only silence behind him. He must turn. He must see!

Then the high heels stamped against the parquet. Back across the long living room. Down the short flight of stairs. Pierce heard the door open and close. The heavy thunk of the camel bells died away instantly.

Weakly he slumped against the railing. But he could not give way to his feelings yet. No, not yet.

He listened intently, letting his heartbeat subside.

Finally he turned and faced the balcony door. Minutes passed before he took short, reluctant steps across the patio.

Back into the living room, moving cautiously, until he drew near the stairwell.

A tiny leaden sound. The camel bells had been lightly bumped.

Oh, Christ!

How easy to have shut the door. From the inside. And waited there, crouching. Till Pierce came back in from the balcony.

He felt rooted to the parquet. Could he make it back to the balcony before those footsteps mounted the stairs? Could he move at all?

He saw he was exactly at the spot where Corinne had stood on the butcher block table. Exactly.

A thin, scraping noise. Someone becoming impatient down there? Tensing? Ready to spring back up?

"I have a weapon," Pierce said. The voice sounded like someone else's.

"It's an iron pipe. It was on the balcony. I'll use it. You won't find it easy to take me. I warn you."

God, wasn't it plainly obvious he was bluffing again? So damned obvious?

Once more, an all-pervasive silence. Silence so thick, he could swear he was alone in this place. Sworn he was talking to himself.

Am I?

Talking to the walls? Imagining? Hearing things? The memory of Corinne, dangling right here where he stood . . . Had that set off hallucinations?

"I haven't seen you," he said quietly. "I'm not a threat to you. Not if you leave now."

Who the hell you talking to? There's nobody there. Can't be!

The camel bells rattled. The door below opened and closed.

"I'm sorry. I'm going back tonight."

Sally helped him stow his pack-cloth two-suiter in the backseat.

"I'll drop you at the Drake," he said.

"Just to check out, Whit. If you're going back, so am I."

He fumbled, attempting to insert the ignition key. She eased him over to the passenger seat. He carried a bulky goose-down jacket across his lap. Under it, she noticed, he held a large kitchen knife.

"There was an intruder," he told her later as they left the Kennedy Expressway.

"Shouldn't you have called the police?"

"I didn't get a good look. Nothing to report. I left the door unlocked. Dumb. Thought I'd just be a couple of minutes."

If he had looked down at the base of the stairs, what would he have seen there under the camel bells?

The lady in the purple dress?

But to look would have meant death. Only yards from where Corinne died.

"While you were waiting, did anybody else come out of the building?"

"I didn't see anyone. Was it a man, Whit?"

"I don't know. I'm sorry, Sally. Your weekend . . ."

He stared vacantly out of the windshield. Seeing lights endlessly flashing by.

Once over the Wisconsin line, they encountered a light drizzle. The day that had begun with such golden radiance was dying in dampness and murk. Sally flipped on the wipers, and as they swished from side to side, there came into Pierce's mind a refrain that echoed in cadence with them: "The big lady in the purple dress . . . The big lady in the purple dress . . ."

In La Soeur he insisted they drive first to her house. He was, he told her, quite able to make it back to Aunt Amy's on his own. As he moved over to the driver's seat Sally set down her overnight bag and touched his cheek.

"Make yourself some warm milk. And get right to bed, Whit."

"Okay, teacher. I apologize. But it's something I can't . . ."

It was just past two A.M. when he parked the Sunbird in the garage. With the flashlight he swept the backyard and the path to the back door. Inside, the knife still in his hand, he paced off every room of the house, from basement to second floor.

Looking for what?

He slumped into the rocker. Watching the rain patter against the front window. The street and sidewalk deserted. He laid the steak knife against his thigh. It was eight inches of stainless steel with a wide blade and a handle of oak. Part of a costly set of flatware from Corinne's Crocks and Crafts.

La Soeur? Chicago?

The lady in the purple dress? What was the link?

Someone who was as familiar with his home in Chicago as the countryside of La Soeur.

Someone who bridged both those worlds—Chicago, La Soeur.

He slept sprawling in the rocker, his hand on the knife.

Chapter 24

On his way to meet Hugh Karlstrom Pierce stopped at a sporting-goods store and surveyed its stock of target pistols. He selected a small-barreled .38. State law required filling out a form, and there would be a forty-eight-hour wait until the information was verified.

"Fine," he grunted, signing his name to a document attesting to the fact that he had never been convicted of a felony.

If he'd only had a weapon on his balcony in Chicago . . .

If he could have swung around, pointing a pistol, confronting whoever stood there . . .

"You can pick it up Monday, sir," the clerk said.

"Thank you."

Only a handful of drinkers lounged around Meadowbluff Country Club's long mahogany bar. Karlstrom was in quiet conversation with the bartender, a black Russian sheltered in his corded hands. There was not even the pretense of a smile as there had been the week before.

"I think we covered it all," he said curtly.

"I want to go over a few more points."

The abrupt tone turned abrasive. "Why, dammit? You know about Angela and Corinne. They're both dead. What kind of kicks do you get going around and shoveling up dirt? You know about Corinne and me. Corinne and Angela. You like hitting yourself in the head?"

All trace of civility had disappeared, and Pierce was sure he knew why. Britt was gone, and it was Britt—and, through her,

Ralph—that Karlstrom was afraid of offending. His status at the club and his status in La Soeur hinged on the continuing good favor of Ralph Hungerford and a small group of the city's other power brokers.

But now, without Britt as his intermediary, Pierce was merely a bothersome outsider, asking impertinent questions.

"There's more I want to know. How did Angela feel when she heard Corinne was dead?"

"You do get your rocks off on this, don't you?" Karlstrom's once ruggedly handsome face was heavily flushed and his voice belligerent.

"I just want an answer."

"There was hardly anything. It was just that this lady from Chicago who'd come to see us a couple of times was dead now. That's all it was to her."

"Angela never went to Chicago to see Corinne?"

"Not that I heard of."

"You're sure?"

"She never mentioned any such thing. That's all I know."

"She never called Corinne? Never talked to her on the phone?"

"Not that I know of. Why would she? She didn't know who the hell Corinne really was."

"What about you? Ever come to Chicago to talk to Corinne about Angela?"

Karlstrom let his eyelids close for several seconds, shaking his head in disbelief. He smiled disdainfully.

"So now it comes out. What's really chewing on you. Did I go down to Chicago to see your wife? Would I tell you if I had? No. For whatever good it does you, I didn't have something going with your wife. Satisfied?"

"Did you know if Corinne ever saw anybody else here in La Soeur? During her trips up here to talk to you?"

"How would I know? The trips were all about Angela. Well,

she did say something once. About calling on this old friend of hers. Winnie Stabo. You know, the wife of that sportswriter."

"When was this?"

"Oh, some time ago. Not long after she started calling me about Angela. My God, look at that!"

He gaped at the couple entering the bar. It was the attorney, Max Fischer, and Ruby Lee Cutler.

Karlstrom's face turned even more florid, so that his dazzlingly white eyebrows stood out like barely healed scars. He made a shuffling move, as if to advance toward the newcomers, then seemed to change his mind. He threw back his head, finished off the black Russian, and slammed the glass down on the bar.

"Can you be more precise? About when she called on Mrs. Stabo?"

Karlstrom ignored him. Riveted, he watched Fischer and R. L. approach. When they passed, ten feet away, Karlstrom spat out hoarsely, "Get her out of here!"

R. L. Cutler spun around, lips curled in a snarl.

"Hugh—" the attorney responded.

"Get her out of here!"

"Hugh! Please! She's a client and . . ."

Karlstrom stared at R. L. Cutler in livid, hypnotized loathing.

"Murdering cunt!" he whispered.

She stepped toward him, thick shoulders outthrust and rolling.

The attorney hurried up beside her. "Let's go, Ruby Lee."

"Angela would be alive if she never met you." Karlstrom breathed the words into R. L. Cutler's face. "You're filth."

R. L. Cutler jerked the cigarette from her mouth, hurled it to the floor, and crushed it under the stiletto heel of her star-patterned cowboy boot. She snorted smoke out through her nostrils.

"Lay off, mister! You don't know what the fuck you're talking about. You didn't know fact one about Angela, and you didn't give a rat's ass about her. Don't come on now like you did!"

"You . . . piece of—"

"Lay off!" She pushed her craggy jaw close to his face, and her eyes burned like glowing cinders. "I don't take shit off losers like you!"

Karlstrom lunged at her. She twisted away, and her balled fist flew up and smashed his nose.

The lawyer grabbed R. L. and pulled her back. Karlstrom roared and heaved himself at her. Pierce caught both of his arms. The tensed muscles were like steel cables as he tried to pull free. The bartender hurtled over the mahogany bar and also pinned Karlstrom.

"Settle down, Hugh. Settle down."

Blood streamed from Karlstrom's nose and onto his lips and chin.

"You keep away from me, mister," R. L. warned. "You keep away from me or you'll wish you had."

Chapter 25

"Sorry, Whit. Winnie's not in."

"When do you expect her back?"

There was a pause that Pierce guessed was Al Stabo sucking on his cigar. "I don't know, Whit. She goes out in the evening sometimes. I don't know where she goes. Ever since Jennifer, you know. Was it something important?"

"I wanted to ask her something. Yes. Something I have to know."

"You know how she is. She goes to see people I don't really want to know. Mediums and psychics and people involved in funny kinds of rituals. I get awfully worried when she's out at night like this. Especially after what happened to Britt Hungerford and all. But I don't want to interfere. If it helps to take the pain away."

"I understand, Al. Thanks."

The Pitch? Again?

The sad, frightening recollection recurred: Winnie chanting in the night, "Jenn-if-er! Jenn-if-er!" It was probably better if Al never knew.

As he went to his car he waved at his neighbors. The Sorensons were closing their garage door. This was their Saturday night at the movies, away from the children. They had just returned.

"You met your guest all right?"

"Guest?"

"The lady who was waiting. On your front porch."

Pierce walked to the edge of the flowerbed that divided Aunt Amy's property from the Sorensons'. "When was this?"

"About eight. We were just leaving. I don't think you were home."

"I wasn't."

"She stood by the tree in front of the house for a long time, looking in. Then she went to the front door and tried it. She sat down in the swing on the front porch, so we figured it must be okay."

"A lady?"

"Yes. A big lady."

"Thanks."

Pierce sped toward the eastern outskirts, along Highway 82 past Meadowbluff Country Club, and turned off on the winding road to Frenchman's Pitch.

"A big lady."

The big lady in the purple dress?

Waiting in the swing on the front porch?

If he had been home, would he have let the caller in?

Had Corinne?

She'd always kept the door locked. But that day she'd opened it. To whomever it was who had been back there yesterday, there with him in the town house in Chicago. He'd known it. He'd heard it. He'd felt death breathing on his neck.

Would Corinne have opened the door to *that*?

He crawled upward at the posted ten-mile-an-hour limit. At night the narrow, black-topped, two-lane could be treacherous. When he reached the parking lot at the peak, he drove around it in a slow circle. There were no other cars in the lot. But there was a small clearing just off the road a fifth of a mile back near the rest rooms. It was possible to pull in between them, and a car parked there could not be seen from the two-lane.

The sky above Frenchman's Pitch was a seamless black. Pierce took his flashlight with him, letting the light play over the stone pathway, not hesitating to make noise. If Winnie was here he wanted her to know someone was approaching. He did not want to surprise her in the middle of some rite she would not have wanted an outsider to see.

The park had been officially closed for more than an hour. Few ever came here on cold November evenings. Even desperate lovers could find more congenial places to park.

He followed the cyclone fence that ran along the southwestern edge, near a sheer drop-off overlooking the city. Then he turned sharply to the northernmost limit beside a wooded copse. The crisp, fallen leaves were thick along the fence, blown into piles by the wind.

"Winnie! It's Whit Pierce! Winnie!"

He cast the beam of the flashlight past the fence as he made his circuit. But the light was weak and whole sections of the outermost ledge were still obscured.

Pierce eased past the edge of the fence near the trees and picked up the footpath. The going was slow, and he paused every ten or twenty yards to call out Winnie's name. He passed the rubble of the small, nineteenth-century artillery dugout and continued along the hard-packed earth of the western face. Soon he reached a point where the path dipped below and around the jagged edge of a large boulder.

The spot was familiar. Just beyond was the ledge where he had seen Winnie. Pierce moved forward along the path.

He sprayed the ledge with light. It was empty.

"Winnie!" Shouting again, letting light leap over the crevices, shrubbery, and rocks.

She was not here. He decided to follow the path the rest of the way around to its southern extremity. But it was clear there was no one out here tonight.

Where was she then? Somewhere down there?

He stepped off the worn path to the lip of the bluff. La Soeur sprawled below, a grid of twinkling lights chopped off cleanly to the west by the black, coiling Mississippi.

The lights of La Soeur. From here they were the same lights

212

he and Corinne had gazed down at so many years before. From here, how little had changed.

Once more he felt—here on this height more powerfully than anywhere else—the sheer, crackling life force that had been Corinne's.

And so that question. Again.

What had driven someone with such a savage thirst for life to that final, despairing act?

But now the answer was plain.

He knew it with certainty. Not as a premise to be challenged and tested. But a fact. He knew it with a conviction that he experienced to the core of his being.

It came with an almost physical thud. A sensation that had its source deep in his viscera.

Yes! Of course!

He would never discover why she had hanged herself . . . *because she hadn't.*

There could not have been reason enough in the world for Corinne to have done so.

His certainty was absolute.

Corinne, I understand.

It was as though he could reach out his hand and clasp hers. He closed his eyes and saw her as she had been then.

Saw her.

Vividly. In detail.

"Oh, God, Corinne," he breathed.

The picture was clear—those sea-green eyes dancing with delight.

It was the Corinne he'd been unable to remember since August. The real Corinne. Not that foul horror he had lived with for so long.

From behind his closed lids tears came. Tears, real tears.

The tears that had not come in August. Or anytime since. Not once.

Never could he erase that last glimpse of her. But now that

was but one of many images of Corinne. And the other images —happier images, truer images—would always be accessible.

Behind him on the footpath there was a sharp intake of breath.

Pierce whirled, lost his footing.

A tall figure stepped up to him. In the dense darkness he was conscious more of movement than of any visual impression.

A hand groped at his shoulder. And some frail shard of light from the city below glinted on an upraised knife.

Pierce leaped backward, feeling his feet teetering on the periphery of nothingness and seeing only the blur of the blade rushing by him. He dropped to a crouch, tried to pivot, and one leg skittered off the edge. Now the knife swished overhead, poking for him as if it, too, were blind in the darkness but attempting to sense him through some batlike radar. Every stab was propelled by a gust of breathing—heavy and quick—from some invisible source so that it seemed that the breath was that of the knife itself.

On hands and knees Pierce scrambled backward, knowing he must keep low, away from the insatiable thirst of the blade. Now it plunged downward, because it knew he was close to the earth, clawing desperately like a burrowing animal, and it would not let him scurry away that easily. He scuttled backward even more frantically, but the blade danced forward, cutting downward and outward so that Pierce wondered if it was toying with him, capable of catching him whenever it chose but prolonging the chase briefly to permit him to cling to the frail hope that escape was possible. And then, his own breath gurgling in his throat, Pierce lost the glimmering of the knife for an instant and wildly searched for it. Instead his fumbling hand found a large stone, closed on it even as the knife reappeared, angrily hissing, and he spun around. The knife was gone before he felt the tiniest kiss of contact on his cheek, and knew he had been grazed.

He got to his feet as the light-speckled blade appeared above him, motionless. He swung his fist, gripping the rock, perceiving only a dim presence hovering near the knife. Pain coursed down his arm and he cried out, knowing he had smashed his hand into a solid outcropping and the rock had fallen. At the same moment he knew the knife would drive toward him now, bringing death, because he was standing, a full and open target. There was movement as if a large slab of black rock had torn loose, and for the first time he saw a hand, clammy, white, and insubstantial as mist. The hand that had brought death before and yearned to bring death again, the hand attached to the knife, and it was as much an absurd revelation—almost a surprise—to detect it as it would be to glimpse the hand of a puppeteer manipulating the little bodies of his puppets.

Now this hand thrust forward and behind it there was a harsh expulsion of breath. The knife was swung at gut level, tilting up slightly.

Chapter 26

Pierce pitched sideways. The ground crumbled under him, and he felt himself falling.

His body struck something hard. Then he was tumbling. An avalanche of pebbles, rocks, shrubs, and branches crashing down around him.

His hip slammed into a sharp outcropping. A white bolt of pain racked his body, but the contact broke the speed of his fall. He grabbed a knobby branch rooted in the thin soil of the rockface, and held on.

The last rock cascaded far down the slope. Silence returned.

Pierce grasped the branch with both hands. The incline was steep and it was all he could do to hang on with the little strength remaining in his arms.

He couldn't hear anything up on the ledge.

The needles of a fir tree tickled his ear and cheek. They oozed a rich, resiny tang—the smell of a newly cut Christmas tree.

The silence was broken by the faint cough of a car engine. Still, Pierce waited. Finally the numbness began to leave his body. He grew aware of the angry throbbing in his right hip and leg. He shut his eyes, allowing more time to flow past.

The fingers of one hand gave way.

If he let go he might slide to the safe, lower reaches of the bluff. Unless he was hanging over a high drop-off. He remembered that long-ago incident of the rock climber who died on these slopes.

He began climbing. Pushing with legs and feet. Hauling with

216

weakened hands, shoving with arms and elbows. Leveraging his body against boulders and tree trunks. Scrambling while stones, leaves, and branches slid beneath him.

At last he reached a slanting stretch of rock on which he could walk. Pierce struggled to his feet. His right leg could not bear much weight and tottered feebly at each new thrust of his body. In the utter blackness he could not even tell if he was going in the right direction.

Suddenly Pierce stopped, arms outstretched. Ahead of him a rock wall—chill and slick—nearly perpendicular. Desperately his fingers searched for a small shelf, a spur, a crevice. Anything. There was only the unbroken smoothness of stone.

A light went on, full in his face, just above his extended arms.

"You're almost there, Mr. Pierce," Emil Gatliffe said.

Staring up, Pierce could see only a thin strip of nearly horizontal rock winding higher toward the top of the bluff.

"You going to just wait there? Till when? Till the Texas Rangers come and rescue you?"

"Get out of here."

"If I go my flashlight goes."

Pierce followed the light that Emil threw just ahead of him each step of the way. The ribbon of footing trickled away at the base of a pitted boulder. The light picked out each foot and handhold. Chest and belly flat against the boulder, Pierce pushed his way up along the route traced by the finger of light.

Near the top Emil's hands gripped him and tugged him the rest of the way up.

Pierce pulled away and staggered onto the footpath. Then he crumpled. The flashlight swept his body from head to foot.

"You hurt bad?"

"Keep away!"

"Just tryin' to help."

Emil bent over him, touching his face. "Let's just see what the damages are."

"Keep back! I'm all right . . . damn you! Keep . . . back!"

Emil chortled. "Oh, that's a hoot! Look who he's afeared of —gentle little me!"

"Where's . . . your . . . mother?"

Emil swung his flashlight in wide, rhythmic loops, a pinwheel in the blackness. "Do you see Manda? Anywhere here? Manda's home. Where else? Manda's a homebody. 'Cept sometimes. Didn't you know that, Professor Pierce? Professor?"

Pierce's eyes clamped shut. But they still saw lights and colors, whipping back and forth. Shafts of light like spears that tore sickeningly through every organ of his body. He fought to hang on to consciousness. He could not.

It was the pain in his right leg that roused him. A draft of icy air swept over the back of his neck, and he saw that he was in the front seat of his car. Emil was driving. In the light of the dashboard the youth wore a rapturous smile.

"Surely hit the jackpot on the Pitch tonight," Emil bubbled. "And only came up 'cause things was so dull down there in town. Don't worry, Professor, Manda'll fix you up fine."

"No!"

"You be surprised how good she'll take care of you."

"No! No, dammit!"

"She's good at healin'. That cat of ours got hit by a car once and Manda like to brought her back to life. Put you on the couch and she'll have you good as new in no time."

"You're taking me home. Got it?"

"Manda's got salves and things. An' she's got her ways."

"No!"

"Let me tell you, she can do things with her hands. She's got power there. Anyways, don't know if you're in any shape to say no."

Pierce ran the window up. "God, it's cold. What the hell were you doing up there?"

"It's fun to go up there at night. Never know what you'll see. Take tonight! Well, it's not usually that exciting. But there are

218

people parking. And can you guess what they're doing to each other in those cars? Oh, my! Oh, my! Naughty! And you'd be surprised who the people are! Oh, it's fun! To find out what people do up there when the rest of the town's asleep."

"You saw what happened?"

"To you? No."

"What do you mean, 'no'? You were there."

"Ah, but 'tis a dark an' dreary night, sir. I was over by the trees an' I heard something. Like somebody falling. That was you, sir, no? Then somebody else. Walking along on the pathway to the parking lot. Not running, don't you know? Walking along, kind of noisy. I was going to turn the flash on, but I decided not to. You never know if people will be too thrilled about that. Up there at this time of night."

"Was Amanda there?"

Emil took both hands off the steering wheel and clapped them loudly. "Oh, he's got Manda on the mind! No, she weren't. But ask her yourself."

"Did you see a car? Whoever it was had a car."

"Negative, Captain. I checked the lot. Saw your beautiful Pontiac. Heard another car leaving. Must've been parked down by the outhouses."

"Where's your car?"

"Didn't bring it. Hoofed it up here like I generally do."

"All the way up the two-lane?"

"Up the shortcut. Starts way down near the golf course. Goes straight up through the woods an' comes out near where the fence starts. Only takes twenty minutes or so to get up it. An' about ten minutes goin' down."

"Your car wasn't up there at all?"

"You still think Manda was up on the Pitch? An' took off in our car? Oh, sir, so suspicious. You an' the heroic deputies. They were back again today. Askin' the neighbors whether they saw Manda out last Saturday night. None of 'em did, 'course. Then they asked Manda some questions."

"Oh?"

"Don't think they got much. Manda's back in the pink again. But she don't talk yer ear off, 'less she takes a shine to you. Oh, they asked her what you wanted to know so bad."

"What's that?"

"If she saw a face on the lady with the purple dress."

"And?"

"What I told you. No. Just a big lady in a purple dress. Nobody she knows or recognizes. Can't describe her any better than that. Ain't it a cryin' shame?"

"Turn here."

"Why don't I just keep goin' an' let Manda take a look at all those—"

"Turn here, dammit! You're taking me home!"

Emil's shoulders twitched in silent laughter. "Righto, sire."

Once back at Aunt Amy's, Pierce locked the back door and filled a tumbler with White Label. When the two front door chimes sounded, he picked up the steak knife.

The door was a solid frame, without glass, and anyone standing in front of it could not be seen from the living room window.

When he eased the door open a matter of inches, the knife was behind his back.

"Whit! Oh, good God!"

Sally Berwyn pushed him through the foyer to the living room. "Your face! Your shirt's torn! You're bleeding!"

Dragging his right leg, he lurched to the rocker and gently let himself settle into it. He dropped the knife on the floor.

"We've got to get you cleaned off."

"Let me finish this." He pulled at the Scotch again.

Sally slung her coat over a chair and hurried to the kitchen, returning with a pan of hot water. With a clean dishtowel and a bar of soap she began removing the dirt and blood from his face.

"I was parked across the street. Waiting. I kept calling you

220

today and there was never an answer. Whit, I'm sorry, but I was concerned after the way you acted in Chicago. And then I saw your car drive up. And Emil Gatliffe getting out and slinking away."

Pierce's head sank back wearily against Aunt Amy's well-worn antimacassar.

"Somebody just tried to kill me. I think it was whoever was in my place in Chicago yesterday. I think it was somebody who killed my wife."

She did not pause, daubing carefully at the slash where the knife had broken the skin, just beneath his right eye. "What's going on, Whit?"

"Wouldn't be a good idea to involve you."

"Whit, I've earned the right to know."

"Earned? Well, maybe you have." He sighed. "Sally, you may be sorry you asked."

He spared nothing, except the extent of his relationship with Britt and except for his having discovered Britt's body. Eyes closed, occasionally sipping from the tumbler of Scotch, he permitted the facts, the fears, the fantasies to stream out. Above all, he told her of Corinne. Afterward he felt purged, empty.

Sally sat on the floor, legs folded under her, holding his hand. "You're not going to report this attack tonight?"

"What would Vigo Lustgarten make out of it? I was jumped on Frenchman's Pitch at midnight? Why was I there? Did I see who it was? Even if they believed me it could've been some random assault. Some junkie or misfit waiting up there to rob whoever came along."

"But you don't think it was random?"

"No. And why should I be killed? The same reason I think Britt was killed—the idea that we must have damaging information. At first I thought that was a possibility in Britt's case. Just a possibility. Now that I'm a target, too, I know that's got to be why. I'm next, apparently. That means there's a connection."

"But you said you don't have any damaging information."

"Not that I know of. But Britt said she found the purple dress. And Britt and I were partners. So the supposition must be that she told me who wore it."

"Then why wouldn't you have told the authorities?"

"Maybe I'm saving the evidence. For what? To spring it in my book? Until I get more substantial information? For purposes of blackmail? I don't know. But it's getting pretty clear that I'm supposed to be privy to something. Something I can't be allowed to keep walking around knowing. Could you get me a refill, please?"

"Here you go." She laid her palm over his forehead. "You're feverish. Do you feel really awful?"

"Aching like the devil. But finally starting to pass out, thank God."

His voice was fuzzy now, his thoughts wandering. "There's a connection. But what? Jennifer. Angela. Corinne. Britt. All dead, all connected. All in La Soeur, except Corinne. But Corinne came to La Soeur. Corinne and her daughter. Corinne and Angela, together, on the day Jennifer died. But what's the connection? Why was Corinne killed after that? And Angela after that?"

"Whit, we'd better get you upstairs."

"Corinne and Angela and the Maserati. Angela drove the Maserati. The day Jennifer died. Corinne let her drive it."

She hooked her arm around him. Uncertainly they climbed the creaking staircase. Sally guided him to the bathroom, began running water in the tub, and removed his clothes.

"That leg is black and blue. And your hip!"

She helped him into the tub. He shuddered and grunted loudly.

"Cold water's best, Whit. For relieving the swelling. That's the current thinking. I took a course."

"Of course, you did. Anything you haven't taken a course in?"

"Just put up with it for a couple of minutes. That's a good soldier."

At last she turned on the hot-water tap. As the warmth intensified Pierce leaned far back, all but asleep.

"Jennifer was first," he mumbled. "On the day Corinne let Angela drive the Maserati. What happened? Somebody saw the Maserati? And thought it was Corinne? Who saw it? Whoever killed Jennifer Stabo? Mistaken identity? Whoever killed Jennifer thought Corinne was in the Maserati and thought Corinne saw something? Saw Jennifer being killed? And so Corinne was killed? Is that the connection?"

"And then," Sally said, "realized later that Angela had seen it—not Corinne? So that Angela was murdered, too?"

"And then thought Britt found out. And so Britt was next. And then thought I found out . . ."

Sally half-pulled him out of the water and dried him thoroughly.

"But Corinne didn't blame me. . . ."

She led him to his room, lifted his legs onto the bed, covered him with sheets and blankets.

"Sally, get out while you can. . . ." His head burrowed exhaustedly into the pillow. "While you—"

"No, Whit," she said very softly. "Rest."

Instantly he was asleep. Sometime before dawn he came awake with a start, shouting. It had been a nightmare. He could not recall the details, but he had been frozen with fear.

Sally touched his face soothingly. He felt her body tight against his. He let his hand glide along her skin—the long, smooth, warm flow of her back, her hip, her thigh.

It had been a nightmare, a not-quite-seen entity reaching, reaching for him out of writhing shadows while he was powerless to move.

Had it been a woman? A big woman in a purple dress? A force, a presence? Something more than human, more than any one human?

Whatever it was had dissolved.

Whatever it was.

But it had not been Corinne.

Not her green, staring eyes.

It had been a nightmare. But not the nightmare he had lived with since August.

He shifted slightly, moaning at the pain in his stiffened leg. Lightly he kissed Sally on her throat, her shoulders, on her firm, consoling breasts. She held him closely as deep sleep washed over him once more.

The bedroom was dark when he awoke, and she was gone. He looked at his watch. Six fifteen. He had slept all day Sunday and on into the evening.

His entire body was sore, but was he immobilized? There was a quick flash of fright as he remembered his dream and how, in it, he had seemed paralyzed.

He flung back the covers and tentatively raised his right leg. It was racked with pain, but it was still flexible. He swung his feet onto the floor, and one arm clumsily struck the small lamp on the nightstand. It banged onto the floor.

Almost at once Sally appeared. "Oh, the patient is up and is *he* grumpy. Honestly. Throwing things to get attention!"

She picked up the lamp, saw that it was unbroken, and replaced it on the stand. Sitting on the bed beside Pierce, she brushed her lips across his, then felt his forehead.

"Fever's gone. Able to get up?"

"We'll find out."

"Time for Sunday brunch. Late, late brunch. Bacon, toast, eggs, orange juice. Would you like it served in bed or shall we be formal and retire to the dining room?"

"I've got to get moving. Can't be laid up. So let's be formal."

"You won't let me pamper you? So be it. You look so much better. True, like you've been through a barroom brawl. But compared to last night, so much better. Seems to me you always ordered your eggs scrambled at the A-I. Is that okay?"

He was hungrier than he thought. Sally laughingly retied an apron around her waist and prepared a second batch of eggs. She had pulled her flowing red hair back and knotted it at her neck as she did at the Appleland Inn. It heightened the little-girl look of her freckled cheeks and the creaminess of the skin over the long, fine bones of her face.

"It's marvelous, Sally. Look, thanks for listening to me last night. And thanks for not telling me I'm imagining half of it. And for . . ."

He paused, wondering how to express this. Wondering if he should. The silken delicacy of her skin so lightly touching him that it did not in the least aggravate the soreness of his body. The sweet softness of her against his lips in the utter blackness. All this was now like a dream. A dream that offset the other dream, the ugly, constricting dream.

She sensed his hesitation. "Well, honestly, you're not imagining what happened to you up on Frenchman's Pitch. Do you remember what you were saying last night? Before you conked out?"

He scowled, industriously applying marmalade to his toast. "About connections. The Maserati."

"And someone seeing Angela in it. Thinking Angela was Corinne. And thinking Corinne saw Jennifer's murder."

"That means Angela saw something. Maybe even saw the murderer. Why didn't she say something? Report it?"

"I don't know. But if any of this is so, everything started with Jennifer Stabo's death."

"Jennifer's death triggered it. A chain. Leading from Corinne to Angela to Britt to me. A logical sequence. Versus the idea that it's some maniac running wild, slaughtering people willy-nilly. *A* plus *B* means *C* must die. Right now, *C* is me."

He finished his orange juice and patted his lips with a napkin. "Well, I'm not going to sit and wait for it."

Sally brought the coffeepot in from the kitchen and filled both their cups. "A doctor ought to see that leg."

"It's going to be all right. I can't be laid up. Not now."

"Ready to talk strategy?"

"Strategy? The only strategy is to go out looking. Looking harder. Let people know it. Start turning over more stones. Any goddam stones. There are a lot of people to go back to. Tougher questions to ask. Anything to get a handle on the connection between *A* and *B* and *C*. Anything to push the killer off balance. Any idea, any ploy. I don't care how crazy."

She poured cream into a tablespoon, dunked the spoon into her coffee.

"The book is on again," Pierce said very quietly and deliberately. "That's it. The book Britt and I talked about. That's my pretext. For asking questions, buttonholing people. Letting the killer know I'm looking. Because, by God, I am. Yes, the book is on."

"What can I do, Whit?"

"I don't want—"

The phone jangled. It took five rings for him to hobble to it.

"Hello, Whit. I understand you wanted to talk to me."

"Winnie?"

"Al said it was something important."

"It could be. He didn't know where to reach you."

"He's a dear, but he shouldn't worry so much. What did you want to know?"

"Corinne visited you . . . within the past year?"

"Oh, yes. Just briefly. We had a lovely little visit."

"Winnie, did you ever visit Corinne in Chicago?"

"No, never. I'd wanted to. To see both of you, of course. But it never seemed to work out, did it? And we were—"

"Winnie, listen. When Corinne stopped by to see you, did she mention whether anyone from La Soeur had been to see her in Chicago? Please think."

"Oh, I remember well. She said Angela had come to see her."

"Angela?"

"Oh, yes. Angela and her friend. I can't recall her name."

"Cutler? Ruby Lee Cutler?"

"That's it. Corinne said she didn't care for the friend much. But she entertained the two of them one afternoon. Of course, Angela didn't know that Corinne was . . . Well, she'd met Corinne here in La Soeur and taken a liking to her. So she and her friend just drove down to Chicago one day and dropped in. Didn't Corinne tell you about it?"

"No, she didn't. Thanks, Winnie."

"Something helpful?" Sally asked.

"Very."

The phone rang again. Sally lifted the receiver and passed it to him. He talked several minutes, then rejoined her in the dining room.

"You volunteered to help. Maybe there is something. I'm not so sure I'm able to drive. If you'd be good enough to do some chauffeuring?"

"Sure. Where to?"

"That was Ralph Hungerford. Wants me to come over tomorrow night. To talk about plans for the future. His future in Washington, I presume."

Pierce stopped, looked intently at Sally, and went on. "I was going to back out of it. Then it occurred to me. Craziness. Wild as hell. But I said I'd follow up any idea. However desperate. It's an idea Emil had. Weird. But I don't care anymore! He wanted me to get hold of something of Britt's. So Amanda could 'read' it. Something associated with Britt's death. I know that sounds like complete idiocy . . ."

"But it's *something*, Whit."

"Damn right. Idiocy. But it's the only thing left."

227

Chapter 27

While Sally waited in the car at the South Side Shopping Center, Pierce picked up the Smith and Wesson .38, a holster, and a box of ammunition.

He didn't tell her what was in the package. But that evening when she drove him to Ralph Hungerford's, the gun, loaded, was nestled in the roomy pocket of his down jacket.

From his appearance, Ralph Hungerford might have been hosting another party such as the one Pierce had first attended here. He wore the same scarlet cashmere jacket, a silk broadcloth shirt, and a paisley silk cravat. Smokey, the Finnish bear dog, frisked and snuffled beside him.

"Welcome, Whit. So good of you. And . . ."

"This is Sally Berwyn."

Hungerford nodded, then stuck his large head forward almost into Pierce's face.

"Good heavens, man!"

"Took a nasty fall. I'm healing."

Ralph offered to take his coat, but Pierce hung it in the closet himself. Once again he stood in that spacious room in which he and Britt had lain together through one long night.

Ralph went to the mahogany side table. "White Label for you, if I recall, Whit. And Miss Berwyn?"

"Perhaps some white wine."

Hungerford mixed a Manhattan for himself and stood over them, his smile artificial and unconvincing. "Cheers!"

The dancing light of the fireplace cast into sharp relief the deep folds running from his nose to the corners of his mouth and the tucks and seams in the heavy mounds of flesh hanging from his jaws. There was music playing on a stereo unit somewhere in the house: distant, Mantovani-like standards, totally unobtrusive.

"Sally was kind enough to come along because I wasn't up to driving over by myself," Pierce said. "As far as any political matters we might discuss, she's assured me she'll keep it to herself."

"Not a problem. Yes, it is about politics. But what I told you in confidence a few weeks ago is soon to become public knowledge. That is to say, I will be officially tossing my hat into the ring. In early December."

He shot one wrist out from beneath a French cuff in order to consult a thin, silver-tone digital watch. "December ninth, to be precise. The day after my speech to the National Economic Forum in Chicago. In the interim I believe it will become fairly obvious as to what's about to happen, since Len Durban will be building our campaign organization. The only point of confidentiality is as regards you, Whit. That is, what your role might be."

"Let me be one of the first to wish you luck, Ralph."

"Thank you. This is moving the announcement up earlier than I expected. Frankly, that's due to . . ." He sat down heavily, across from them, automatically pulling up his trousers to keep the knees from bagging. "To the tragedy regarding Britt. I welcome the start of this campaign. It's going to engross me. It's going to tax all my energies. It's going to wear me out. Fine. I want that. It's going to keep my thoughts away from . . ."

His arm moved in a half circle, a gesture that vaguely included this high-ceilinged room, the elaborate staircase, the gallery above. "In fact, I wanted to announce at once. But Len said to give it a month at least. For the sake of propriety."

"Mr. Hungerford," Sally said, "we've never met before. But I want to tell you how sorry I am."

"Eh? Thank you, young lady. The memories are so hard to ignore. All these familiar surroundings. But she's not a part of them anymore. Whit, you must know what I mean?"

Pierce was silent a long while. "Yes."

"Well. What I said to you in my office in a general way I now repeat, more specifically. I need a professional on my staff who knows how to deal with the media, who can write well and do it under pressure. The bottom line is that I'd be enormously pleased to be able to welcome you to our team."

"Sounds intriguing, Ralph. Whether it's right for me, I'm not sure."

"You've been deferring your decision, Whit. It's an option that will not always be open. I would like to be certain of the key people on my staff when I make the announcement December ninth. And I'd like to get started as soon as possible on some position papers, some overviews of various topics of the day. There's no other major project occupying your time, is there? Now that you've dropped the book."

"I haven't dropped it, Ralph."

"Oh? Sheriff Lustgarten told me you had."

"I've reconsidered since I talked to him. The book is on again."

Hungerford pulled back the mesh fire screen, picked up a brass poker, and nudged the logs. Tongues of flame sizzled.

"So much for Sheriff Lustgarten's accuracy. Another example of his inadequacy."

"You've been rough on him in the *Sentinel.*"

"Britt used to tell me he was incompetent. I pooh-poohed it. We always endorsed him for reelection. No more. I see now she was right. Oh, he's put on a show of great zeal and activity. Yes, he had a line of men out there on the course last week, starting at the fourteenth green and covering every inch of ground for half a mile. No results. It's not lack of energy. It's lack of expertise, starting at the top."

Pierce shifted his leg and uttered a soft grunt of pain. Sally looked at him, sharply, anxiously.

"Privately I've been talking to the United States' Attorney's office," Hungerford went on. "Trying to get some federal investigation going. So far they say it's not within their jurisdiction. So we are left to the mercies of Vigo Lustgarten."

He peered intently into the depths of the blaze. "Vigo's not a power in the party, even though he's held that job forever. It wouldn't disrupt party unity if I pushed for somebody else. In fact, it would bolster my campaign. A fighter for progressive leadership across the board—both in Washington and in La Soeur. Out with the fossils, in with the professionals. You know, they've had only one original idea. And it wasn't the sheriff's. It was one of his deputies."

"What's that?"

"Smokey. Britt had taken Smokey out that night. He was discovered beside her body. Possibly he saw who . . . attacked her. Maybe he could identify this individual. React in some way. Lunge or bark or *something*."

"That makes sense," Sally said.

"They had Smokey down there today, some vagrants and local ne'er-do-wells parading in front of him. Nothing so far, I'm told. But they'll keep it up. At any rate, Whit, Lustgarten isn't up to the job. But isn't this book idea of yours totally quixotic? Not to mention dangerous?"

"I'm committed to it, Ralph. And I'd appreciate your cooperation."

"Of course. But I don't know how I can help you."

"There is a way. I know it sounds bizarre. But I'm pursuing a particular line of inquiry. Is there anything Britt had with her . . . that night . . . that I could take a look at?"

Hungerford's massive, fleshy face appeared to settle more solidly into his powerful shoulders. He seemed saddened. There was hurt in the blue eyes that fastened incredulously on Pierce.

"Why, Whit?" he said at last, in a stage whisper. "What would be the point? Except to wallow in morbidity? At Britt's expense. Something to stir up ghoulish titillation? Oh, really, Whit."

"No, that's not the point. I can't explain why. But there's a chance—a small chance—that it might prove useful."

"He's right, Mr. Hungerford," Sally interjected. "It might come to nothing. But it's not just . . . titillation. Honestly, does that sound like Whit? It's nothing disrespectful to Mrs. Hungerford."

"Ralph, I assure you this request is germane to my research. I just can't divulge the reason. Not right now. But I'm asking for your trust."

"Whit, it's not worthy of you. And I have nothing to produce, at any rate. The authorities confiscated everything on and around her person."

"Any jewelry?"

"They have it all. Her ring, her bracelets, her earrings, her watch, her purse and whatever was in it. Her clothing, her shoes. Everything. It was all tested at the state crime laboratory. They learned nothing. I don't understand what you, as a layman, could discover that they could not."

"Will her belongings be returned to you?"

"Soon, I've been told."

"Do you know how soon?"

"Probably the end of the week. I asked that her clothes be destroyed. I don't want to see them. Her valuables I may send to her parents."

"Ralph, I'd be grateful if you'd call me when you get them back. I'd like to borrow them. Just briefly. I'm asking it as a favor."

Hungerford's broad back was to them as he stood before the

fire, hands knitted together behind him. He shrugged his shoulders in resignation.

"Very well. I'll call you."

"Thanks, Ralph, and would you—"

From elsewhere in the house, from the other wing, there was barking. Sharp, loud, and vicious.

"Smokey!" Hungerford shouted.

The barking grew more frantic, turning to snarls. Angry, savage.

"Smokey! Stop it!"

Then a scrambling, clattering sound.

Pierce sat bolt upright, head cocked.

Then three agonized, high-pitched yips.

Distant, stamping footsteps and a slamming door. Then silence.

Hungerford's face was slack. He looked, as if slightly puzzled, from Pierce to Sally and back to Pierce.

"Excuse me, please." Hungerford strode toward the rear of the house.

Pierce limped to the closet and pulled down his coat. Sally had already started after Hungerford.

"Hold it," Pierce commanded. He took her arm. Together they hurried through the formal dining room, through the sun room, into a spacious French country kitchen.

Directly ahead, in the back hallway, Hungerford was stooped over something.

Now his face was ashen, beaded with sweat. The object on the floor was Smokey.

"Oh, no." Sally moaned softly.

The big dog was dead, legs splayed, jaws agape. Blood pumped from the artery in its neck and gushed from stab wounds in its chest and belly.

Slowly Hungerford got to his feet. He searched Pierce's face, his jowls shaking.

Pierce yanked open the back door, his hand on the butt of the revolver even while it still rested in the pocket of the coat thrown over his arm. He went outside.

Be there, damn you!

Be there and come at me!

Let me see you this time, God damn you!

But there was nothing. Only the wide, decked terrace and the smooth sea of lawn falling away toward the woods, mantled in silence.

Sally followed him out, and with her beside him, he circled the house. Over the deck, past the garage, across the front driveway, and back to where they had started.

Hungerford stood exactly where they had left him. He stared solemnly and questioningly at Pierce. Pierce shook his head.

"Poor Smokey." Ralph's tenor voice strove to be composed and dignified, but it was tremulous.

He saw Pierce examining the door. "The lock's not broken. There are no chisel marks or anything else. Nobody forced it. It must have been unlocked. The cleaning lady . . . she was in today. I've warned her that there's always the possibility of prowlers. Now look . . ."

"Prowlers?" Sally repeated quietly, and looked at Pierce.

"We have them at times," Hungerford said. "That's one reason we bought Smokey."

"Ralph, you'd better be calling the sheriff's department."

Several splotches of blood led to the back door, Pierce noted. Small, regularly spaced. The intruder had not been able to avoid some contact with Smokey's blood. It might have been a heel that stepped in it.

A high heel?

Pierce heard again in his mind the precise, ringing quality of the click-click-click on the parquet tiles of his Chicago home.

Hungerford twisted the bolt on the back door firmly into its mortised slot.

"First I'm having another Manhattan. Miss Berwyn, would you mix it for me? I'll admit it: I'm shaken. Very shaken."

When Sally and Ralph had left, Pierce bent over the mutilated carcass. Deftly he unloosened the leather, rhinestone-embedded collar.

Pierce found Sally alone in the living room. Her arms were crossed tightly against her body.

"It was so hideous." Her voice was tiny, all but inaudible.

He touched her arm reassuringly. "Where's Ralph?"

"Gone to call." Despite the warmth of the fire, she was shivering. Her lips were parted and she looked dazed. Strands of russet hair tumbled over her forehead. Pierce brushed them back, pulled her to him, and held her.

"I've talked with Len Durban," Hungerford announced, emerging from a doorway on the second floor to stand on the gallery above them. He had drunk virtually all of the Manhattan, and color had returned to his cheeks. He descended the stairway carefully, one hand on the rich, oaken handrail.

"Len's handling it. Calling the authorities. And coming over himself. I've told him to expedite the installation of a security system in this house. I should have seen to it before."

The timbre of his voice was again firm, melodious. But he moved slowly, wearily. He pulled back a fold of the drapes and looked out into the night.

"I'm sorry this evening had to end so badly. I'm afraid I'm not disposed to resume our political conversation."

"I understand, Ralph."

Hungerford rested his forehead against the windowpane, making no attempt at further conversation. Sally sat close to Pierce. He took her hand in his, and her fingers clutched him tightly, urgently. They were ice-cold. He noticed that she could not keep her eyes from straying continually to the dining room doorway, to the passage that led to the kitchen.

And what, Pierce wondered, if the dog had not been there to intercept whoever had entered through the back door? Or had Smokey been the intended target?

"Here's Len's car," Hungerford said.

He turned to his guests once more. "Whit, remember. You're getting back to me posthaste on the matter I brought up tonight. I'd hope to hear one way or the other by the end of this month."

"You will, Ralph."

"Miss Berwyn, a genuine pleasure."

"If we can do anything else—"

Pierce tugged her arm. He did not want to linger until some deputy sheriff examined Smokey. And possibly asked Ralph if his dog didn't normally wear a collar.

"Take care, Ralph. Good night."

Chapter 28

Tuesday morning was clear and cold. Pierce groaned as he wedged his body behind the steering wheel.

Backing out of the garage was particularly difficult, but once on the street his confidence grew. He had to drive cautiously and concentrate on using his left leg, which wasn't accustomed to manipulating the accelerator. Still, he was managing. And this was better than having Sally drive him. Better than getting her more inextricably involved.

The Mustang was not parked outside Amanda's mobile home. Not only were the curtains drawn once more, but now a shade had been placed over the small window in the front door and the wilted Christmas wreath had been removed.

Pierce pounded on the door. As he waited he put his hands in his jacket pockets. In one pocket was the .38 and in the other was Smokey's dog collar.

Two small children came out of a neighboring aluminum-skinned home and squinted curiously at him. Possibly, he thought, this was one of their favorite pastimes—staring at whoever paid a call on the crazy lady next door. In the window of the children's home was a hand-lettered sign: WORMS, REDWORMS, NITE-CRAWLERS 4 SALE. The sun was blinding.

The door opened and Amanda hovered over him. Her off-center eyes registered recognition, and with urgent, jerking movements of her arms she motioned him to enter.

He followed her along the narrow corridor between the heaps of clutter. It was uncomfortably warm, stuffy, and dim. There were two table lamps lit, but this warehouse of a room was filled with shadows that hid and distorted the shapes of the furniture and bric-a-brac.

"Mrs. Gatliffe, I've come to ask a favor of you."

Through a flurry of hand signals she indicated he was to wait where he was. She disappeared into the next room, moving rapidly despite her precarious, thin-heeled black satin evening slippers, despite the fact that her body seemed thicker than the passageway. When she returned, she held a hairbrush in her large hand.

"Emil," she said.

"This is Emil's?"

She nodded. The words emerged slowly as though spoken by someone not familiar with English. "I want to tell you. What I see there. Not good. Sometimes I read things Emil has. To see how he is. I don't tell him. But I want to see. How he does. To see is he okay. I want you look out for Emil. Take care he don't get in trouble. Take care he stay all right."

She ran her hand up and down the handle of the hairbrush. "I see it here. Bad. Black clouds. All around Emil. I never see that before. And I see you. Looking. Near to Emil. While all black comes over Emil."

"Mrs. Gatliffe, did you come to my house? To talk to me?"

"I go to your house," she said, straining to put her thoughts together in words. "Ask you help Emil. I don't know how. But the clouds come over Emil. And you there. You look out for him."

"This was Saturday night?" he asked.

The huge head nodded. Just then there was the clink of a key turning in the front door lock.

"Not tell him!" Amanda burst out, hastily pushing the brush out of sight.

A gruff voice boomed, "Who's been sitting in the big bear's chair when the big bear's out to lunch?"

Emil bounded in, the bean-pole body loose and flopping. He grinned and applauded.

"Bravo, Mister P.! You've done it! Up out of your bed of pain to pay us another visit! Can't keep a good man down, ain't it? Can't believe you're out an' about so soon. Not after our little whoop-de-doo on the Pitch t'other night. Oh, what a tumble that was! Jack fell down an' broke his crown. But it only hurts when you laugh, yes?"

"I'm here to see if your mother will examine something for me."

Emil smacked his lips with satisfaction.

"Something from the late, lamented Mrs. Hungerford? Something to read? Like I asked you?"

"No. Something else. But I'd appreciate Amanda's cooperation."

"Well, course! Manda, have you offered our guest some hospitality? The best in the house of Gatliffe for him! Take off your coat, Herr Doktor. Have a seat."

Elaborately he whisked a handkerchief over a peeling, discolored rattan chair. "Refreshments are on the way."

When Emil returned with a tray and three glasses of cider, he was less frenetic. Portraying a waiter of polished elegance, he remained aloof as he served Amanda first and then Pierce.

Pierce nodded curtly and tentatively tasted the drink.

"Does it suit your palate, sir?"

"It's very good."

"La Soeur's finest. From our magnificent orchards." Emil's smile was sly, knowing. "Did you think there'd be something else in it, hmmm? Something . . . unusual? Another little trick, like the one I played on you last time? Would I do that to a guest? Here, I'll trade you glasses."

"No need. This is fine. Mrs. Gatliffe—"

"Manda, you'll read something for Mr. Pierce, won't you? Now? That's my good girl."

Pierce reached into his coat for the dog collar and handed it to her. Emil leaned over, peering excitedly.

"I know that!" he cried. "I know where it's from!"

"Oh? Where?"

"The Hungerford house. By Meadowbluff. And I know who wore it. But I won't say now. Don't want to influence Manda."

"How do you know the Hungerford house?"

Now Emil's smile was mysterious and inscrutable. "Oh, I've been by it. I've looked it over. It's fun to see how the royal families live."

The face in the window during Ralph's and Britt's dinner party, Pierce recalled. "What you mean is, you're a peeping Tom. Isn't that it?"

Emil smoothed his yellow locks of hair with exaggerated fastidiousness. "I like to know what's happening. It's fun to drift around at night when people don't know you're there. You learn a lot." He giggled. "You know, you weren't the only one visited Mrs. Hungerford out there by that tree at night. Not by a long shot. Did you think you were?"

"That's enough."

"Oh, that wasn't nice of her. Sneaking around like she did." He swirled cider in his glass, tasting it reverently as if it were vintage wine. "But then, Mr. Hungerford has his secrets, too."

Pierce felt the rush of anger that Emil inevitably seemed to produce in him. But he curbed his irritation and asked, "What do you mean, secrets?"

"Aha! You see, it's fun to know what people are up to at night."

"God damn it, Emil, just what do you mean?"

The answer was given in a conspiratorial whisper, Emil cupping his mouth with one hand. "He has a friend. A tall lady. Strolling across the golf course. Late at night. She lets herself in the back door. Isn't that juicy?"

"A tall lady? Who?"

"Never been close enough to tell. Just seen her twice. On very

240

dark nights. I think she only comes to see him then. When it's really dark out. Ain't that romantic? And ain't that sneaky?"

Oblivious to their conversation, Amanda sat placidly, motionless. Her legs were spread, and her hands lay clasped in the folds of her lap around the dog collar.

"Story time!" Emil exulted in a high, piccolo voice, clapping his palms together. He dropped to the floor by Amanda's side and sat hugging his knees against his chin, tilting his face up.

Amanda held the collar in her right hand while her left stroked it gently, almost tenderly, from buckle to tip. Gradually her eyes closed. Then the hand stopped moving and lay still, thick fingers half-curled around the collar.

The misshapen jaw fell open, baring the stained and worndown teeth. For a moment Pierce wondered if she'd gone to sleep. He stared closely at her face: the total incongruity of the features—the swollen right side, the sunken left, the nonalignment of the eyes, and the uneven slanting of the eyebrows.

He watched for some flicker of movement, and there was none. Then words came, from somewhere deep in her chest cavity, hollow words completely without inflection.

"There is dog . . . Big dog . . . Mostly black . . . Some white . . . He has the collar on . . . He is barking . . . At a door . . . Door opens . . . Dog barks more . . . He backs away . . . Now runs forward . . . Shows his teeth . . . Tries to bite . . . He tries to bite the legs . . . Strong dog . . . Barking loud . . . Hands come down . . . Grab dog . . . By throat . . . Dog fights . . . Sticks knife in dog . . . One time . . . Two time . . . Three time . . . Four time . . . Then in throat . . . Dog is bleeding . . . He lays down . . . Now wipes off knife on dog . . . Boot steps in blood . . . Legs walk away . . . Door closes."

There were no more words. Emil continued to gaze raptly at Amanda.

Pierce looked sharply at him. "Can I ask questions?"

The youth nodded.

"Can you see the person's face, Mrs. Gatliffe?"

A long pause.

"Just legs. Blue pants."

"Is it a woman or a man? Can you tell?"

"Just see legs. Pants. Boots."

"What kind of boots?"

An even longer pause. "Pretty boots . . . Brown . . . Little stars . . . All over them . . ."

"Stars? What color?"

"Blue and red. Blue and red stars."

Pierce pulled back, upright in the chair. "Do you see anything else?"

There was only silence from Amanda.

"Thank you, Mrs. Gatliffe," he said. She opened her eyes, her face still wholly impassive.

"You know those boots, don't you?" Emil sprang to his feet. "I do, too. But I can't remember where. Somewhere in town. I've seen them. Somewhere. You know, don't you?"

Pierce stood up. "Mrs. Gatliffe, I appreciate your help."

Shrillness filled Emil's voice. "We did what you wanted. Manda read for you. She saw something. You know what it was. It's only fair to tell! It's only fair!"

Pierce took the collar from Amanda and walked to the door. Emil hurried after him, gesticulating wildly.

"Not fair! To hear our story and not tell us what it means! Not fair! You have to tell! You have to tell what you know!"

Pierce looked past him, back at Amanda.

Furtively she held up the hairbrush for him to see.

Emil clutched at him. Pierce pushed him aside and left.

Chapter 29

The Adult Book Store remained open till nine, the only shop on the far western edge of the downtown district not to close by six. These early evening hours, in fact, were apparently the busiest of the day.

Pierce watched a small but steady procession of clients entering and leaving. Initially men in business suits, professional-looking types, stopping by after work. Later the customers grew both younger and older and, in both cases, noticeably scruffier.

There was no doubt in his mind anymore. The boots that Amanda had seen were R. L. Cutler's. So what was the strategy? Tell her he was on to her? But if R. L. was the big lady in the purple dress she already suspected he was on to her. And that's exactly why she had made two attempts on his life already.

No. There was only one thing left to do. Fasten on to R. L. Cutler. Follow her. Haunt her. Until she made a mistake. Until he knew it was R. L. who killed Corinne.

He had parked across the street, half a block away. The hours dragged by slowly, but he was patient. It had been three months now since Corinne's death. Months of anguish and horror. He had endured those months, and he was prepared now to invest the time it took to destroy the creature who had sown that anguish and horror.

At two minutes after nine, R. L. Cutler emerged carrying a briefcase. The usual cigarette jutted from her mouth. She locked the front door, walked to the end of the block, and then down an alley. Pierce started the engine of his car and began inching forward.

A van rocketed out of the alley, turned left, and sped off. He recognized it from the time Deputy Nehemiah Evans had pointed out R. L.'s farm home. The van—tan-colored with two orange, pouncing pumas painted on the sides and rear—had been parked in the yard.

It was not difficult to keep her in sight. He followed at a considerable distance and was able to let other cars move ahead of him without fear that he would lose the van.

Soon it became apparent that she was driving home. Traffic thinned and all but disappeared on the asphalt county highway. Pierce dropped even farther back.

She steered the van into the long driveway of her farm. Pierce drove slowly past the spanking-white two-and-a-half-story house, the barn, and the other outbuildings. The pickup truck he had seen before was still there, parked in the dirt driveway.

He drove past three more farm homes, then swung around in the entrance of the fourth. Approaching from the north, he killed his lights five hundred yards from the turnoff to R. L.'s and rolled to a stop on the shoulder of the road. A high-voltage lamp was lit above the door to the one-story extension abutting the larger part of the house. From here he had a clear view of anyone coming or going.

Cold crept quickly into his car. Intermittently Pierce switched on the engine and heater. At eleven ten, R. L. stamped out of the house and got back in the van.

She cut directly west at the first crossroad until she picked up Highway 35, paralleling the Mississippi. After traveling ten minutes at seventy miles an hour, she exited and almost immediately swerved onto another county blacktop. It was a lonely road with not another vehicle to be seen on it. Pierce permitted her to widen her lead.

Then the lights of the van turned right and were lost to sight. Pierce accelerated until he reached the spot and saw she had pulled up beside a tavern. Again he swung around and parked on the shoulder, facing north, assuming this was the direction she'd take back.

Like so many rural taverns, this had once been a farmhouse. It was a modest frame structure, clapboard-sided. The sound of a jukebox blasted jarringly through the quiet, country air.

Only one diffused light shone through the curtained second floor, which was probably the owner's residence. Blue neon letters in the front window announced beer on draft. The weathered sign above read: VI'S TIP TOP TAP. There were a half-dozen cars in the small gravel lot.

Two women left together in a Winnebago just before midnight. Pierce pulled his jacket more closely around him and shifted his body about, trying to get comfortable. He stretched out his right leg, which had become cramped and ached intensely.

He was not conscious of the car that eased up behind him until he heard a door slam. Then a powerful light went on in his face and a hand rapped on his window.

Pierce caught a glimpse of a uniform and, looking back, a star on the sedan parked there. He rolled down the window.

"Good evening, sir," said Nehemiah Evans.

"Mr. Evans."

"This is not where I'd expect to find you, Mr. Pierce."

"No. But is there anything illegal about it?"

"It's not an especially good place to be parking. Across from Vi's. After midnight. Considering the sort of thing that's been happening in La Soeur lately. May I see your driver's license?"

"Of course. But, look, Mr. Evans—"

"May I see your license?"

The voice was cold, impersonal. There was no ring of familiarity in it, no hint of warmth in the hard, scowling face.

"Of course."

"We are checking more closely than ever, Mr. Pierce. We are

under orders. Anything irregular. Anyone acting in an unusual manner. May I ask why you're parked out here at this hour?"

"It's . . . personal. I can't go into it. Look, you're aware that I've been doing some investigation on my own. You've cooperated with me, to an extent."

"Which is why I'm on nights for the indefinite future. Now, what are you doing here at this hour?"

"The fact is I am here as part of that ongoing research."

"Would you step out, please?"

"Yes. But I assure you—"

"Step out, please."

"All right. For a writer, Mr. Evans, you are one helluva hard-nosed cop."

As Pierce struggled to get out of the car his injured leg buckled. It had been hours since he had stood on it, and the unaccustomed weight proved too much. He fell toward the hood of the Sunbird and threw out his hands to catch himself.

The revolver slid out of his jacket pocket and onto the shoulder of the highway.

Evans bent slowly to pick it up. He touched only the barrel and examined the weapon carefully.

"You registered to own this?"

"Yes."

"Can I see the papers?"

"I don't have them on me."

"I'll have to take this down to the Safety Building. This all part of your research, Mr. Pierce?"

"Yes. I think I'm entitled to defend myself."

Evans trained the light full on Pierce's face, taking in the effects of the fall from Frenchman's Pitch. "Mr. Pierce," he said, and for the first time his voice had softened, "is there anything you'd like to tell me? About why you're here and what you think you're doing?"

"I can't. Not now."

"I don't have a choice, you know. I'll have to report this."

His forehead creased with angry wrinkles. "Listen, get yourself home, will you? Right away."

Pierce climbed back in his car. Evans leaned down to him. "This is no place to be. Here, at this time of night. Mr. Pierce, use a little common sense. You know what I'm sayin'?"

Pierce drove off, watching the lights of the patrol car in his rearview mirror until, finally, the deputy turned off at the next road junction. Pierce went on until he reached a wide intersection. He made a U-turn and returned to his post across from the tavern.

The van was still there, but within minutes R. L. Cutler came out. She was between two other women—a slight, angelic-looking brunette scarcely out of her teens and Jan Laughlin.

R. L. opened her passenger door and motioned the younger girl in. Jan also tried to enter, and R. L. shoved her away. Jan raised her voice, and Pierce could hear the high, tinny protests, but he could not discern the words. He ran the window down and heard R. L. holler, "Fuck off, will you!"

Jan pressed forward again, trying to put her foot inside the cab.

"Fuck off!" R. L. repeated.

With both hands she seized Jan by the shoulders and hurled her aside.

"I'll tell!" the tall girl shrilled. "I'll tell everybody!"

R. L.'s speed was dazzling. She planted her fist solidly in Jan's midsection and withdrew it just as rapidly. Jan squealed and sank lazily into a heap. She was like a broken alabaster statue—blond hair, fawn coat, white boots—alone in the ebony darkness of the parking lot.

Cutler started the engine with a belch of exhaust and backed out in a burst of gravel.

Pierce lagged far behind, alert to the chance she might make an unanticipated turn but not really expecting it. She did not, and at one forty she and her companion entered the farmhouse.

Once more Pierce parked opposite the silver mailbox that

stood beside the driveway. He knew his car was invisible against the dark fields and the black sky.

Soon the downstairs lights were extinguished, and the lights in the square tower flashed on. At three twenty these lights, too, winked off. R. L. Cutler's farmhouse, outbuildings, and the surrounding pastures lay dark and slumbering under a vast panoply of stars.

A sense of unreality clung to him—one he knew he must combat because there might be many more nights such as this.

I am here, he thought, because a deranged woman saw stars on some boots in an image that took form in her mind.

How do I know that's what she saw? How do I know what she saw has any bearing on who killed Smokey? How do I know if who killed Smokey is trying to kill Ralph and is trying to kill me?

But if not this, what else? Who else?

At four A.M. he decided he could safely assume there would be no more observable activity at R. L. Cutler's until after daylight. He pulled away.

I'll be back, R. L. Damn you, I'll be back!

Chapter 30

His leg throbbed viciously as he limped from the garage to the back door. Obviously he'd needed another day or two of rest. He was exhausted and frustrated.

His first night of surveillance and the only notable occurrence was that he had been relieved of his weapon.

A totally inept performance.

He had left the kitchen light on, largely for psychological reasons. It gave him a greater sense of assurance anytime he returned during the hours of darkness. And dawn remained more than an hour away. He slammed the door shut and fastened both locks.

He heard the rocker creak and footsteps pad across the living room carpet.

Pierce froze.

"Whit, it's me." Sally entered the kitchen, her face clouded with anxiety and strain.

"God," he whispered, feeling as if the breath had been knocked out of him.

"I'm sorry. I didn't mean to . . . I never thought of how it might startle you. I've been waiting. And knowing what could happen. Here. Give me your coat. Are you okay?"

"How did you get in?"

"Come in and sit down. You look frazzled."

She eased him into the rocking chair and pulled the ottoman over for his right leg to rest on.

"I made hot chocolate. Like some?"

"How did you get in?"

"I took the extra set of keys. The set you had made up for Aunt Amy. I found them Sunday, while you were sleeping. I just thought . . . Well, they *are* Aunt Amy's. She'd want me to have them. And, I don't know, Whit, if there might be some emergency. If something might happen that I'd have to get in the house. To help you in some way. Just in case . . ."

"I just wish you'd told me."

"I'm sorry." She stood behind him, lightly massaging his neck and shoulders. "What happened?"

"Nothing, really."

"Nothing? All this time?"

"Nothing for you to be concerned about."

"I'm entitled to know. Remember? We agreed."

"I don't want you involved."

"I am involved. Up to the earlobes. I was at Mr. Hungerford's. I saw what happened there. I know what you know. That means I'm involved."

Pierce shook his head in resignation. There would be no way to fob her off indefinitely without an explanation, since he would probably be out all night every night for some time. And he was too tired to argue with her.

"What I'm doing is keeping an eye on R. L. Cutler." Tersely he described Amanda's reading of the dog collar and the strategy he'd based on that reading.

"R. L. Cutler! That could account for one problem. Excuse me. I'll get the chocolate."

"What problem?"

"Why Angela Karlstrom didn't report whatever she knew about little Jennifer. You said Angela and R. L. Cutler were very close. So if R. L. was connected with Jennifer's death and Angela somehow witnessed it, chances are she wouldn't have said anything. But maybe Angela finally threatened to tell what she knew. Or R. L. just thought it wasn't safe to have her around anymore."

"If R. L. started all this by killing Jennifer," Pierce said slowly, "what was the reason? I suppose Jennifer could've wandered in on some drug transaction out there in the woods."

"You're still not going to report any of it?"

"Any of what? Should I report Amanda's latest shaggy dog story? What if they even half-believed it? What would the sheriff do, give R. L. more of a grilling? That'd just warn her to lay back and bide her time."

He gripped his leg and shifted it to a more comfortable position. "Dammit, I don't want her to lay back! If she's it, I want her to commit herself. To do something. To make her move. And I want to be there when she does. I want to see it. Beyond any doubt. I don't want her to just fade away. There are debts to be paid."

She placed a saucer and a cup of hot chocolate in his hands. "You'll be getting in this time every morning? It's going to be grueling. I imagine you could use a little breakfast before you turn in."

"No, Sally. I don't think you ought to be waiting around here in the early hours every day."

"I don't mind. You need some moral support. You can't go it alone. Not totally alone."

"No!"

She crouched beside him, her soft voice patient. "Whit, I'm here voluntarily. I—"

"Listen!" he shouted. "It's a contagion! Britt thinks she knows something, she dies. I'm Britt's partner, so I'm supposed to die. Ralph is Britt's husband, so he's supposed to die. It's a contagion! For God's sake, don't let it rub off on you, too!"

"I only suggested that I'd be happy to be here when you return, that maybe you could use—"

"Jesus Christ, must you always be so goddam *accommodating?* Are you going to spend your whole life *waiting?*"

Her head snapped up, and she stared at him in shock. She seemed to uncoil, slowly, dazedly.

"Waiting for me to come back every morning! Waiting for a teaching job to open up! Waiting for that principal to get a divorce! Waiting for your father to die! Waiting, waiting, waiting!"

Her face had turned chalk-white, so that the sprinkling of freckles shone like red welts.

She grabbed her coat and walked swiftly toward the kitchen door.

Pierce flinched as the door slammed shut.

Chapter 31

Vigo Lustgarten leaned across the desk, his hands folded in front of him. "Time we had another talk, Pierce!"

"That gun was legally registered to me, Sheriff."

"That's right. We checked. But it's kind of peculiar for a man to be sitting outside a tavern in the middle of nowhere in the dead of night, carrying a handgun. A tavern frequented by lesbians. We'd be remiss for not interrogating anybody under those circumstances."

"If you're thinking of me as a suspect, let me point out that I was carrying a gun, not a knife. No gun was used in any of those killings."

"I didn't say you're a suspect. I said I got damn good cause to get you in here to answer some questions."

"When can I pick up that gun?"

"Tomorrow. At two. In my office. And bring along the rest of those stories."

"What do you mean?"

"We've been back to see the Gatliffe woman and her son. I understand she turned in a story to you every week. You gave us two. Should be two more."

"They weren't relevant, it seemed to me."

"Let me be the judge of that, Pierce."

"I thought you weren't giving her stories much credence. That every murder brings some crackpots crawling out of the woodwork."

"Crackpot or no, we're checking everything."

"You've been looking for a purple dress?"

"That's right."

"You went through Mrs. Hungerford's things?"

"Damn sure did. Hungerford gave us access to everything of hers. We went through the whole house. Found a couple dresses in shades of purple, but all in her size. She had 'em for years."

"And you looked elsewhere?"

"Of course."

"Where?"

"I ask and you answer, Pierce! Tomorrow at two. And bring those stories."

He considered calling Sally but instantly rejected the idea. The look on her face was one he would not forget. It was as if he had inexplicably slapped her with all the force he could muster.

At least now she was out of it. That was the essential thing. But, Lord, that look!

As if nobody she trusted had ever been cruel to her before. *Dammit, kid, grow up! What are hurt feelings? Compared to . . .*

Compared to what the lady in the purple dress could do.

He cruised past the farmhouse just before noon, but the van with the snarling pumas had already left. He found it parked in the alley behind the shop. He assumed R. L. was inside, but there were no signs of her all evening. Pierce was certain, from the occasion when he and Deputy Evans had visited the shop, that there was no exit other than the front door.

At nine he switched on his engine and, with it, the car radio. Heavy snowfall later tonight or early tomorrow, a voice reported. Possible accumulations of three to five inches. A travelers' advisory.

As the five-minute newscast ended R. L. appeared. The door seemed to stick, and she pulled it fiercely, giving it a kick after it closed. She scuffed along the sidewalk in her elegant, stitched boots, hands thrust deep in the faded jeans. She walked with a slight forward slouch, shoulders rolling aggressively with every step.

Cutler vanished in the alley, only to rush out moments later in her van. Tonight she drove north and then west, stopping at a lounge on the periphery of downtown.

She was there twenty minutes, then off to a bowling alley eight blocks farther west. She went in through the bar entrance and remained there forty-five minutes. The Stetson was pulled lower over her face when she left, and she seemed absorbed in her own thoughts. Pierce didn't worry that she would notice him in the innocuous brown Sunbird.

Looking neither right nor left, she pulled away. At once she screeched to a stop. A station wagon—which clearly had the right of way—beeping wildly, had nearly sideswiped her.

"Motherfucker!" she screamed, jabbing a finger at the other driver.

Gunning the engine she wheeled the van down a side street that funneled into Archer Avenue, which bore straight past the silos of the brewery to Wharf Row and the river. Within ten minutes she was at the Ace High.

Pierce parked diagonally, close to the ancient warehouse adjacent to the tavern. The nose of his car faced the street, so he could follow instantly without having to back out when R. L. reappeared. From this spot he also had an unobstructed view of the side door of the bar and of R. L.'s van.

Was she having a couple of quick ones, he wondered, as she had at the first two bars? Or was she settling in for the night? It was at the Ace High that she'd spent so many hours the night Angela Karlstrom was killed. The night of the questionable alibi.

He glanced at his watch, and when he looked up, he saw a tall, slender woman in a blue parka, the hood pulled low over her head. She was crossing the lot briskly. Her face was averted.

With a shock he realized it was Sally. He opened the car door, startled and undecided. Did he dare call to her? Before he could decide, she had gone in.

Had she just chanced to stop by for a drink? She'd never mentioned coming to the Ace High. It was a rather dubious place for a woman to go alone.

But what did he *really* know about Sally and where she went when she wanted a drink? So she makes it to the Art Institute in Chicago. Does that mean she's too dainty for the Ace High?

But why tonight? Why when R. L. was here?

His mind raced. Did R. L. know her by sight? Had they ever met?

Not to his knowledge, not since he'd been back here. But if that had been R. L. Cutler in his town house in Chicago, he may have spotted Sally. Or if R. L. had been observing him at Aunt Amy's house in La Soeur, she could have seen Sally.

But would Sally know R. L. by sight? At first glance? Would she know what the hell she just walked into?

Pierce got out of the car. He would not be able to wait. Checking his watch every thirty seconds. Drumming on the steering wheel. Staring at that door. Wondering what in God's name was going on inside.

He pulled the collar of his jacket up as high as he could. Three things were in his favor: the barroom was long, it was crowded, and it was dim. Newcomers would not be especially noticeable.

Before the spring door had closed behind him he recognized R. L.'s broad back, almost at the far end of the bar near the rest rooms. Pierce drifted leisurely toward the front entrance where the largest concentration of customers had gathered.

Here the bar stools were all occupied, and standees were packed three deep. He sidled behind a group of convivial dockworkers and carefully let his eyes wander down the bar to R. L.

She was in semiprofile, hunkered over, elbows on the bar. She glared straight ahead at the shelves of bottles. In front of her was a shot glass and a stein of beer.

With an abrupt burst of movement she downed the contents of the shot glass and followed it with a long swig from the stein. At once she pushed the whisky tumbler forward for a refill. Her eyes remained riveted to the rows of bottles.

And Sally? Pierce began to survey the room, segment by segment, but something pulled him back to the end of the bar where R. L. sat.

It was Sally's red hair. She had let the hood fall back, her hair like a beacon. She was almost next to R. L. Only one customer sat between them—a mustachioed young man in a cable-knit sweater. Already trying to strike up an acquaintance, chatting amiably, his head close to Sally's. She nodded, an unenthusiastic smile on her face.

Cutler was oblivious to Sally and the young man. One hand plucked the cigarette from her mouth, and the other raised the shot glass. The whisky disappeared. She took a long swallow of beer, snorted, and clamped the cigarette once more between her teeth.

Sally pretended to be unaware of R. L. She toyed with some mixed drink, and the young man beside her nudged it from time to time, evidently urging her to quaff it so he could buy her another. Occasionally she made some brief remark, seemingly in response to a question of his.

Coincidence: R. L. and Sally here at the Ace High on the same night, sitting almost together? Of course, this was not much more than an overgrown small town. There were only so many places to go on an evening out. But, still . . .

Then Sally pointed to the vintage lithograph of the *Belle of La Soeur* on the wall. The young man looked at the river steamer and shrugged.

As he did so she hopped off the bar stool and stepped toward the side door. The young man gawked after her.

R. L. Cutler, Pierce saw, had not noticed Sally leaving. He

walked rapidly after her, brushing past some new arrivals at the door.

She was running toward her car, yanking the hood up over her head. Almost with one movement she unlocked the Toyota and slipped inside. Pierce grabbed the door just before she could swing it shut.

"What the hell goes on?"

She said nothing, but pulled the door. Pierce held it open.

"I said, what goes on?"

She studied him coolly, almost appraisingly. There were no laugh lines at the corners of her eyes.

"I'm not just sitting and waiting anymore. That's what goes on."

"But why did you stop here?"

"To see R. L. Cutler."

"You came here to see her? How did you know she'd be here?"

"I followed you. It wasn't hard."

"Jesus Christ! I told you not to get involved!"

"If I'm not going to spend my life waiting, I have to get involved. Please close the door, Whit."

"But why? Why did you go in there?"

"For this."

She held up an object, and Pierce bent to get a closer look. It was a quartz cigarette lighter, diamond-plated, some zodiac sign engraved on it.

"It's R. L.'s. I took it when she wasn't looking. Easy. Her mind was somewhere else. But I've got to get out of here. She may notice it's gone. She may remember me and come tearing out."

Sally turned the ignition key.

"But why did you take it?"

Her face remained utterly placid. "Isn't it obvious? Why did you take Smokey's collar?"

"For Amanda?"

"It's worth a try, isn't it? It's worth finding out what she reads in this. R. L. always carried it. If what R. L. has done rubs off on anything, it'd be on this lighter. It's crazy. But no crazier than what you're doing."

"All right." He extended his hand. "It's worth trying. Give me the lighter and I'll check it with Amanda."

"No. I will." Her lips were drawn in a tight line. She darted a glance at the tavern. "I've got to get out of here."

He put his shoulder against the door, preventing her closing it. "Look, I'm sorry. What I said to you last night . . . I didn't mean it to come out that way."

Framed by the parka hood, her face had the silver pallor of a waning moon. But it was set in firm determination. "You were right. I guess that's why I took it so hard. It's easier to be offended when you know the other person's right."

"No. I was worn-out and fed up. And scared. I didn't mean what I said."

"But you were right. I just never thought about it. I guess I have wasted a lot of time waiting. Well, from now on—no more. I'm making things happen."

"Okay. But not with this thing. This is no way to start, this stunt you're pulling off tonight."

At that, a wisp of a smile broke through her implacability. "Are you advising me to run my own life or aren't you? You can't have it both ways, Whit. Anyway, I'm full of ideas about how to make things happen. Case in point: I did some snooping this afternoon. Did you know that R. L. has no alibi for the night Mrs. Hungerford died?"

"No. Of course, I assumed that. But—"

"She closes her shop at six on Saturdays. She said she was home between six thirty and the time they found the body. But she says she was there alone. No witnesses to confirm it."

"How do you know?"

"I called Nehemiah Evans. He's given you information, so I

figured I could ask, too. He'd taken a look at the reports the investigators filed."

"I should've thought to check that point, although I'm not sure Mr. Evans would be so cooperative with me anymore. All right, hang on to the cigarette lighter. We'll go to Amanda's tomorrow and get a reading. The two of us."

"It's not much past eleven. She may still be up."

"Look, I'm keeping an eye on R. L. You know I'm stuck here."

"I know. But I'm not. And why wait?"

The car slid forward without warning. Before Pierce could react, she had pulled the door smoothly shut. The headlights went on as she crept toward the exit.

"Sally!" he shouted.

She lowered the window, and her voice was taut, urgent.

"Whit! She's coming out! Be careful!"

Sally drove off. Pierce stepped into the shadows between two cars.

R. L. walked steadily and with belligerent certainty, her heels ringing on the concrete. There was nothing in her heavy, precise gait to indicate that the boilermakers she'd drunk had had any effect.

Once her back was to him, Pierce returned quickly to his Sunbird. He stopped and swore.

The left rear tire was flat.

Squatting, he examined it. A long, jagged wound. Someone had stabbed it with a sharp, bladed instrument and then turned the puncture into a slash.

Peering up, he saw R. L. Cutler's van roar past him and out onto Wharf Street. As she passed him her face was pointed dead ahead, the rocklike jaw tight with tension.

With fumbling fingers Pierce began removing the bolts from the wheel. It was a slow process. He flung open the trunk and lifted out the spare tire. Laboriously he assembled the parts of the jack and cranked up the rear end of the chassis.

Nearby a man groaned. One of his tires was flat, too.

"They all are!" the woman with him shrieked.

"Kids," the man grumbled. "West High won the championship tonight. The kids are running wild all over town."

Pierce let the ruined tire lay where it was and, with near frenzied haste, dumped the jack back in his trunk.

R. L. had turned left out of the parking lot, heading north or east.

Returning home? That would be the first supposition, although he didn't think it was the case at all. It wasn't late, and she hadn't looked ready to call it a day.

Twenty-five minutes later he found he was right. Only the pickup truck was parked beside her farmhouse.

Where now?

Ralph's house? Or mine?

His own home was closest. He coasted slowly down the quiet streets he had gotten to know so well, conscious of the irony involved.

Was she trying to stalk him while he was trying to stalk her?

The van was not parked anywhere on his block. The lights were on in the Sorensons' family room next door, and Mr. Kendrick's house was completely dark. Pierce had left the kitchen light on again at Aunt Amy's. He could see that the garage was empty.

Of course, she would not be so obvious as to park where his neighbors would see the van. He threaded his way up and down the adjoining streets for nearly half an hour. Nothing.

Ralph's then? Pierce accelerated sharply as he left the city limits. It was now more than an hour since he'd lost contact with R. L.

Moisture spattered the windshield. Motes of whirling white, indistinct, evaporating on impact. The anticipated snowfall was almost on schedule. He turned on his wipers.

In his mind's eye he saw again what had happened to

Smokey. And he thought of the star-patterned boots that Amanda had described.

Amanda.

Did R. L. know Amanda?

Sally would be at Amanda's now, if she meant what she said about getting a reading immediately.

Could R. L. be aware that it was Sally who took her cigarette lighter? And somehow have gotten onto Sally's trail?

He slowed, looking for a turnoff, instantly possessed by the need to turn back toward the river, back toward Amanda's. God, did Sally even suspect what could be happening?

Suddenly he was shaking. Recalling Britt's butchered body. Recalling Corinne's tortured face.

Seeing Sally—just for a moment—bloodied, twisted, staring blankly full into his eyes.

No! Please, God! *No!*

The Pontiac veered off onto the shoulder and he fought the wheel. The car swerved back onto the highway.

He let his arms go limp for a moment, let the trembling flow out of him. He blinked away the images that had blazed up before his eyes.

A side road loomed ahead.

No. He was almost at Ralph's house. Logic dictated that he take a look there first. Then race like hell to Amanda's.

Pierce kept his speed down once he reached Kimberley Drive, passing the wide lawns and quarter-of-a-million-plus homes illuminated by the amber gaslights the residents had erected on every corner. Just before the dead end, he swung his car into the long, familiar entranceway.

Lights glittered from the upstairs windows on the far side of the house fronting the golf course. The first floor was dark. He drove along the arc of the driveway past the front entrance and on to the garage.

There were no vehicles outside. Pierce got out of the car, leaving his engine running. His eyes took in the house—no evidence of anyone gazing down—and he walked quickly to the garage.

Through a porthole-shaped window he could make out Ralph's Cadillac, Britt's lemon-colored Mark Six, and a Land-Rover. But no van.

Could R. L. actually have spotted Sally?

Pierce went back to his car. He drove back to Kimberley Drive, and then impatience got the better of him. He streaked along the deserted, tree-shrouded street to the wider road that in moments brought him to Wisconsin 82. Here he pushed the accelerator to the floor and kept it there.

His eyes were fixed on the city ahead, and he passed the Kennilworth Motel without consciously noticing it.

From out of nowhere a question shrieked for his attention.

Didn't you park at the Kennilworth when you went to see Britt?

So what?

Wouldn't somebody else? Somebody who wanted to go to the Hungerford's and not be noticed?

Okay! Okay, dammit!

At the next exit Pierce swung off, spun around on the darkened side road, and hurtled back onto 82. Within seconds, tires squealing, he peeled off at the entrance to the Kennilworth Motel.

First he drove along its westernmost length, past the place he had parked the two times he'd gone to meet Britt. He glanced quickly at the long row of cars. The snow was falling harder. There was one van, but it was powder blue, decorated with a red sunset.

Recklessly he circled the main building and swept past the vehicles on the other side. It was even less plausible that she'd park here, because it was farther from the edge of the woods that led to the golf course and to the Hungerford home.

Then he saw it.

Nestled tightly between two cars so that only the tail of one of the pumas was visible. Nestled so closely as to seem to be trying too hard to look inconspicuous.

He slammed on the brakes and squinted, examining the van intently. It was without a doubt R. L.'s.

So she'd gone on foot to Ralph's. That had to be it.

Either that or checked into the motel?

That possibility could be investigated later. After he had checked Ralph's.

With a jackrabbit start the Pontiac bolted forward and whipped around the corner. How long would it take to get back to Ralph's? Five minutes. Maybe six?

Cutting through the woods had never taken more than four. It wasn't much more than a quarter of a mile. And, jogging, he could do it even faster.

He pulled his car up at the western edge of the motel lot and walked quickly across the long stretch of lawn, tugging on his gloves. The snow was stinging his face.

When he came to the first trees he broke into a half-run.

Here it was much darker, and he could not see the ground clearly. The branches acted as filters so that there was hardly any trace of snow. It was silent within the woods, as if he had entered a room and closed a door behind him.

He had a vivid recollection of the last time he had made this journey, the night he discovered Britt under the hanging tree. Then the leaves had been fresh on the ground, crackling and brittle. Now they were pulpy, rotting into compost.

A hushed tranquillity filled the center of this scraggly grove. Pierce slowed to a walk. He was breathing heavily, the air frosty in his lungs. He felt tinglingly alive in a place that was restful, sheltering. Here he was secure and enclosed. Away from what lay behind him, safely cut off from whatever awaited him ahead.

Pierce began running again. Already the spell of the woods was disintegrating. A yellow light took form in the distance. It seemed to flick on and off, but he knew this was the effect of the thinning clumps of trees that stood between him and the Hungerford home.

Once he stepped into the clear, it was with a sense of reluctance. A great weariness suddenly overcame him, as though he were passing from alert wakefulness into some vaporous, paralyzing dream. The glittering flakes that surrounded him were wetter and thicker than they had been even minutes before.

The walk across the front lawn seemed to take even longer than had his passage through the trees. The low-hanging sky was sooty. The snow gave the night a shimmering opalescence, and every detail of the house was drawn with surprising clarity. The rough texture of the cedar walls, the chimney spouting smoke, the silver maples fingering the roof.

Like a scene on a Christmas card, he thought, then reversed himself: Hell, no. No. Not a Christmas card. It was like a stockade, with its high and boxlike facade, its second-floor balconies girding the building as if they were parapets.

A goddam fortress.

A watchful, wary place.

Because Britt no longer lived there.

Because of what had happened to Smokey.

Because of who might be there now.

Pierce went up the small porch, tried the door, and found it locked.

Of course.

He stepped back down and onto the flagstone path to the rear entranceway. The balcony overhead blocked any view of the second floor. Yet light spilled weakly out onto the lawn from some upstairs windows. Curtains covered all the wide glass panels on the main level. On his right he could see the pale contour of the gazebo.

And ahead, at the far end of the back lawn—past the phalanx of hedges where Ralph's property ended—lay the slatey blur that was Meadowbluff golf course. Pierce halted at the corner of the north wing of the house, staring in the direction of the hanging tree. He was unable to distinguish it through the screen of snow.

It was just a few feet past the threshold of the back door, he reminded himself, that they had found Smokey. He wondered if Ralph had had a new lock installed.

Then he noticed that the door was ajar.

"Hands come down . . . Grab dog . . . By throat . . . Dog fights . . . Sticks knife in dog . . . One time . . . Two time . . . Three time . . . Four time . . ."

He reached out to push the door open further. . . .

Pierce took two steps in. The spacious hallway was unlit and so was the kitchen adjoining it.

He was about to call out "Ralph!" but stopped.

Maybe it was best not to make his presence known. Not yet.

But, my God, if Ralph's waiting up ahead . . . panicked, ready to shoot anybody who walks in unannounced?

Ralph would certainly have wondered if whoever killed Smokey might be back. Wouldn't he take some precautions? There'd been talk of a whole security system in the house. Had Ralph left the door open himself? Or had someone else . . . ?

And what if that someone's waiting—and it's not Ralph?

The stereo was playing somewhere in the house. Very muted, almost imperceptible.

He wouldn't be able to pick up his .38 until tomorrow. At the earliest.

Tomorrow! An eternity away.

Pierce removed his gloves. He needed some kind of weapon. Anything.

Something from the kitchen? A steak knife?

No. He didn't know this room, and he did not want to be fumbling through drawers in the darkness. Nor did he wish to switch on a light. He held his breath and walked swiftly through the kitchen, almost on tiptoe, as if the red Spanish tiles were a bed of coals.

He paused at the edge of the sun room. Blood pounded in his

temples, but he knew his hearing was at that instant more acute than it had ever been in his life. He detected nothing . . . nothing within breathing distance of him. Silently he went on to the open doorway to the dining room.

He studied every swirl and pocket of shadow in the room, his senses keyed to recognize any subliminal shifting or stirring. The long, narrow French Provincial table was concealed beneath stiff, formal linen that grazed the floor. A mammoth bronze and ormolu candelabra sprouted from the exact center of the table. In one corner was the Louis XV commode, emblazoned with dizzying scrollwork, and atop it a Baccarat bowl filled with fresh violets.

The silence of the room was stifling, a silence intensified by the oppressive, muffling presence of the closed damask drapes that blotted out the window wall.

Beyond, the music was growing identifiable: "Poinciana," a vapid, overly sweet orchestration. The music seemed to have no source. It was just there, floating in the air as it had always been.

Less cautiously this time, aware that the thick carpet cushioned his steps, he went to the tall arch that connected the north wing of the house with the cavernous living room.

The melody was branding itself on some lower level of his brain. Foolishly a fragment of the lyric—or something resembling the lyric—raced through his conscious mind.

"Poinciana, your blossoms sing to me of love . . ."

In two quick, jerking motions he swung his head from side to side, taking in everything from the fireplace to the stairway and back again.

No one there. More deliberately he scanned the room again. No lamps were on, but they were not needed because of the power of the light streaming from the second floor.

Still there was silence, except for the sprightly notes emanating from nowhere. "Your blossoms sing to me of love . . ."

Once he set foot in the living room he knew he would be

clearly visible from anywhere along the length of the gallery above.

The recollection of the gentle woods he had just traveled through flooded him. To be back there now, while the snow sealed him off from the world. From this house.

He must leave now, slipping out the way he had entered. Or shout Ralph's name. Something. Anything. The emptiness of these rooms was a desolation.

His hands flexed and opened helplessly. He stared at the poker.

Yes, by God, the poker!

Pierce strode rapidly to the fireplace and picked up the solid brass rod. In his haste he let it scrape loudly against the tongs in the galleried base stand.

He whirled, faced the balcony overhead.

No one peering down. His eyes jumped from one to the other of the four doorways set back from the hallway.

But something caught his attention at the lower edge of his field of vision. To the carpeting at the far end of the balcony.

A hand protruded between two of the thin, beveled, oaken balustrades.

The palm was turned up, fingers outstretched.

Blood trickled between each of them, dripping onto the keys of the piano directly below. Half of the keyboard, Pierce saw, was soaked.

He stepped backward hesitantly, back toward the curtained picture window, so as to bring more of the upstairs gallery into perspective.

A wide swath of blood coiled across a wrist and bare forearm and the cuff of some checkered garment. Past that, the angle of the balcony obscured his view.

Pierce moved slowly, like a sleepwalker, across the room. Eyes locked on that hand and forearm. Still he could see nothing beyond them. Still there was absolute silence except for the music. Then he was at the base of the curving staircase.

He placed his weight very gingerly on each step of the grass-green carpet before he went on to the next. The top remotely distant. He held the poker in his right hand, high over his shoulder.

At a point halfway from the second-floor landing his head reached a level with the body on the floor of the balcony.

The face was buried in the nap of the carpet, but the mane of yellow hair and the lank, spidery limbs were easily recognizable. It was Emil Gatliffe.

Emil's back was to him, the shirt stained with dribbles of blood. But a solid, iridescent pool had settled around the shoulders, head, and midsection. Apparently from wounds not visible from where Pierce stood.

He hesitated, and his left hand groped for the support of the sturdy, smooth railing. Then he mounted the last of the steps with difficulty, as if a thick bog sucked at his feet.

He could not wrench his eyes from the tall, frail form curled up at the end of the hallway. So profoundly still. The immobility was so unlike Emil.

Emil the hoaxer, Emil the trickster. Was this some elaborate ruse?

Pierce paused at the top of the staircase, looking intently at Emil. Straining to detect any movement, the slightest shiver. Another of his games? There was a deafening, shattering roar.

Emil! Jesus!

Another roar. A door slammed open. The master bedroom, a few yards to his right.

Ruby Lee Cutler came out into the hallway and moved toward him. She moved fast, mammoth shoulders rolling, head flung back, the tendons of her thick neck taut.

Instinct jerked his arm far back, the poker poised above his head.

Her body smashed into his. One hand, with incredible power, dug into his arm, blocking his blow. The force of her momentum staggered him. A hurtling, grinding, onrushing ferocity pushed him backward.

From her mouth, gaping open inches from his face, poured a roar that rose and rose to a keening screech. Her breath enveloped him in a foulness like vomit.

The eyes glared into his. They bulged, the pupils mere pinpricks, the whites crisscrossed with squiggly, crimson lines.

Her fists and elbows pummeled him. The hard, heavy legs moved in choppy steps, propelling her forward.

Pierce felt one foot dangling in the air. He tried to lower it to the first step of the stairway. Her forearm slammed viciously against his nose and mouth.

Pain blinded him momentarily. He toppled backward; his single conscious thought was to wrap his arms around her and carry her with him.

Noise thundered in his ears. But there was no more pain. Yet he heard a sharp scream and he knew, though there was absolutely no sensation in his body, that the scream was his. And that he had fallen on and twisted his already damaged right leg.

Fingers clawed his face, gripped his throat.

Pierce's eyes opened. She lay beneath him, wriggling, groaning.

Somehow his arms moved, and he fastened on her wrists, attempting to pull her hands from his throat. The poker had flown from his grasp. He had no idea where. The balustrade on the main floor loomed over him. They had rolled the length of the staircase.

He forced one of her hands to her side. How wet it was, her hand. So very, very wet. Covered with blood.

As was the front of her denim jacket. Her torn, slashed jacket. Slimy, bubbly, bright red.

Her face was contorted, knotted. But the eyes were half-closed, filmy. He noticed for the first time that blood was gushing from her mouth.

Then the eyelids rolled up, and she was squinting at something beyond him, above him. At once the eyes became alert—hard and malevolent.

Her mouth moved, an incoherent mumble. She inhaled—it was a racking, rattling sound—and spat a great gout of mingled phlegm and blood. Her slobber-flecked lips twitched.

"Behind you," she snarled.

Chapter 32

Pierce wrenched his body around. To his dazed eyes the steps were a shifting, fluid pattern of green. As though he lay at the bottom of a foaming, spray-filled waterfall.

Then the illusion was gone. The haziness hardened into solidity. Two feet had approached the head of the stairs. Pierce's vision came into sudden, sharply defined focus.

The feet were encased within silver-and-pink ankle-strapped slings. The heels were very high, slim, and contoured. Each step was taken slowly, cautiously, yet with smooth, confident grace.

Every detail was incredibly clear to Pierce, as if he were looking through a microscope and as if there was all the time in the world to examine each component of whatever was affixed to the slide beneath the lens. He was aware of nothing else. Only each small segment of the whole, each segment that was to be scrutinized with patience and growing fascination.

The ankles were thick and the calves heavy, straining against the black, fishnet stockings.

There was a dinner dress of dazzling buttercup yellow lace, just touching the knee with swirls of scallops. A long-sleeved jacket of the same color, yards of gossamer intricately worked into it. The four buttons were undone, permitting full display of the pearl necklace that had been doubled again and again until it was a ropelike, glowing choker.

The elegant dress was snug but not ludicrously so, and the jacket was peplumed, softening the silhouette of the huge hips.

There was pride, even imperiousness, in the way the stylishly cut clothes were worn.

The face was haughty, too, the vividly rouged mouth drawn in a prissy moue of displeasure. Piles of upswept spun-sugar hair, streaked glossily in a half-dozen shades of blond, lustrous as the pelt of some exotic, fur-bearing Arctic animal.

It was no one Pierce had ever seen before.

Yet someone who was familiar. Certainly. He groped for a name.

Idiotic of him. Idiotic. Like meeting an acquaintance at a party and the mind momentarily going blank. When you know who it is and you know you know who it is. But the conscious mind balks at making the connection.

Irresistibly his eyes dropped back to what he had observed in his initial, almost clinical, inspection of the figure gazing down at him.

Back to the knife in the right hand. The long-bladed knife coated with blood. The knife held away from the body almost distastefully, as though to prevent it from dribbling even more on the sunflower dress. Already there were spots on the skirt, near the hemline, and on one sleeve of the jacket.

The hand that held the knife was large and fleshy, the wrist hairy. The fingers of the other hand toyed with the pearl choker, languidly, almost with boredom.

"You understand why I could not let it be known," Ralph Hungerford said in his resonant tenor voice.

Pierce stared at that face. Still not quite seeing Ralph in it. Still not matching the voice and the features.

"The way people are—the way they react—you understand why I simply could not countenance having it known."

Sweat shone on his forehead, and mascara was seeping from the corners of his violet-fringed eyes.

"Cruel of them. So damnably cruel. But that's how they are. To a man in my position. If it were someone else they'd say, 'All right, it's eccentric, but he's doing no one any harm.' Which is true. No harm at all. Britt didn't mind. We had an understanding."

He burst into full, rich, resounding laughter. It was the laugh that had rung out so freely at the dinner party he and Britt had given in October. Suddenly it stopped.

"Let me be blunt, Whit. We go back a long way together, and can't we be frank? I am not a homosexual. You understand that, don't you? That people can be eccentric and nothing more? What harm did I ever create by indulging myself this way?"

The eyes boring down into Pierce's were pleading. "But they would have laughed at me, ridiculed me. Ruined me. How could I have run for public office?"

Pierce pushed himself up on his forearms. Pain, fear, rage— all exploded from him in three words.

"You killed Corinne!"

Ralph was humming lightly, melodically. "A terrible mistake. Believe me, Whit. I thought I had to. With the others, of course, I had no option."

He began walking down the stairs in a stately manner, holding the knife before him as if it were a lighted candle carried in some processional rite.

"Nor have I now," he said evenly.

There was no clumsiness in his descent. He moved expertly in the high heels. Pierce watched the powerful calf muscles bunch at every step, the body erect and perfectly balanced.

"The big lady in the purple dress puts her fingers on the little girl's throat. The big lady squeezes . . .

"The big lady in the purple dress bends over and sticks the knife in the girl's throat . . .

"The big lady in the purple dress stands on the table and ties the rope to the ceiling . . . The pretty lady is hanging there. Her eyes are open. Her eyes are green . . ."

Pierce flung himself around, crawling furiously over R. L. Cutler's body. She moaned, almost inaudibly. Her eyes were shut, her face floating in blood.

Shooting out his elbows and kicking with his good knee, Pierce wriggled away from the staircase.

The poker! Where?

His right leg was worthless, dead weight to be dragged behind him.

The brass poker lay beside a lamp four yards away.

"No farther, please."

The rustle of a skirt. The sling sandals planted themselves beside him.

Pierce, gritting again, looked up into the sagging face and the clear, azure eyes. The blond wig was slightly askew, and one of Ralph's ears poked through the glossy strands of hair.

"I have no option, Whit. Surely you see that. I regret it exceedingly because I was wrong about you just as I was about Corinne. I thought Corinne knew about me and had told you. And that you were blackmailing me. That's why I cultivated you so assiduously when you came back to La Soeur, presenting you with every opportunity to give yourself away. That's why I went through your notes. Oh, yes. I got the key to your house the day you visited my office. I took it from your coat and walked down the street and had a copy made all the while you were talking to Len Durban."

He went to the poker, picked it up, and took it back to the fireplace.

"All a mistake. I thought you were blackmailing me. And I wanted to put a stop to it. That's why I followed you to your home in Chicago. And up to the top of Frenchman's Pitch. That's why I invited you here two nights ago. I didn't expect you would be leaving here alive."

He opened the fireplace screen and absently prodded a smoldering log. "But you brought the young lady," he called loudly across the room. "And I had no idea of the extent of her knowledge or whether she'd told anyone you were visiting me. And then, of course, Smokey was so foully slain."

He pulled a lace handkerchief from his jacket and dabbed at

the perspiration and the running makeup streaking his face. "Naturally I realized that whoever killed Smokey was probably the same person who was blackmailing and threatening me. And I realized then that it couldn't be you."

Hungerford sauntered back to Pierce, poised and casual, maintaining his perfect carriage.

"I want you to know that, Whit. I realize now that you wouldn't be guilty of anything so repellent as blackmail. No, the blame lies with this odious creature."

With the knife he pointed toward R. L. Cutler.

"It was this travesty of a woman who precipitated it all. This R. L. Cutler! She! Because Angela Karlstrom saw what happened to the Stabo girl. Out joyriding in Corinne's sports car and she'd parked there—to take dope probably. Saw me and the Stabo girl. And told R. L. Cutler what she saw. And Cutler induced Angela Karlstrom to blackmail me. That's why I had no choice but to do what I did to Karlstrom. She set up a payoff in the cemetery that night, so I met her there and I thought that ended it. But then the blackmail notes started again. I concluded it was you, Whit. I apologize. All the time it was this . . . this abomination!"

Hungerford pivoted and violently kicked the sharp pink-and-silver toe of the sling into R. L.'s ribs.

His large body trembled, folds of flesh quivering at his jawline. He bent over Cutler and ducked his head, listening for the scratchy intake of breath.

"Damn it! She's gone! And I so wanted it to last longer."

The big man in the yellow dinner dress stood over Pierce.

"I'm sorry you had to witness this, Whit. It doesn't concern you. I'll deal with you quickly, I promise. It will be instantaneous. Not as it was with Britt. For she betrayed me. We had an understanding. My wife, whom I considered my closest friend. Then she found the purple dress, which I'd carefully concealed. And she betrayed me. For Britt it was not instantaneous."

Pierce grabbed for the stocky legs in the fishnet stockings.

He clasped them just behind the knees. He jerked with all the weight of his body.

You killed Corinne!

Hungerford toppled. Pierce rolled toward him, reaching for the hand with the knife.

A slippered foot caught Pierce flush in the mouth. He reached for the foot. It swung away.

Pierce hurled himself again at the knife hand. But Hungerford skittered sideways across the carpet, the skirt upflung. A flash of flabby thighs and pink, floral-patterned panties.

Hungerford lurched to his feet, stepped forward, and lashed out with another kick.

It struck just over Pierce's right eye, and in a crescendo of flame and noise all vision ceased.

Pierce heard the voice as though Hungerford were whispering in his ear. It was a vibrant tenor once more, soft and melodious.

"What a trusting fool I was. They won't leave you alone. Ever. They sneak around and spy on you. The Stabo girl. She saw me and she knew me. I knew she'd tell her parents. I knew they resented me for what I'd achieved. I knew they'd spread the story. I knew I had no option. And the Gatliffe boy. Always prying, always skulking. I've seen him at night lurking at the edge of the fairway. And tonight. Brazen as can be. Staring in. Seeing me. I invited him in. I knew I had no option."

Pierce blinked, frantically, desperately, trying to see.

"God damn you!" he cried.

"Corinne was a terrible error, Whit. I simply traced the license number of the car and it was registered to her. So what could I assume except that she was the one who'd seen me with the Stabo girl? And chose to blackmail me? It's a logical assumption, isn't it?"

Pierce thrust out both hands, clutching for the source of that voice.

The voice pulled back. It was soothing, lilting, comforting.

"Don't thrash around so, Whit. I can't be sure it will be instantaneous if you do that. Be still. That's right. Steady. Ah, now we're ready. Believe me, you'll never even know. I'm that fast and that good. I've learned."

Chapter 33

Running footsteps clicked somewhere, distantly, in the house.

"Whit? Whit, are you here?"

Sally Berwyn stepped hesitantly into the living room. She saw Hungerford and stopped. He walked toward her and said hospitably, "Come in, please."

Her eyes widened in disbelief. She looked from Pierce to Cutler and back to Hungerford.

"Please come in," he said more severely. "I'm sorry. But, you see, I have no option."

Other heels echoed. Heavy, clopping footfalls crossing the kitchen.

Hungerford inclined his head to one side, listening. The sound ended. There was silence for several seconds and then a slight creak. The creak of a floorboard under the dining room carpet as a considerable weight pressed upon it.

Hungerford edged back toward the stairwell, staring past Sally.

Another creak and the massive body of Amanda Gatliffe filled the doorway.

There was no pause in her stride. Her old, brown greatcoat was sprinkled with snow. Her wheat-colored, stack-heeled pumps punched moisture into the thick carpet at every step.

The twisted, uneven features of her face were as empty of expression as the ridges and crevices of a boulder.

Hungerford moved one foot behind him, placing it on the

first step of the stairway. He jabbed the knife in Amanda's direction.

"No farther!"

It was a hoarse whisper. There was no melody, no harmony in his voice now.

Amanda marched steadily across half the length of the huge room. She halted and, without hesitation, looked up to the second-floor gallery where Emil lay.

Her black, button eyes dwelt on the sight with unwavering absorption.

"Get out!" Hungerford choked.

"I come for my boy."

The immense body turned and began trudging toward the stairway.

Hungerford moved awkwardly, backing up the stairs. He switched the knife to his left hand in order to cling to the rail with his right.

"No farther!" The knife swung threateningly from side to side.

She reached the stairs and immediately started up.

One of his feet missed a riser at the point where the staircase made its grand, sweeping curve. He teetered and quickly caught himself.

She was only three steps from him. He lunged, feinting, with the knife.

The gesture did not deter her even for an instant. The off-center eyes never left his face.

Hungerford half-turned and ran up the remaining stairs. At the second-floor landing he spun around to confront her once more. Spun too soon. One high heel caught the edge of the last step just as he shifted his weight onto it.

The heel collapsed under him.

His body thudded against the wall. Desperately, with both hands, he pushed himself upright.

By then Amanda stood over him.

He tried to bring the knife up, but he was still off balance.

She clamped one hand on his wrist and the other went under his right armpit.

She lifted him up. He uttered a faint, drawn-out, strangling hum, as though searching for the proper tonal quality before choosing the appropriate words.

She carried him four unhurried steps along the corridor, toward the body of her son. Her arms moved upward—without urgency, without haste—and raised the body in the sunflower dress so that Hungerford's head was high above her own.

She hurled him outward, over the magnificent red-oak railing running the length of the hallway, onto the blood-splattered piano in the living room below.

Sally squeezed his hand with all of her strength, as if the warmth and pressure could numb the racking pain. He lay on his back on the soft pile carpet, listening to a deep, anguished, roaring groan. It went on and on, an endless animal wail.

"What the hell's that?"

"Amanda," Sally answered. "They're trying to lead her away. She won't go. She won't leave Emil."

"Oh, my God. Why'd you come here, Sally?"

"Amanda. She knew what happened to Emil. She *knew*. I went to see her, to see what she'd make of Ruby Lee's cigarette lighter. Instead she had something of Emil's she was touching. She saw what was happening to him. And she saw who was making it happen."

In the background he heard Sheriff Vigo Lustgarten's loud, harried shouts.

"Shut up that yowling! And I told you to leave Hungerford's body where it is! Christ's sake, let the technicians get the photos taken!"

Then the voice was closer, volleying down on Pierce.

"I want your statement. Now, Pierce! Beginning with why you showed up here tonight!"

Sally snapped back at him instantly, with anger and authority. "He needs medical attention. Now!"

"It's on the way. First I want a statement!"

"No! You'll get it after he's been taken care of!"

"Listen, lady——"

"After! And get that ambulance here. We've waited long enough!"

"I'll check on it," Lustgarten grumbled, moving away.

"No more waiting?" Pierce said with a grimace that was meant to be a grin.

"No more waiting, Whit. Hush now."

He struggled to form his words. "Sally, I haven't mourned, and now I have to. What there was till now wasn't mourning. I miss her and it hurts. . . . I have to mourn her. And the book is how I'll do it. That's how the grief will come out. . . ."

"It'll be a fine book, Whit. I know it."

"It's going to free me, Sally. Of all this . . . of the past . . ."

"They're here, Whit. The medics."

"I haven't thought about the future. For so long. Sally, we've got so much to talk about. . . ."

"I know, Whit." He felt her cool lips brush his forehead.

She walked beside him, still gripping his hand, as they carried him through the vast living room and the long, paneled foyer.

He could still hear Amanda's inconsolable, bellowing dirge as the front door slammed shut behind him.

**Sheer terror...
and the uncontrollable urge
to keep reading await you
in the suspense novels of**

MARY HIGGINS CLARK

Imagine yourself finally settled into your large Victorian home. Life in your charming, quaint New England village is a dream come true...until the dream turns slowly into a nightmare. And you must confront evil forces *you don't even believe in*...and cannot stop.

Just like the families in these 3 novels of horror and suspense. By the *master* of supernatural terror,

DUFFY STEIN

_____ **OUT OF THE SHADOWS**	16826-0-05	$3.50
_____ **THE OWLSFANE HORROR**	16781-7-10	$3.50
_____ **GHOST CHILD**	12955-9-19	$3.50

At your local bookstore or use this handy coupon for ordering:

DELL READERS SERVICE—DEPT. B1499B
P.O. BOX 1000, PINE BROOK, N.J. 07058

Please send me the above title(s) I am enclosing $_____ (please add 75¢ per copy to cover postage and handling.) Send check or money order—no cash or CODs Please allow 3-4 weeks for shipment.

Ms./Mrs./Mr._____

Address_____

City/State_____ Zip_____